The Attic

By

Richard McMaster

ISBN 979-8-218-44858-5

August 24, 2025

Reviews

- McMaster's characters are so vividly portrayed that they practically leap off the page. Byron Kelly's struggle to rebuild his life while facing insurmountable odds is both heart-wrenching and inspiring. **Hemi Loomis**

- McMaster's portrayal of corporate greed and the devastating impact it can have on individuals and society as a whole is both timely and thought-provoking. The Attic is a wake-up call to anyone who believes that the pursuit of profit should come at any cost. I would recommend it! **Cecil McGuire**

- The Attic is a beautifully written novel that explores the complexities of human relationships in a world that often seems cruel and unforgiving. McMaster's prose is both lyrical and haunting, leaving a lasting impression on readers long after the final page.
- **Juana Chandler**

- McMaster's exploration of the intricacies of the justice system and the lengths that people will go to protect their secrets is both riveting and thought-provoking. The Attic is a must-read for anyone who enjoys a good legal thriller. **Lashaunda Chase**

- The Attic is a tour de force of storytelling. McMaster's ability to seamlessly blend elements of suspense, drama, and emotion makes for a compelling read that will keep you on the edge of your seat. Loved it! **Carol Coleman**

Dedication

The inspiration for the character Sybie, was known by many in my high school as Tic Toc, a disabled victim of NPS, nail-patella syndrome, a rare genetic disorder. Not everyone called her that but knew her by that name. I doubt few people remember her real name but recall seeing her struggle to get from class to class. Based on my brief time knowing her I hope she would approve of my fictional character.

About the Author

Before embarking on a writing career, Richard was a healthcare executive, heading up three different start-up companies, one ranked fifth largest of its kind in the United States. A native Iowan he was blessed to live twenty years in beautiful Coeur d'Alene, Idaho, and now in Arizona. He is a member of the Phoenix Writer's Club, The Authors Guild, the Arizona Author's Association, and the Arizona Traditions Writing Club, a local club he co-founded. He is a Surprise, Arizona Police Department volunteer citizen patrol officer.

He is the author of novels, *Aaron's War*, *A Love Divided by Time*, *Voyage of Life*, *The Other Half,* and *The Attic*. He just completed his sixth novel, *The Guts of Life*. A summary of these novels can be found on the website Richard-McMaster.com

Other Books
by Richard McMaster

Voyage of Life. The Voyage of Life story is told as the Thomas Cole *Voyage of Life* paintings are described: *Childhood, Youth, Manhood, and Old Age.* The paintings are a metaphor for Sean's life. In early manhood, he thinks Maddy, his one true love, has left him for another man and spends his life wondering what happened.

The Other Half. Twelve days before Christmas Luke loses his job and his wife is called away to care for her dying mother. Left alone at Christmas time, of the major traumatic life events—being fired from a job, fearing divorce, plotting murder, the death of a family member and jail time, any one of which can threaten your very existence—he faces them all.

Aaron's War. Aaron's War is about a young soldier who can't kill, overwhelmed by the horrors of war, conflicted by religion, and ravaged by memories, who makes the painful choice to leave his wife and child. Later, when he confronts the German soldier who spared his life, he faces a life decision that could take him back home.

2018 runner-up fiction book of the year
Arizona Author's Association.

A Love Divided by Time. Forrest and Allie believed they found love in a previous life and being born again was a game of hide and seek to find each other in plain sight, seeking their better halves, united and whole. When tragedy strikes, Forrest makes a pact to find her killer, raise their daughter, and find peace by joining her in the ever after.

2019 finalist unpublished book of the year
of the Arizona Author's Association.

For information on other novels go to
www.Richard-McMaster.com

Chapter One

Turning the car around and returning home was not an option. Byron Kelly sold everything, and there was nothing to go back to. He left behind painful memories, a lost job, lawsuit, and criminal charges—all now in his rearview mirror. His attorney said the judge would see the criminal complaint as a vendetta, but the two civil suits were more challenging. Going up against the deep pockets of Oreves, Inc., an international investment banking company, was daunting, and a negotiated settlement when the stakes were personal offered little hope.

He would have fought the claims and cleared his name if he had any fight left. Byron wasn't going to show up in court and listen to Valentin tell lies and spare no expense to strip him of his honor and destroy him. *Doesn't he understand what I went through, that he can't hurt me anymore?*

Byron, the youngest senior partner ever in an industry of silver hairs, was recruited by Oreves, Inc., an investment banking firm in Seattle, Washington. He graduated from the University of Washington at the top of his class with a double major in computer science and finance and a master's degree in commercial banking and risk management. The perfect recruit—well-groomed, fit, and trim with his dad's dark eyes and sandy hair of his mom's.

Byron's boss, Valentin, the owner of Oreves, inherited the billion-dollar business from his father, Victor Deroche, who passed away in 1975, along with Uncle Scrooge's amounts of money. Victor's self-taught hard work success came by frugally applying his hard-earned money, and his son Valentin, a Harvard graduate, was the living proof an apple can also rot on the stem.

Victor wore the same suit every day for the first ten years while he transformed businesses through financial restructurings, acquisitions, mergers, or expansions. He was admired, even loved, internationally for his humor, philanthropy, and most of all, the highest closing ratio and results few companies could match. Valentin, his son, on the other hand, wore the most expensive Italian suits, drove the fanciest Italian cars, and unlike his father, was universally disliked.

Byron's gaze broke free of the gray pavement just beyond the hood of his car and with a nod, recalled his life was already falling apart when the police showed up at his condo. He leaped to his feet when the doorbell rang but arrived at the door at the same time as Sybie. The policeman's stiff, solemn expression softened as he steadied his gaze on Sybie's deathly ashen appearance, pale and gaunt with sunken eyes, her Capri jeans and sweatshirt two sizes too big. Byron tenderly placed his hand on her shoulder, "I've got this."

Sybie turned back to Byron, alarmed but too weak to argue, and like a zombie, retreated in the shadows and disappeared back into the condo. Byron motioned and stepped out to the lawn, not wanting to alarm Sybie and hoping not to be arrested.

The policemen removed his hat and began, "I'm Bill Hill. Are you Byron Kelly?"

Byron nodded.

Officer Hill offered his hand, a nice disarming touch, then looked at his notes said, "Mr. Valentin Deroche has filed a charge that you assaulted him." Officer Hill was a tall, thin man, guessed to be in his forties, wearing a bulletproof vest for safety or exaggerated appearance, making him appear a bodybuilder muscular man who could take care of himself. Dressed in his tactical navy-blue uniform, his belt strapped high around his waist, heavy with his handgun, radio, handcuffs, and mace. His smile conveyed he policed more on the benevolent side and would be easy to talk to but be leery of. Byron avoided offering a lot of information but wanted to cooperate.

"How do you know him?"

No doubt officer Hill had the answers to most of the questions, or at least a version of them, so Byron cooperated.

"He is the President and CEO of the company I work for. Worked for."

"Oreves, Inc. Is that the name of the company?" Hesitating, looking up from his notes, "Does it mean something? Somebody's name?" His non-confrontational manner was disarming.

"Nay. It's a made-up word…French. The founder was French. Gold dreams. Something like that."

Looking back to his notes, Officer Hill continued, "What do you do there?"

"I'm a senior partner…was…it's an investment banking company."

The questions flowed, covering his role in the company, his relationship with Valentin, the incident, whether he attacked him, and what prompted the altercation until Sybie's sudden reappearance at the front door. She stepped outside.

"Sybie, this is Officer Hill. He's just asking a few questions. It's nothing important. "It's about the company. Everything is okay. I'll be in in a minute." Byron made eye contact with Officer Hill, hoping for cooperation. "Sybie is about to be my wife."

The officer studied her, and his lips parted as he nodded, unmistakable she was gravely ill. "I won't be long, Ma'am."

Sybie leaned against the door jam. "Is everything okay, Byron?"

Placing his hand on her shoulder, nodding, he said. "Everything is fine. I'll be in in a minute."

Sybie wanted to say something, sighed, couldn't find the energy to respond, turned, and disappeared inside.

Officer Hill cleared his throat, stiffened, and looked to the closed front door as he mulled questions about the woman who just disappeared into the house, unsure whether to ask as he evaluated its pertinence to the investigation.

"She's not doing very well." Byron offered. "We are getting married tomorrow."

Officer Hill hesitated, trying to get a fix on the situation—she was frail and very sick, but they were getting married the next day. He decided to lighten the moment. "Hope getting married isn't making her sick."

Byron felt some chemistry with the police officer and tried to address what he thought was on his mind. "She has cancer." Not wanting to linger on her situation, he quickly added, "The altercation was about business. Valentin was upset about a client we lost, and we had words. No doubt I overacted…"

Before Byron added anything else, the officer broke in. "It sounds like your disagreement got out of hand. You know I'm not the final word, but it sounds like he sought you out, so it wasn't like you were pursuing him, right? You didn't invite him here, did you?"

"No. He gets a little carried away sometimes. Look, I'm not sure I should admit to shoving him, but I did want him to leave."

Officer Hill wrote a few notes and closed his notebook. His narrowed gaze added importance to the question, "Did you hit him?"

Byron hesitated and locked on to his eyes, "Yes, I did."

"I don't know how far he'll pursue this, but no doubt there's more you'll have to deal with." Hesitating, pondering what to say next. "I interviewed Mr. Deroche. Let's just say he seems to be carrying a grudge, and he's…well he's a handful." Putting his hat on to leave, he added, "You don't look like the kind of guy who needs advice, so we'll just leave it if you want to get an attorney, you will. Here is a copy of the complaint. A warrant will be issued for your arrest, and you will be required to appear in court to answer the charges."

"This is a bad time to be going through all this," Byron humbly offered.

Officer Hill looked aside toward the closed front door. Rubbing his chin, he said, "Yeah. Getting married, huh? I'll do what I can to delay things. But you will have to answer to this."

Officer Hill gripped Byron's shoulder, "Good luck."

Byron clenched his jaw and held out his hand. "Thanks."

Chapter Two

Starting out on the same route of a memorable trip with Sybie a few years back, Byron motored through Snoqualmie Pass and across the Columbia River to Coeur d'Alene, Idaho. There he resisted the pull of the car to turn north onto Highway 95 toward Banff, Canada. Instead, he stayed on Highway 90 through the Bitterroot Mountains and crossed the Continental Divide at Homestead Pass in Montana.

The Pacific in the rearview mirror, he reached the dark side, east of the Cascade Mountains, where Sybie said night came from. She wouldn't want a broken heart to be his lasting reminiscence, so he stiffened his resolve to leave her memory on the sunny side of the mountains.

Driving through Montana felt like wandering across a desert of brownfields as the highway ate away at his anger and sadness—the perfect transition to anonymity. All day, the sky was clear and wide—the only clouds on the horizon were forming their own mountains. His memory of the trip would be the gray pavement beyond the hood of his Blazer, the hum of tires and engine, and the occasional familiar auto companions—sometimes, they were in front of him, sometimes behind.

His Blazer didn't have a CD player, so it was just the radio and the view out the window. When one radio signal was lost, he found another. He tried to avoid news channels, which mostly looped day-old stories speculating on a recession, troops to Uganda, and the announcement Steve Jobs died at the age of fifty-six, the founder of Apple. T. S Elliot said the radio was the only medium of entertainment that permitted millions of people to listen to the same joke at the same time and yet remain lonesome.

The used Blazer was new to Byron, a trade-in for his Mercedes. He smiled as he recalled the car salesman's expression when he told him what he wanted to do—trade his Mercedes for a used Blazer. Not having a CD player was the last thing on his mind. The salesman figured Byron's expectations were too high to make such an improbable deal, then stifled a grin when Byron said, "Whatever you think is fair." They did the deal on the spot, titles exchanged, and the salesman threw in new floor mats and tires.

The further from Seattle, the more Byron questioned his decision to leave against his attorney's advice. Before meeting Nicholas Baer, the attorney recommended by a former Oreves colleague, Byron received a white-collar warrant demanding a court appearance the following Wednesday and separately a copy of the lawsuit. Reading through several pages of allegations and damage claims, he wondered how a simple case of revenge could require so many pages.

Nicholas Baer's office was on the thirty-fourth floor of the Columbia Center in downtown Seattle. A middle-aged man, likable, athletically built—and judging by the array of memorabilia in his office, a fanatical Seahawks fan. Byron was numb and in no mood for friendly banter, but the run-up to business conversations was small talk, so he fidgeted in his chair for several minutes as the attorney droned on about the Seahawks and the new coach, a college coach no less. His voice faded in and out as Byron braced himself, rehearsing his story, hoping to minimize his time there. It occurred to him he'd better like this attorney because he didn't have the time to search for another.

As the attorney skimmed through the documents, Byron described the criminal complaint, feeling it explained a lot about the lawsuit, emphasizing the background, including stories about Valentin, his ego and controlling ways, and how they had been feuding. He admitted shirking some responsibilities when taking care of his sick wife but was still contributing to the company.

"I was a senior partner, for God's sake. When Sybie, my wife…" It felt nice saying that. "When she started having serious health problems…" It was still hard to say cancer. "She had cancer. Valentin was upset about how much time I spent with her. Then, when the Sunnyside deal fell through, he blamed me. There's more to it, but that's the gist. He came to my condo and started haranguing that I wasn't following orders... anyway, we had words, and he said some things about Sybie, how she was dying, and I couldn't do anything about it...what did he know anyway...I shoved him a couple of times." With regret, Byron added, "I punched him." Then, shaking his head, louder, with some conviction, "Yeah, I punched him. He wasn't hurt. He drove away."

For fifteen minutes, Nicholas sat emotionless and waited for Byron to get the whole story out in his way. When finished, as casually as talking about the Seahawks, Nicholas asked, "Cancer, huh?"

Byron wanted to avoid talking about it. Nicholas had no idea what he had endured. Shrugging his shoulder, stifling tears he learned were a breath away, refusing to give in, he drew his lips up tight and narrowed his gaze. Angry and determined, he nodded.

After a series of questions and occasional side trips to explain legal principles, the attorney offered his best guess how things would proceed. There was the assault charge and two civil cases, one arising out of the assault charge and the other out of Byron's purported abandonment of the company and negligence.

"Winning on the criminal charge is important to their strategy," Nicholas continued. "So, they will go all-in to win. They are counting on the assault charge to prop up the civil suit for abandoning your duty as an officer of the company. Valentin will no doubt make all sorts of outrageous claims. His civil suit will not merely be about the money, although he will claim significant damages, which we can beat down. It's all a setup for the final suit, the one they claim you damaged the company. By the sound of it, this will be more about winning and crushing you. Of course, they can win the civil suit without winning the criminal one."

Byron was pretty good at getting to the bottom line. Valentin would spare no expense to destroy him and ask for the stars if he wanted the moon. Even the moon would be a significant amount.

At first, the attorney exuded confidence they would win the lawsuit. He said Valentin had a weak case. "You were taking care of your sick wife, for God's sake. We'll attack Valentin's management style—his attorney will explain all this to him. This was a vendetta." Though, as the discussion continued, Byron's confidence waned. He figured attorneys always talked about winning but had settlement on their minds.

"Byron…Byron…are you listening to me?"

Byron shifted his gaze from the window and dark brooding clouds forming on the horizon over the Sound—rain was coming again. Shaking his head, Byron looked slowly back to Nicholas. "Yes. Yeah, taking care of my wife."

"Beating the assault charge and civil suit will be important to winning the big one. You were caring for your wife." He repeated, nodding his satisfaction, "This is an awkward transparent vendetta against you at the worst time of your life. We'll even bring Valentin to tears with our sob story. Oh, we'll win this."

Byron swallowed hard and gazed at Nicholas. *Winning? Sob story?* Nicholas rose and moved around his desk and sat in a chair nearby, and put his hand on his shoulder. "We have a good case. We'll win," he repeated.

The meeting shifted. Nicholas lowered his voice. "There are other things to consider." Of course, by duty, attorneys lay it all out, then a little by design after telling him they would win, they express the realities and unreliability of the law. In between the lines of the good and bad news, it was going to be costly. That was how it worked—big companies like Oreves, with endless resources, always knew the cost of winning favored them and factored into their strategy. He didn't say it, but Byron knew he wasn't going to be cheap, and of course, finally, the punch line came when he reminded, they could lose, too. That message always came at the end, like a footnote. Meetings with attorneys never start with, "We could lose this."

Sure, the attorney's duty was to lay out all the legal disclaimers. That was what attorneys did, as much marketing as law. They loved to spew out rehearsed college classroom arguments to the lively music of a fox hunt. In reality, after so many years of practicing law, attorneys avoided wasting time in court—take the easier route and settle—not about right or wrong, make the client feel like he won something. A Settlement; Byron hated the thought. Paying money for nothing, but just to feel pain.

Nicholas summed it up. "With all that, we hold a wild card."

"Wild card?"

"Something beyond the law. Beyond the humdrum…outside the usual predictable legal arguments we hear over and over. We have your wife's illness. There is the law, but in real life, everything is emotional, and in this case, it could govern the outcome. Wait and see."

Byron turned away and took a deep breath. *No matter what Nicholas said, Valentin wins.* He turned his thinking to other options and began to formulate a plan.

"By the way, Byron, how's that wife of yours doing?"

Byron reacted stone faced, "She died. Sybil. That was her name. She died."

***

Byron returned his focus to the roadway and shook off thinking about the meeting. He saw it on Nicholas' face when he told him his wife died, how it made things so easy for him, so theatrical. The attorney would never say it. But he'd thought it… *she died, even better.*

He hadn't driven a car this far in his life. Chicago, Illinois, was two thousand miles away. Exhausted, but not wanting to stop for the night and just mid-way through Montana—*I can't believe the state is so big.* Outside of Billings, Montana, he turned south on Interstate 90, looking for a place to stop; he wearily continued on the longest stretch of highway he faced all day until urgency met necessity. Still, in Montana, he passed accommodation signs for Lodge Grass and Forty Mile Colony, but they seemed to be miles off the highway, and he pressed on. Nearing the Wyoming border, he committed to stopping in the first Wyoming town, no matter what. If he couldn't find a motel soon, he would sleep in the car.

In Wyoming, there wasn't much to choose from but exhausted and dreading another twenty miles to Sheridan, he elected to stay in the Ranch Motel for forty-nine dollars. There were two cars in the parking lot. A lumpy mattress, noisy heater, a flickering neon vacancy sign outside his window, the inescapable thoughts of the past few days and gruesome realities he faced made for a short sleepless night.

The next morning there was frost on the ground, so he unpacked his brown Bass and Ringneck car length hunting coat his dad had given him. Gassing up, he saw an Army soldier with a troubled look on his face studying the gas pump across from him. He recognized the soldier as a car traveling companion, mile after dreary mile across Montana. He noticed Byron right away but avoided eye contact.

The soldier looked troubled, so Byron stepped to the other side of the pump. "Everything okay?"

"Sure, everything's fine." He looked away, so Byron returned to his side of the pump. A few minutes later, the soldier appeared. "There is a little problem. I don't have enough gas to get him home. I'm on leave and had a flat tire outside of Billings, had to buy a new tire. It cost more than I expected. I won't make it to Rapid City. There's a lot of miles left."

"Damned big state, huh?"

"If you could loan me some money, give me your address, I'll repay you."

"Are you kidding? I'll do one better. I'll fill your car and call it a thank you for your service."

The soldier smiled awkwardly. He didn't like asking for help. Soldiers were used to doing the helping. "Thank you, sir."

Right now, it felt good to be called sir.

After filling his car with gas, Byron moved to the other side of the pump, shook the soldier's hand, and gave him a hundred dollars. "Here is a little something else." Byron never knew this end of generosity could feel so good.

It didn't take long to sink back into his routine, gobbling up the highway and warding off memories of Sybie and Valentin. But unavoidably, random thoughts of Sybie bubbled to the surface in a burst of movie-like scenes. He was irresistibly aware of her picture in his backpack on the seat next to him, the one he had taken on that memorable trip to Banff. He quickly pushed aside recollections of the trip, but his resistance waned, worn down staring at a horizon and hundred miles to the next town road signs that never changed.

***

Details of when he met Sybie, were always there, dry tender, a spark away from a roaring inferno. On that fateful life-changing day, still a young man, he had no way to know the future.

When he woke Friday morning, his senior year of high school, something was different, like yesterday he was a boy and today a man, but not quite. Byron felt more grown-up today, but it didn't seem right. Manhood happened more slowly than overnight, came on more like creeping tide.

He felt something was going to happen, not impending doom, far from it, but a tugging expectation of the new, something extraordinary. High school graduation was a few weeks away, and time crawled by. For ten days in a row, late spring rains blocked out reminders of the sun. When it wasn't raining hard, it was misting gloom.

Rainy days weren't unfamiliar to Cascadians of Work, Washington, where he grew up, a mere two hundred feet above sea level caught between Mount Rainer's shadow, a capturer of fourteen thousand foot passing clouds and the Pacific Ocean. More than friendly eye candy, Mount Rainer was better known to locals as one of the world's most dangerous volcanoes.

It wasn't the weather getting him down. His father always said quarreling with the weather was like arguing balls and strikes. For the first time since he was eight years old, he wasn't playing spring baseball, an unfamiliar feeling, not entirely explained by last fall's football injury. That didn't explain his mood shift, either, although having his boyhood football stardom dreams dashed was partially responsible.

Monday morning, he intended to rise early and catch Mr. Frazer before classes. On the way to school, his 1981 two-tone rusted Chevy C30 pickup his dad gave him puffed blue smoke out the exhaust pipe. No, that didn't explain what disturbed him—not the football injury, not playing baseball, the blue smoke, or wasting his time with the notorious Mr. Frazer. It was a girl. Not even a girlfriend.

When Byron arrived at school, he found Mr. Frazer sitting at his desk wearing one of his several white shirts, head resting on his hand, flipping through papers. When he looked up, he saw Byron standing before him, no doubt waiting to hear the same thing he told hundreds of students before.

"Mr. Frazer, are you giving me a B in history?"

Drawing up off his elbow, "Mr. Kelly, why would you think that? Do you deserve a B?"

"Because you never give students an A in your class, and because you gave me a B on the final exam."

"That sounds like a B grade to me. And, I did give one of my students an A."

Byron was going to graduate at the top of his class. For sure, a B in history wouldn't change that. The vice-principal had already asked him to speak to the graduating class. That meant he was valedictorian. Still, Mr. Frazer gave him a B in history because he missed a couple of dates on the final exam.

"Byron, I gave you a final grade of B plus."

"For missing a couple of dates, actually transposing a couple of digits." It didn't seem fair for missing two dates—transposing two digits. Why was it so important to get the exact dates on a test? How important was that to his future? What did it have to do with anything? It was about as important as missing a comma on an essay.

"So, maybe you deserved a B for your carelessness. What's wrong with a B plus, anyway? Not many other kids got that grade."

"This is not a class on carelessness," Byron retorted. "It's not an A, and all of my other grades are A."

"So, I should give you an A because all your other grades are an A?"

Shifting from foot to foot, feeling trapped, sensing there wasn't a thing left to say, but still he wanted to tell him how unfair it was, or something he might regret, or worse, start sounding like he was begging.

Biting his lip, Byron looked back to the clock hanging above the door. Startled, he gasped, turned, and without a word, rushed from the classroom and raced down the hallway dodging in and out of other students. When he rounded the corner, his worst fear realized, there on the floor sat Sybil Kobak, among papers and books scattered on the floor, her leg brace just beyond her outstretched hand. Students standing nearby watched her, slowly moving to help.

Dropping to his knees, Byron pulled her leg brace up to her. "I am so sorry; I'm late. Crap, I'm having a bad day."

"Yeah, bad day." Her sarcasm was obvious.

Byron gathered up her papers and stacked them on top of her books. Looking at her for the first time, he stared awkwardly at her blue eyes, magnified by thick corrective lenses with one eye angling off to the side. Sybil was a junior and new to Work High School. He had seen her in the hallways a few times recently. When he added his name to the list of volunteers who helped her get from class to class, he learned her disabilities prevented her from attending school until now. He wondered how severe her disabilities were, or maybe she was afraid. Who would blame her?

Byron had second thoughts about putting his name on the help Sybil list, afraid, fearing what he didn't know. Today, he helped her get to and from class, the cafeteria at lunchtime, and her ride after school. At lunchtime, he helped her through the cafeteria line and found her a seat where she could set her brace on the floor out of the way of foot traffic. Afterward, he went through the cafeteria line and joined her.

She looked surprised when Byron took a seat across from her. "This isn't part of the deal, you know."

Byron's mouth dropped open. "What deal?"

"Helping me. You don't have to eat lunch with me."

"Is it okay if I do?

Sybil answered with a nod.

She wasn't what he expected. Looking past her disability and corrective glasses that magnified the bluest blue eyes he had ever seen, pretty, without any makeup, her face was round, her complexion polished, her black hair pulled back in a ponytail. "So, do your friends call you Sybil?" Immediately the question felt dumb.

A smile crept into the corner of her mouth and spread across her face. "Friends? You can call me Tic Toc like the other kids if you want."

Byron wondered if she detected his embarrassment, no doubt aware behind her back kids called her Tic Toc because of the way she shifted back and forth as she walked. Was it a serious comment? Maybe she would smile and laugh it off.

"No. I'll call you Sybil."

"That was a joke." Sybil smiled.

Byron returned her smile.

"Sure, you can call me Sybil. So, Byron Kelly, the next great quarterback for the Washington Huskies, what do they call you?"

Grinning, he answered, "They call me Byron. You a football fan?"

"My dad took me to a few of your games."

Maybe a football knee injury didn't seem like a big deal to her. She must be the only person who didn't know the extent of his injuries. Like everyone else in Work, expecting him to be the town's football hero, the next great Husky quarterback. "Not going to happen. No football in the future. Never. I'm too small and too slow. Nah, my glory days are behind me. I know that."

"Where are you going to school? Sybil asked.

"Washington U. I always wanted to go there, and we can't afford out-of-state tuition or private college." Byron pondered, wondering whether to ask about her plans and decided to ask anyway. "What are your plans?"

"I'm going to art school…" Sybil hesitated and with a hint of sadness, continued, "If I learn how to… how to…well, everything. I can't go to school and expect people to wait on me."

"I hope you do."

Byron wanted to get off the subject, for her sake and his. Still upset with his conversation with the history teacher, he asked, "Do you have Frazier for history?"

"Yes. He's one of my favorites. He goes out of his way to help me. Getting an A in his class."

Byron shook his head and bit his lip to hide his irritation. "Really? Must be he just doesn't like me. Maybe he doesn't like football players." Looking away to hide his disgust and then back to a smiling Sybil, as if she didn't have a care in the world. It should be hard to have such a nice smile in her situation.

My Sybie. The woman who always counted her blessings with the knowledge every day was borrowed and with angel hands, painted his favorite watercolor—A Lonely Cloud and Field of Daffodils. It turned out to be a blessing growing up under a cloud of ridicule, as Tic Toc, and then be granted life as a beautiful, successful woman, the woman who taught him perseverance and love.

"Oh, Sybie!" The sound of his voice broke the car silence and startled him.

The sign, 'Welcome to Iowa, Where the Tall Corn Grows,' flashed before him. Seeing the sign triggered the realization he was on the wrong road, not entering Minnesota as planned, heading south instead of east. Slamming his hand against the steering wheel and jerking the car to the side of the road, he opened the highway map.

How did I miss the turn and end up in Iowa? I must have been sleep-driving. When Byron figured out what he had done, he decided not to backtrack. And, when he looked down to check the time, his watch wasn't there. The Shinola watch cost him a thousand dollars, and he left it on the motel nightstand. No matter, no schedule to meet—nothing but time. It was just a watch.

How could life take such a radical and permanent turn? No matter who you are or what you are doing, you never know what is around the next corner. His dad told him, "You can be on top of the world and in a minute fall to the bottom. Take nothing for granted. Tragedy is pitiless and doesn't give one damn who you are." All the success, all the money in the world couldn't change that one fact.

Chapter Three

Manhood consequences. As a young boy, Byron recovered from mistakes with ease, and sloughed them off. Now in manhood, he was supposed to know better, consequences enlarged, and recovery more challenging. Yeah, he chose this path, or anger picked it, but he never imagined anger would be a determinate of his path in life. He'd do it all again. He didn't regret a thing. If he had known where life would take him, he still would have punched him. He went down like a first-round knockout. Oh yeah, he wished he had punched him harder.

Byron's career ended with no future in sight, and so many memories—the past and future incompatible, his only plan now to get lost.

He continued on Interstate 29 South, connected with Interstate 80, and turned to east, which would take him to Chicago. He couldn't remember why he picked Chicago, except as a place he enjoyed traveling to, and with a population of over three million people, he could get lost there—a city where dead people voted, and he could change his identity.

Five hundred miles to go. Flipping through news channels, he quickly picked up on the journalistic genres, opinion, sports, hard news, each one catering to a bottom line that required feeding listeners' desired slants on the news—not always news, sometimes fabrications. Some even buried stories that didn't fit the corporate narrative of their media niche. Byron felt it was unethical for a purported news station to be so slanted. If a company couldn't win ethically, it shouldn't be in business. He felt ethics should be a required standard and refused to be one of the millions of people who blindly pledged allegiance to a political party or a favorite bought-off talking-head—talking-head millionaires reading news off a teleprompter.

As for personal finances, Byron traveled with enough money to get by for quite a while—a long while, but it wouldn't buy invisibility. Before he left, he obtained three cashier's checks with no payees, akin to carrying a suitcase of cash. Anybody who got their hands on these cashier's checks could cash them, and there wouldn't be a thing he could do about it, so he purchased a lightweight passport travel pouch he wore around his neck under his shirt.

There were other challenges to cashing the checks once he arrived in Chicago. Banks might be suspicious of a large, very large cashier's check made out to cash, so he obtained the checks from a large national banking firm—branch banks were less suspicious of their own cashier's checks. Also, a bank would be less suspicious of money deposited rather than cashed, so he planned to open an account and needed a new identity and a job.

It was Fall harvest time in Iowa. He passed white farmhouses, red barns, and mile after mile of fields of golden corn, the color of Iowa, combines poked their heads out over the top of corn stalks. Time, facing an unknown future, and memories were an unwelcome amalgamation.

***

Byron leaned his head back onto the headrest and smiled, recalling he had been a full partner of Oreves, with the pick of clients, large and small. Inexplicably he opted to handle the remodel refinancing of the Sound Tower, prime real estate in the heart of Seattle, three blocks up the hill from Pike's Market and not far from his office.

The image now so real, standing alone, sipping a glass of Champaign, Byron scanned the lobby approvingly. Italian leather sofas and granite tables were arrayed around the room atop quarry tile. Brazilian marble walls handpicked for their subtle swirls had to be cut and pieced together like a giant jigsaw puzzle. A 200-inch flat-screen television spanned the wall behind the security reception desk flashing landscapes in brilliant colors and hues.

The invitation described the affair as a formal occasion, so most of the men were dressed in tuxes and the ladies in gowns. Byron didn't have a lady to bring, and since he worked only a few blocks away, it was too much of a hassle to change clothes. He meant to wear a dark suit to work, but it was Friday, with nothing important on the calendar, so he wore a blue blazer and silver and navy rep tie. He was glad he wore the white shirt. Starting his career, how he dressed seemed important, but success and time had a way of clarifying what was necessary.

The three-story domed ceiling featured an indirectly lit mural of white puffy clouds and blue sky. The glass three-story windows on one side provided variations of light throughout the day and added much-needed daylight—this part of the country was famous for dark days. In the center of the room, a forty-foot-tall modern sculpture drew admiring looks and dominated conversations. A string quartet played classical music.

Standing in a crowded room, seemingly invisible to others, he watched the other guests and admired the results of his financial dealings. The financial aspects of the project weren't all that challenging, but he enjoyed local work so close to the office. Alone for the first time all day—in a crowd of hundreds, he thought back to high school daydreams of playing quarterback for the Huskies, wondering if the two inches of height and twenty pounds he added since then would have made a difference. No one threw a tighter spiral than he did.

Being a football player wasn't meant to be. But life worked out better than he dreamed—better than being the quarterback. It hadn't turned out badly for the famous Huard brothers either.

Byron's unrivaled rare feat, rising to the top of an industry crowded with tenured, well-established older men and few women before turning twenty-eight, came somewhat fortuitously, not so much for the guy who hired him, his mentor, Walter Simpson, second in command under Valentin. Walter hired him right out of college and immediately assigned him to work with on the biggest deals.

Halfway through the merger of two powerful tech companies, Walter had a heart attack. Fifty-seven, overweight smoker, and a heavy drinker, a doctor could have just looked at him and known he was heading for a heart attack. An annual physical would have detected his clogged arteries, or so would have an autopsy. Lucky for him, coronary artery bypass grafting of five arteries saved his life. Walter always bragged, a cigarette hanging from his mouth and drink in hand; he'd be ready when his name was called. Now, in his recovery, he said he ought to quit smoking.

There was never a good time for a heart attack, not for Walter especially, and not for Oreves, but not so bad for Byron. When the merger of two tech giants was about halfway to the goal line, the largest deal Oreves ever handled and the largest of Walter's career, he was struck down suddenly while standing at the bar, drink in hand. There were others in the company more qualified than Byron to carry the ball over the goal line. But Byron had been with the project from the start, and his education provided more understanding of the tech industry than anyone else in the company.

The deal stalled, and Byron received a lot of credit for saving it. The original deal ran into some anti-trust issues, then it became a political issue, as everything always does, usually requiring a pay-off like in third world countries, until he navigated around the politics and convinced both camps no one was going to be a winner, except the merger itself. He was surprised how quickly the deal came together when the politics cleared. A year later, he achieved full partner status.

As Byron scanned the lobby for familiar faces, he saw a college classmate friend standing in the center of the room next to the sculpture. Just beyond him, a woman formally dressed in a silky, flowing ivory-colored evening dress, adorned with a chandelier pendant rhinestone necklace and matching earrings. Her long black hair was layered in a French twist updo. She looked vaguely familiar. He watched her throughout the evening, and each time their gazes connected, she smiled coyly like there was a secret. He strained to conjure up her image, again and again, trying to connect it with a name or previous meeting.

Byron weaved his way toward his friend, through the guests, waiters, and waitresses offering Champagne and hors d'oeuvres on silver trays, stopping once to shake hands with the president of Pacific Bank Corporation toward his friend Charles Wardlaw, Chip. He couldn't recall the origin of his nickname. He was standing in the middle of the room admiring the modern, twisted Mobius strip—mirror-polished stainless-steel sculpture, entitled Perseverance. Chip earned an advanced degree in aeronautics and engineering and was now working for Boeing. Like Byron, he was a drop-in and not dressed in formal attire.

As Byron shook Chip's hand, he peeked over his shoulder at the woman in ivory. Slapping his friend on the back, "I expected I'd see you here with all the free food and drinks." It was a familiar joke between old fraternity brothers historically enticed by occasions of free food and drink. Two minutes into the conversation, choosing between rudely not listening to his old friend or making a quick, honest exit, Byron interrupted. "I'm sorry, but there is someone I have to say hello to."

"No problem. I have to scoot anyway. Dad will be wondering what happened to me. We need to get together."

"Next time you come down, call me. Let's have dinner. Bring your father."

Without shifting his gaze from the woman in the ivory dress, he walked toward her. She was so familiar, yet he couldn't recall her name or even meeting her before. When he arrived, a sudden glimmer of recollection struck him and left him momentarily speechless. The stunning woman standing before him was no longer a girl. Could this be Sybil, the girl they called Tic Toc?

"I know you," Byron said, still lacking confidence. It all seemed so improbable. It was meant to be a question. What to say next tumbled over and over in his mind. "That's a beautiful dress you're wearing."

She looked at him curiously. "It's the only nice dress I own. If you ever run into me again at another formal occasion, I'll be wearing this one."

And I'll probably be wearing this sport coat, he pondered. "I hope I do. Sybil!" Byron burst out with confidence. "It's you. Sybil. Look at you. You are all grown up." His mind raced. Again, it wasn't what he intended. He wanted to say, 'You are a beautiful woman.' Was it okay to say that?

The string quartet finished one Rachmaninoff piece and began to play Rhapsody on the Theme of Paganini. As they were talking, Byron's gaze angled away to the 'Perseverance' sculpture. The sculpture looked different from this angle. He noticed a straight rod rose vertically through the modius mirror-polished twisted sculpture. From this angle, it resembled a human figure. Looking back to Sybil, "That's so cool. That sculpture."

Without looking away, Sybil smiled, "Thank you."

"Did you have something to do with that?"

A mischievous smile swept across her face. "Why do you ask?"

"It reminds me of something."

"Or someone? Yes, I commissioned it. I was the lead interior designer on this project."

"You work for Sally McSally Interiors? Good company. Good for you. Perseverance, that's you."

"Nobody, not another person, will understand. I don't think anyone from high school would even remember me. Oh well, that's fine with me."

Looking back to the sculpture, and with a wave of his hand, Byron said, "That's you for sure. "Perseverance," he repeated.

"Yeah, sometimes we all need a little bracing up."

Chapter Four

Byron didn't contact Sybil for three weeks after he obtained her telephone number. Two of those weeks, he was in Paris, France, and returned with a head cold. He intended to call her but recalled their parting conversation every time he pulled the phone out. He felt like a schoolboy when he asked for her number, and she was reluctant to give it to him. She didn't say no, but the warmth between them went suddenly cold. A serious, contemplative look swept across her face and left him speechless. It was like proposing marriage and being rejected. Before separating, she gave him her number, hesitantly.

He assumed there was someone else in her life, and she didn't want to complicate things or tell him he was too late. Byron decided to call anyway. When he finally called her, she seemed excited to hear from him and quickly agreed to meet. As it turned out, they both lived north of the Seattle loop, so agreed to meet at a nearby coffee shop near the Lake Union Marina.

Relationships can evolve over time or suddenly like the striking of a match. Their relationship progressed more like building a house—laying the foundation and then walls, the roof, the interior, and furnishings. For several weeks they met for coffee and lunch, then once a week official dates: a Friday night movie, dinner at the Osprey Restaurant near the Bitter End Marina on the Jib Sail on Lake Union, an evening of dancing at a popular downtown nightclub with live entertainment, a play at the Sound Theater Company and Sunday matinée performance of Les Mis at the Paramount Theatre, the third time for him, the first for Sybil. He tried to cover up his tears, but she bawled, and afterward, standing outside the theater, they held each other for the first time.

Still, there was an invisible barrier between them. It felt like the relationship was settling on being best friends, the last thing Byron wanted. They enjoyed their time together, texted back and forth like teenagers, laughed at each other jokes, after a while finished each other's sentences, and giggled at the concurrence of it. Being her brother was the last thing he wanted. When he touched her arm, sometimes she stiffened, and when he took her hand walking along the marina, it was cold and stiff. Every time he attempted to probe her feelings, she cleverly changed the subject.

Months of rainy, cloudy days blotted out the sun, finally yielded to lingering blue-sky days. The Northwest was at its best in the summer. To celebrate, Byron and Sybil ferried to Friday Harbor, the San Juan Islands, toured the fine-art galleries and specialty shops, enjoyed deli sandwiches for lunch sitting on a park bench near the harbor, and frozen yogurt for dinner.

The bluest blue sea reflected up through the green forested shoreline rising up to snowy mountain peaks across the bay. They felt like poets silently watching white cumulous clouds rush by sailboats returning to their slips. The setting sun transformed the early summer day into a magical evening. Even from this distance, they could see Mount Rainer.

"What are you thinking?" Byron asked.

Sybil sighed. "This view empties your mind. I think this is the most beautiful place in the world."

"I don't remember feeling so alive. It's incredible." Waving his hand toward the snowcapped peak of Rainer, he added. "I was born there, in the shadow of that mountain. I spent my childhood and youth there. Sometimes I feel I've already lived three different lives. I remember as a child wanting my mother to read to me at night when she tucked me in, and then suddenly I'm the football star dreaming of playing in the NFL. Today, I'm a man who works all the time and doesn't even notice what a beautiful place we live in."

Starring off in the distance, Sybil reflected. "I wasn't born there but moved there when I was young. I always imagined climbing to the top of Rainier someday. One of my many dreams."

"That's a nice dream. They say the most beautiful place in the world is Banff."

"I've heard. I'd love to go there."

Swallowing hard, ever so gently venturing his wish, "Would you like to go sometime?"

Without the slightest hesitation, Sybil answered, "I'd love to."

Stunned, Byron asked cautiously, "With me?"

She hooked her arm inside of his and answered, "Especially with you."

Warmed by her touch and the tactility of her soft declaration, he said, "The summer season is short there unless you like to Ski; we'd have to go soon. I'll make the arrangements." Still uneasy, he felt the uncommon warmth of her touch, but it wasn't clear how she felt, "Should I get you a room?" He ventured.

Blushing, she answered, "Not unless you want to."

The next day he began planning the trip. When he suggested they stay a full week, she hesitated but later texted, "Yes. Sure. Let's spend the week." Still, he wondered. Was she afraid of something? Did she have concerns?

Wanting the trip to be memorable, he spared no expense. He was making great money, better, no doubt than she realized. Based on the opulent accommodations he reserved, she would learn of his financial status or be left to wonder if frivolity was a side she didn't know. After all, she knew from high school days his upbringing was middle class, like hers.

Byron picked her up in the early morning to avoid the dreadful Seattle commuter traffic, and they cleared Snoqualmie Pass at sunrise. The drive to Banff was mostly small talk imbued with anticipation. Her great-grandparents fled Hungary in 1917, the year the United States declared war on them. Sadly, her last living parent passed away at forty-five when she was in her twenties.

He learned Sybil never had a serious boyfriend. He didn't press her but discovered she had been without a leg brace for several years and abandoned corrective glasses right after high school. After she told him her daily workout routine, lifting weights, the elliptical, and swimming a mile three times a week, they drove on in silence, leaving him to recall the meager half marathon he ran last year, the high point of his fitness accomplishments.

At the time, it was Byron's most extended driving trip since he purchased the silver Mercedes and drove it to Los Angeles just because it was new. Across the plains of central Washington, over the Columbia River, they headed north along the edge of the Coeur d'Alene National Forest and stopped for coffee in Bonners Ferry, Idaho, before crossing into Canada. When they passed through the narrow high granite canyon walls in Radium Springs, Alberta, Canada, they entered Banff National Forrest—from one world into another.

Byron rented the most expensive chalet he could, luxurious beyond any place he ever stayed. Surrounded by mountains, the Three Sister peak seemed so close they could reach out and touch it. After settling in, they walked along the shops on Banff Avenue and stopped at Evelyn's Coffee Shop for a cookie and hot chocolate, then rode the gondola to the top of Sulphur Mountain to watch the setting sun accentuate deep gorges, glaciers and ice fields, beautiful lakes, alpine meadows, and mineral hot springs.

Leaning on the observation deck railing, breathing in the clean mountain air, sipping wine, Byron wrapped his arm over her shoulder and pulled her close. As if a breath of wind halted their conversation mid-sentence, he turned to her. She looked deeply into his eyes. Smiling, he leaned in, their lips met, briefly, lightly, before they parted, a kiss filled with assurance and anticipation.

Evening shadows outlined amazing hoodoos, the Cascade Mountains, and pyramid rocky tops poking through low hanging clouds looking out over the panoramic valley. At times the clouds eclipsed the sun and advanced early nightfall. Byron peeked at Sybil, who was gazing intently at the clouds hurrying by as if marking the passage of life itself.

Sybil seemed to be in a trance. "It's nighttime beyond those mountains," she said. "It's where the nights come from." The sun was already low enough to see the shadows angling early nightfall to areas of the valley.

Byron wished he could read her mind. There still seemed to be hesitancy about her—he hoped it wasn't him. A thousand times, he wondered, especially at night trying to sleep—*what did she think?* Crazy mixed-up feelings swirled. What was it about her? He hadn't known her that long and yet he was warmer in her presence, tingly, at times breathless. What was that? She was here with him now—that was hopeful. But something bothered her. He knew he should give her time, but life was rushing by, like the clouds fighting to make their way over the mountains to gather on the plains.

Sybil remained transfixed by the mountain views. "I always want to live on the sunny side," she said reflectively.

Tired from the long day of driving and sightseeing, they walked back to their chalet in silence until finally, Byron broke in. "Are you okay? You seem to be someplace else."

"I'm just tired." As she spoke, a tear broke loose and rolled down her cheek. "Tired... a really good kind of tired. What a great day. One of the best days of my life."

Byron nodded in agreement. "There'll be many more."

Later, after dark, she entered the bedroom dressed in flannel pajamas. Byron could see she had been crying. "I'm so sorry. I don't know why I keep crying."

Byron went to her and pulled her head onto his shoulder. "You have nothing to be sad about. I hope those are happy tears."

"I'm scared."

"What are you afraid of?'

"I don't know. I've always been afraid...even afraid of being afraid, I guess. All my life...and, of living, maybe. Of dying. I've always lived in the shadow of wondering how I would be when I woke up in the morning. Now, being with you feels like a dream… and I have to wake up…and will I be wearing my brace?"

Byron wasn't sure how to respond.

Sybil continued. With a wave of her hand toward the bed, she said, "I don't want to…want to fail…to disappoint you.'

Suppressing a smile, Byron responded tenderly. "Please don't be concerned. We can pull the covers up to our necks, snuggle together and sleep like hibernating bears. Sleeping with you beside me is my dream."

Sybil answered forcefully. "No. I want to…want to be a woman. But it's so… I don't know…scary, I guess.

"It can't be about sex. We are surely talking about something else, something spiritual; if it happens, it won't be anything we can mess up."

The next morning the sun hadn't yet crested the mountain tops, and daylight crept into the room. In the night, Byron opened the French doors to the cold mountain air. Wrapped in each other's arms, the white down comforter was pulled up under her chin; her black hair splayed out over the pillow top. The sound of Gray Jays on the patio rail woke them.

Byron woke first, propped up on his arm, and watched as she opened her eyes. "You're awake. I've been waiting for you, Sybie."

"I've never been called that before."

"I could call you Tick Toc."

"Not anymore. You can call me Sybie. I like it."

"I'll call you Sybie then when I am not calling you, sweetheart."

Her blue eyes searched the room and out to the Gray Jays and Three Sister peak as she recalled the night before. Turning to him, she said, "Thank you for last night. I never thought that would happen?

"Never," I asked?

"I mean, never with you. Yeah, never. There was a time when I thought never. I wasn't a normal teenager."

Smiling and leaning in, he kissed her. "You're right. There is nothing normal about you. I remember the first time we met, sitting on the Work High School hallway floor."

Sybie blushed and looked away. "Thanks. Thanks for last night."

Byron chuckled. "Thanks, huh? Okay, thanks. That was a great day. Let's make today even better." No words followed, just a lingering gaze between them.

Byron broke the spell. "Louise."

"Louise? I thought you were going to call me Sybie or sweetheart."

"We had a good day, right? And last night was special." Rolling his eyes. "So special. Ever since you said you'd come to Banff with me, I've been planning today. Let's go to Lake Louise. Are you up for a hike?"

"Depends," she answered cautiously.

"The trail is a little over two miles. It's not technical. You'll be fine."

When they arrived at Lake Louise, no photo, no description, not the words of poets, prepared them for what greeted them. Standing at the water's edge, in front of the Lake Louise Hotel, an end of 19th century mountain castle, with few rivals in the world, they gazed out to an amphitheater of emerald green water, chiseled peaks, and glaciers.

The sun crested the rugged peaks. A man dressed in lederhosen, a brown Oktoberfest alpine hat with braids, and a beer stein purse, greeted the day with the ancient sound of a Swiss Alphorn, a cone-shaped wood instrument used 4,000 years ago as a way to signal the daily activities of shepherds. It reminded them of a Ricola cough candy commercial.

The hike to Lake Agnes took a little over one hour. It began at 6,000 feet, and in a little over two and a half miles, they gained 1,300 vertical feet. The hike was filled with promise, another persistence toward a dream. Along the trail, little white flowers grew impossibly in the shade and out of rocks—noticeably determined to live.

Well along the way, they rested and hydrated beside Mirror Lake. When they heard a small waterfall carrying overflow from Lake Agnes, they knew they were close to the end of the hike. When they arrived at Lake Agnes, they climbed the stairs to a log cabin house, ordered a simple Earl Gray green tea from a menu of over 100 teas, and sat on the porch overlooking the lake. Lunchtime, they ate a bowl of tomato vegetable barley soup and peanut butter and fresh jam sandwiches on warm from the oven whole wheat bread. Afterward, they sat on a bench lakeside and fed the chipmunks who climbed onto their laps and ate out of their hands.

Later they moved to a flat boulder that lined the shoreline to while away the precious moments and delay the end of the hike, clinging to today. Sybie's long glossy black hair rustled in the breeze and across her face.

Byron tossed a pebble far out into the lake.

"Touchdown," she joked.

"I'll never forget that time in the hallway when I helped you with your books…"

"When you were late to help me, you mean," she interrupted.

"Yeah, that time," he smiled. "I saw someone special in those thick glasses… maybe they magnified your soul…whatever. I saw what a beautiful person you were. I'll never forget the moment. Then our lives rushed by…but you know I never forgot. And running into you at the grand opening was like being beamed back to earth, like beam me up, Scotty."

They laughed as Byron reached out for her hand. "And, I rematerialized into reality." They laughed harder, and she laid her head on his chest.

"You're going to find what I'm about to say a bit shocking. I hope we get married someday. Spend our life together."

Sybie stiffened and drew back.

"Oops, don't be offended. I'll make an official proposal when its time."

"Sybie gasped and sat upright, a serious expression swept across her face. "You're right. That is shocking."

"I'm a man who knows what he wants."

"Remember I told you my dad took me to your football games. I saved all your newspaper clippings, pinned them on my bedroom wall. I always dreamed we would go out, but always knew reality ruled. Just like I always dreamed I would overcome my disability but then, at the same time, knew I wouldn't. My mom always scolded me and tamped down that dream. She said boys like you wouldn't date girls like me. So, I never allowed such thinking. Oh, maybe once in a while late at night, but I always scolded myself for such thinking. I was consumed by my disabilities and the desire to be normal. Yeah, that's a nice dream—marrying you. Being normal and living happily ever after is like some fairy tales. But while I wished, I never believed in fairy tales."

"It's no fairy tale. It can happen."

Sybie face turn hard and sad. Sternly, she declared, "It will never happen."

Byron's expression turned serious. "I am not asking you to decide right now. I think we are just right for each other. I get goosebumps thinking about last night."

Sybie was transfixed on a Harlequin duck swimming nearby, his mate nowhere to be seen, poking his head underwater for the longest time. "Me too, but I don't think we can ever marry. That's too hard to believe. You were always the nicest person in high school."

"Nice? Nice has nothing to do with this. With us. With last night. I hope you don't think I was trying to be nice."

Shaking her head, "No, No, that's not what I'm trying to say. I know last night was real…"

I interrupted. "Then what is it?"

Flustered, Sybie dug in. "I'm so sorry. What a beautiful thought, marrying you. I don't know what to say."

"This conversation isn't going as I intended. I'm not asking you to elope tomorrow." Frustrated, he began to laugh, just a little giggle at first, then full-throated. "I sound a little crazy, huh? Of course, I can see that happening…someday. Who knows? I'm sorry. I don't know where that came from."

Chapter Five

As Byron neared the Illinois border, his mind sharpened on the task ahead. If he lived under his real name, Byron Kelly, Valentin would find him in short order, and the whole trip would be a waste of time. He could lose all his money and face jail time.

Coming up with a new name wasn't as easy as it seemed. He considered the names of celebrities, colleagues, college professors, high school and college friends. Familiarity caused him to reject borrowing names of past colleagues. He thought about characters in books, and nothing seemed to work. He didn't feel like a Jordan, Shane or a Jay and certainly not an Atticus.

It's just a name, but harder to come up with than he thought. What did he want out of a name? Just any name wouldn't work. He wanted the name to conjure up an image, not a friendly one, but to evade friendships and fit a new persona—a loner. That was the plan, to lay low and not make friends, start a new life, and see where it took him.

Also, he needed a place to live, so he planned to check into a motel on Chicago's outskirts and begin searching for an apartment. He didn't want to sign a long-term lease—any lease for that matter, not even a contract if he could avoid it. A furnished apartment. Just a security deposit. It shouldn't cost much, given what he pictured.

As he neared the Mississippi River, he passed city signs, Davenport and Bettendorf, on the Iowa side, Rock Island and Moline, on the Illinois side. The Quad Cities. He had been to Rock Island and Moline before to meet with Deere and Company officials, long enough to remember Rock Island was the largest island on the Mississippi. There was a large military arsenal there, one of the biggest in the country.

Byron recalled helping the Army soldier. He assumed he made it home to his family. Army. Did he tell me his name? Would that work...Army? Army...Bettendorf. Bettendorf? He had never been to Iowa, had only seen the

Bettendorf sign, and wasn't familiar with the city. He said the name aloud, "Army Bettendorf." No, it didn't sound right. "Army Bendorf." The image of a troubled loner appeared. Yeah, Army Bendorf. Not sure anyone would jump to make friends with a guy named Army Bendorf. The name sounded so mysterious. Nerdy.

Crossing the border was a milestone of sorts—a new life. As he neared Chicago, the traffic intensified, so he stopped in Hoffman Estates and checked into a Hampton Inn, where they would have good internet access, as Army Bendorf and paid cash. The hotel registrar studied Byron as she assigned a room. His uncombed hair, well past the time for a haircut, disheveled appearance, and travel-weary red eyes were the perfect personas of his new identity.

After breakfast the next morning, he took his coffee to the lobby area. On a single sheet of paper, he obtained from the registration desk, Byron made notes on what needed to be done: access to the internet, a search for schools, apartments, and a job. He needed a computer, at least a tablet. He also needed a phone.

He spent two hours at the nearby Best Buy evaluating options. He knew too much to be swayed by a salesman and asked for a review of all technical specifications. He hadn't had a personal PC of his own since college. In recent years the company IT guys handled the purchase, setup up, and maintained them. He decided the better option was a PC because it fitted into a backpack. He wasn't going to be doing any excel spreadsheets, making any charts, or writing a novel. He wanted access to the internet but wasn't exactly sure what for. He wondered if he would still read financial news, track industry trends, watch the economy and the markets. Old habits are hard to break.

Byron decided on a PC with a prepaid sims card and a flip phone. He didn't need access to the internet on the phone and wasn't going to be taking pictures or sending text messages. Insurance to cover losing the phone or a warranty plan wasn't necessary. As the salesman explained why he should purchase their extended warranty plan, his business consulting background emerged as he wondered how profitable extended warranties were, more margin than the product itself, leading to speculation companies charged what the buyer would pay. He paid with cash and left the store satisfied all his purchases were under the name Army Bendorf.

Returning to the Hampton Inn, he spent the rest of the morning setting up his phone and PC, then opened a new google email account and profile. He also opened a Facebook account and began to seek out online friends in the computer field. His online profile suggested he was a long-time resident of Chicago. Now he needed a local address.

Sitting in the lobby, he searched area computer schools and enrolled in two classroom courses and three online courses. He figured he could easily earn certificates from a locally recognized school and, at the same time, gain access to career placement services. Unsure of what kind of job he could get, he covered his bases. Local certifications were most important. If there was a job open in database management, he figured a certification in Oracle would help. Given what he already knew, he might be able to fast track the training and, if willing to pay, might be able to test out of some classes.

The apartment search focused on areas north of the loop where his computer classes were. There were so many apartments to choose from it slowed his search. His needs weren't great—a furnished studio apartment near the rail line that didn't require a long-term contract, any contract for that matter, with a comfortable bed. That narrowed his choices. He also preferred underground parking, where he could buy a cover and remove the license plate. He wasn't committed to keeping the car but was concerned about selling it.

After two full days, he found an old brick four-story apartment in Evanston, twelve miles north of the Chicago Loop, in its day one of the nicest in the area, but now low maintenance and cheap rent, close to Juneway Beach, and his classes. The apartment building was rundown and poorly ventilated—the noisome blend of fried onions and burnt hamburgers drifted into the hallways but thankfully wasn't noticeable inside the studio apartment he rented on the third floor. The building manager agreed to no contract when Byron offered a year in advance.

By the end of my first week in Chicago, he had enrolled in classes, purchased a phone and computer, and moved into a furnished apartment with underground parking. He bought a television and signed up with the cable provider already hooked up in the room. The cable company offered hundreds of options. There were a limitless number of channel alternatives: infomercials, religion, news, old westerns, new movies, and old ones, sports, romance, crime shows, history, geography, fifties shows—Ozzie and Harriet, Rawhide, Have Gun will Travel, Gunsmoke, and on and on.

No matter how many viewing options there were, the apartment was dark and claustrophobic by the end of the second week. Byron began to take long walks through the neighborhood, all the way to a coffee shop near Juneway Beach, on Lake Michigan, and back to the shops and offices in downtown Evanston. He stopped in a thrift store and bought two shirts, two casual pairs of pants, and a pair of shoes. Before he left Seattle, he donated all of his dress shoes and casual loafers, so the only shoes he owned were the athletic ones on his feet. His Brooks Brothers clothes didn't feel like Army Bendorf, so he gave them away.

It was a clear sunny day; the wind blowing off the lake added a chill to the air. Byron paused in front of one of the shops and looked at his reflection. Smoothing his hair back, he rejected the thought of getting a long-overdue haircut. On the way back to the apartment, early in the afternoon on a Monday, he stopped at a neighborhood bar. The only invitation needed was the simple sign over the door, Buster's, and an old neon Budweiser advertisement. The bar smelled like stale smoke and spilled beer. There were only five patrons sitting in the dim light, two men at oak tables, two sitting on high back black vinyl bars stools, and a woman at the far end of the bar.

Byron ordered a draft Budweiser. This was a beer joint—there were no liquor bottles on the shelf behind the bar in front of a long mirror, only neatly stacked beer glasses and mugs, a display of Slim Jims, a two-gallon jar of boiled eggs, a popcorn machine, and a coffee pot. There were two cold draft beer options—Budweiser and Millers. Later, he learned there were Coors, Bud, and Miller Lite bottles, and one premium beer, Michelob, in the cooler. A small Polish flag hung in the center of the mirror.

Customers came here to drink beer and for the comradery of long-time night friends, catch up on neighbor news, and debate local and national politics. At five o'clock, right before the bar filled up with city workers, bus drivers, firefighters, and street cops, Buster brought out two crock pots of schnitzel. At five, the age distribution tilted toward a younger fortyish crowd. When the five o'clock patrons drifted out, the bar shifted back to the silver citizens.

Byron surveyed the room. It felt like a dive bar out of the forties, dust from a previous time swept up into the corner. There was a jukebox at the far end of the room and a pool table in the backroom. There were several oak tables, chairs, and booths. A large mural, dulled by years and yellowed by smoke, featuring various dogs in humanoid poses sitting at a bar dressed for a night out—a glamorous poodle sipping a Martini in serious tête-à-tête with a dapper Great Dane, a tuxedoed boxer, and a wolfhound wearing a Hugh Hefner lounge jacket competed for the attention of an alluring cocker spaniel enjoying their attention. A chihuahua sat alone on the floor at their feet, looking on enviously, nervously. The shaggy dog bartender appeared to be counseling a sporty terrier.

Not much about Buster's reminded Byron of Sybie. Dive bars were like that, more about forgetting than remembering. She wasn't a beer drinker and only enjoyed an occasional glass of Chardonnay. He wasn't much of a beer drinker either, but Buster's beer was colder than any draft beer he remembered.

During the week, he returned every night to watch the world series and a handful of others who, like him, were neither fans of the Texas Rangers nor the St Louis Cardinals. Buster's was on the north side of Chicago—Cubs territory, and once again, they weren't playing in the series, and neither was his old favorite team, the Mariners. He had attended Wrigley Field games a few times in business travels and grew to love the tormented loyal fans with a long tradition of, "We'll win it next year." Besides, a Chicagoan now, he needed a team. This year the series ended dramatically when the Rangers were one strike away from their first World Series championship when the Cardinals homered to win the game and series.

Every time he entered the apartment, closed the door, and heard the lock click into place, the loneliness struck him in the way he wanted—to be left alone. After a while, he grew accustomed to it and even preferred it. At the same time, he could be alone at Buster's too. There were no suits and ties in Buster's, and everyone left him alone unless he wanted to talk. Everyone but Gabby.

Byron remembered the first time at Buster's a gray-haired older woman sat a few barstools away at the corner of the bar. At times the men outnumbered the women ten to one, sometimes only Gabby. He guessed her to be in her sixties. Thin, with a pot beer belly and long gray straw-like gray hair that climbed down her back like a hippie, she wore no jewelry, no makeup, just black and white patterned cat eyes-glasses.

After a while, he staked out his own barstool. It was a matter of honor that nobody would knowingly take a loyal patron's seat, like Gabby's. She always sat nearby in the same seat around the corner of the bar, perched there where she could see everything going on. She knew everyone by name, and every regular knew her.

Byron avoided eye contact with her, hoping to avoid conversation. He knew from her nickname, Gabby, to avoid her.

"You becoming a regular?" Gabby asked after a while.

Not thirty seconds later, he heard the voice again, louder. "You're becoming a regular?"

Byron knew it to be more a question than a statement, so he nodded and avoided eye contact. Buster drew a draft Budweiser and sat it before him, unordered. It struck him; there was nothing more regular than the bartender knowing what you wanted to drink.

"You from here?" She had a soft, friendly voice. When she smiled, Byron noticed an incisor and a canine tooth missing from the right side of her mouth, and her skin wrinkled from years of overexposure to the sun. He had the impression life had taken a serious turn somewhere along the way, or maybe many turns. Sitting at the bar every night, clean and self-confident; otherwise, she looked to be homeless.

"I'm new to the neighborhood," he answered.

"I'm Lillian. Everyone calls me Gabby. Don't get the wrong idea about that."

They exchanged smiles. She could have been the bar's greeter, the way her eyes narrowed as her mouth stretched out, unabashed that her teeth were yellow and missing two of them.

"Army. My name is Army."

"Army, huh? Dad must have loved the Army?"

"Not really, Mom did."

"She in the Army?"

Playfully, Byron responded. "Nope, she liked Army guys. She liked the uniform. My dad was a draft dodger."

Buster listened not far away, cleaning the bar top, rubbing it like waxing a car. When the bar was empty, and the glasses were washed and wiped dry, the tables and bar top wiped down, Buster started over wiping the tables and bar tops. He moved closer. "Army, huh? Never met a guy with that name."

"Never met a guy named Buster."

Judging by the flag hanging behind the bar Buster was Polish. He was round and thick, with muscles everywhere, in his jaws, his Popeye forearms, legs, and torso. He wasn't bodybuilder muscular, but man strong, his English as good as the next guy, but with a thick tongue. His hair was so black it seemed dipped in ink. He lived above the bar.

Buster laughed, a deep belly laugh. "It's a nickname my father called me, then friends in Pulaski Park. Been carrying the name since. Now my nickname is Mack. "Get me a cold beer, Mack?" Buster smiled. "Okay, Army it is." Throwing the bar rag over his shoulder, he added, "New in town?"

Byron thought about his question. He wanted to be considered local but careful not to be caught in a lie.

Before he could answer, Gabby chimed in, "He's new to this side of town."

Hoping to avoid any more discussion, Byron added, "I just moved into an apartment off Dempster near the L."

Buster leaned on the bar. "What do you do?"

"Right now, not much. I'm taking a few computer classes to get certified. Then get a job."

"Lots of computer jobs, huh?"

"Yep, so I thought I'd get some training. Figured if I learn computer stuff, I'll never be without a job."

***

Byron learned more in his computer classes than he thought he would, but on reflection, he was surprised how fast the technology world had advanced, seemingly replacing itself even before users learned how to use it.

Every night and on the weekend, Buster tended the bar. Even on Christmas day, he opened at noon. Heaven forbid he ever got sick having no friends or family to cover the bar, only two different barmaids to work the after-work crowd.

41

According to Gabby, he lived alone above the bar—no one knew what happened to his wife.

Byron was unprepared for Chicago winter weather. When he was young, it snowed, but nothing like the bitter howling cold wind that came off the lake. He learned the hard way when the season's first major snowstorm hit. It started snowing when he left class, and by the time he exited the train, snow was whipping sideways off Lake Michigan.

The first blizzard buried Chicago area roadways with a foot of snow, cut off power to thousands of homes, and closed dozens of schools. But unlike other districts, public schools in Evanston remained open. The far north and northwest suburbs were hit hardest: close to two feet of snow and strong winds, which downed trees.

Byron's canvas hunting coat was ineffective against the sideways snow and bitter cold, and he didn't have gloves or a hat. Hoping the stores in Evanston were still open, he headed that way and purchased a thrift shop winter parka, mittens, stocking cap, and sturdier shoes. Making his way home, he turned his back to the storm, using alleyways, side streets, and buildings to block the wind.

When he awoke the next morning, more than a foot of snow had fallen, and thousands of homes were without power, many schools and businesses canceled. He called Buster and learned the bar wasn't open, but he'd open it if he came in. When he arrived, Buster was rubbing down the bar, looked up, nodded, flipped a coaster in front of Army's regular seat, and pulled a draft Budweiser. "You're becoming my best customer."

Byron was becoming the best customer of a beer joint, and the remark a friendly gesture, the kind you make to a friend. Still, Byron's plan all along was not to make friends, but he figured being friendly with the bartender wasn't too great a transgression.

Gabby came in the late afternoon. As it turned out, she wasn't so chatty after all. Curious to be sure, but her lonely side was more likely mistaken for wanting conversation.

Curious she was but tight-lipped about her personal life. Byron did learn she was married once, and it ended horribly, which explained why she tuned out discussions about bad marriages—might have been the only subject she avoided. Once in a while, she screamed at the television when the news showed pictures of battered wives, leaving Byron wondering.

Byron sat awkwardly two barstools away from Gabby, the only patron, just the sound of clinking mugs and scraping of chairs. He had the impression operating a bar included habitual quirks of obsessive behaviors—washing and drying glasses, rubbing the bar down, straightening chairs and bar stools, and today sweeping the floors. Finally, breaking the silence, Byron asked Gabby, "Where you from?'

Quick to answer, setting her beer on the bar, she leaned forward. "I'm from the part of Texas that speaks Cajun, the soggy part next to Louisiana—mosquitoes, bullfrogs, and alligators. My kinfolks came from Tevis Bluff, the original settlement of Beaumont, Texas. They call the area the golden triangle. Nothing golden to me."

"Golden?"

"A lot of rich people there but mostly poor ones. It all started with the Spindletop oil strike. The area immediately produced more oil in one day than the rest of the world's oilfields combined. My great great-granddaddy was there when oil geysered 150 feet in the air. "

"You don't sound very Cajun or Texan for that matter."

"My momma could talk Cajun. Of course, not anymore. We moved out of there when I was very young. Momma was what you call enlightened. Left her husband instead of killing him, she always said.

"As the story goes, my Great grandpappy made his money on misery. Toilet facilities being limited, he tried to get rich selling immediate access to a toilet for fifty cents. Funny, can you just picture a guy preying on weak guts. In those soupy days, he sold swamp water for drinking, which caused severe stomach cramps, or what was locally known as the Beaumonts."

Byron smiled and took a drink. She might be gabby, but she was full of personality. He pondered whether to invite more conversation but didn't have to.

"When I was a little girl, my momma ran away, and we ended up in Chicago and changed our name. Never saw papa again. According to momma, I didn't want to. When I was older and adult curious—she warned me he'd kill us both if he found us—it was enough to cool my interests." She looked around suspiciously and whispered, "My name was LeBlanc.

"That plus my grandpa was big in the Klu Klux Klan. They controlled the politics in those days." Her last remark killed the conversation temporarily.

The weather kept the patrons away but didn't keep Buster from feeding us Polish Mistakes. The cold beer and conversation with Gabby took Byron's mind off the bitter cold walk back to his apartment. She did most of the talking. He refrained from asking questions, hoping to avoid encouraging her, and worried the number of beers he drank no doubt affected his memory for whatever lies he conjured.

The image of Gabby as a school teacher to five-year-olds didn't fit. She left teaching because she thought she might kill a kid. "The cure for me having any kid of my own," she said. She lived alone and skirted talking about any husbands or boyfriends.

There were only five patrons in the bar at the end of the day. Byron never met a man named Buster or Gabby, and now Frosty, the fifth patron. Frosty wasn't as old as Gabby but older than him. He guessed him to be in his fifties. His graying hair wasn't as far gone as Gabby's or any of the older regulars. Still noticeable in a forest of aging gray hair was a prominent shock of white hair, no doubt the reason for the name Frosty. Gabby said he lived with his mom.

Frosty usually stationed himself at the far end of the bar, but tonight he headed for the pool room and stayed there.

He was always looking for a game and plugging the jukebox when he wasn't. It was easy to imagine those piercing black eyes staring down the length of a pool stick calling the eight ball in the corner pocket.

Chapter Six

The past winter was ruthless to an unsuspecting Northwesterner. March, the gateway to spring, promised warmer days ahead and elevated his spirit. Byron's focus turned to job hunting. There were several jobs he applied for all over the city, six interviews in all. He learned from each one how to answer the questions and hone his story to fit the expected requirements of an entry technical analyst position. He could have had two jobs, but he held out for something more convenient to the train line. In the end, the job chosen was in the heart of the city.

When Byron arrived at Seven Continents Financial Group for the interview, a large international company with operations on all seven continents, the wind was wiping up, and the mix of rain and sleet stung his face. People under umbrellas scurried along the sidewalk, darting in and out of buildings. The company was located in a sixty-floor building on West Wacker.

After announcing himself at the lobby security station, he was directed to human resources on the thirty-third floor. Crowding onto an elevator, serving floors thirty through sixty, he joined others staring in silence at their feet, and when he arrived, a young man right out of college interviewed him. His sport coat was too big, and his tie too short with a tight knot that bunched his shirt's collar. Byron learned in the small talk before the interview he had been there less than six months.

Byron wasn't impressed but was relieved the interview process was so casual. He had to pass through three interviews. Each interviewer had notes from the previous interviewer, and each followed a set script for the low-level job he was seeking.

When he applied, his resume left off his advanced college degrees and listed only his trade school credentials and that he attended Washington University. He doubted they would check references for a job like this, and his current certifications were more important. If they did check with the University of Washington, they wouldn't find him. Army didn't exist outside of Chicago. He used Washington because he was familiar with the campus, courses, and professors and could bluff his way if needed. One of his fears was to run into someone who graduated there, but given the size of the school, he could handle that.

Byron didn't makeup jobs for his resume—it was too easy to check. Instead, his story was he dropped out of college and moved back home to take care of his mother, who passed away last summer. He dramatized how painful her cancer was and how his brother wouldn't help, leaving all her care with him. The story generated the level of sympathy he hoped, and they hired him on the spot.

When he started work the next Monday, Human Resources issued him a badge, explained security rules, and assigned him a cubical on the fifteenth floor. Alfred Taylor, his new boss, a man about his age on the short path to obesity—his tightly cinched belt on its last notch. Year by year, his youthful lifestyle of no exercise and eating anything he wanted added pounds.

Alfred helped him set up his workstation, logged him into the system, and explained the password procedures and requirements. As he set up a new password, Byron attempted a little friendly banter, knowing from experience he could learn a lot about a person from small talk.

"So, do people call you Fred or Al for short?"

Alfred responded with a silent stare. At first, Byron wondered if he offended him, and he didn't like joking around. His expression softened, and he responded in a kindly voice, "No. They just call me Alfred."

The thing about technical people is they can be so literal. Natural for techy people—their world is precision. Computers don't operate on entering commands close to correct. After orienting him to his new workstation, he took Byron on a tour of the cooled, sterile room that housed the mainframe computer to show off the main hardware.

Computer geeks love to show off the hardware. "Of course, you know we don't like people coming in here without reason. I doubt you will even have the need."

They returned to his workstation. Alfred continued to explain the system in broad strokes—the various partitions, files system, backup system procedures, redundancies, schedule mainframe maintenance procedures, and security policies. Many of the employees were using mainframe terminals with no access to the software or outside world. Support for them was with applications or, once in a while, replacing their terminals. For others, who were using PCs with access to the outside world, he set up their VPN, which required enhanced company security, and updated and assisted with various software programs. Byron had extensive experience with a variety of software applications.

Alfred was a hands-off kind of boss, more a resource than someone who supervised. Brilliant to a fault, he always had his nose pointed at his computer screen. Before leaving, he welcomed Byron aboard again and, with a smile, offered, "Don't hesitate to call me with your questions. After a year of help desk, depending on how it goes, we'll look at what additional training you need and get you some classes. Our legacy system was built over time, so we prefer homegrown employees and are always looking for advanced coders."

Alfred turned out to be the most tolerant boss ever. The guy Byron replaced was a do-nothing malingerer who disappeared the rest of the day when he went out on help missions. It took years before Alfred did anything about it, which suggested the company valued him for his technical skills, not his supervisory ones.

Byron learned Alfred was one of those guys who made good money and didn't spend a dime of it. He owned two shirts, one short sleeve and the other long sleeve; he washed once a week. A private man, he wasn't much for small talk and never talked about himself. He lived frugally and planned to retire at forty, and a shock to Byron, he wanted to live on an island somewhere.

Eventually, sunshine replaced the cold gray days and imposed temporary happiness on fellow morning train computers. The snow melted away, leaving only a few crusty, dirty remnants of shoveled snow.

All winter Byron continued to let his hair grow. Wearing a wool stocking cap enhanced the new look. He even wore it at Buster's and slept in it in his cold apartment. The apartment building was hell hot all the time, so he left the windows open, wore a stocking cap and sweatshirt to bed, and used a thick comforter to keep him warm. The effect of wearing the wool stocking cap produced long straggly gnarly locks of hair—the beginning stages of dreadlocks.

Byron's routine was firmly set, so by eight o'clock in the morning, he settled at his desk, ready to start a new day, and after work, joined the five o'clock crowd of bus drivers, cops, and city workers at Buster's.

His apartment was dark, dusty, and smelly, and even the sounds of the television couldn't relieve the silence, so Buster's became his home away from home. Buster always greeted him with a nod and a draft Budweiser. Gabby was in her usual spot, and Frosty hustled pool in the backroom then took a seat at the bar at eight o'clock when the crowd thinned.

Byron's personal barstool was usually vacant, and when it wasn't, he watched and waited to reclaim it when he could, wondering if it was obvious. Buster said he was going to put his name on the stool.

The job turned out better than expected, not as stimulating as his chosen career and a bit like factory work—the same things popping up over and over. It felt like a game of Wackamo. Five people staffed the help desk, not counting Alfred, who hardly ever came around and frequented his time on the penthouse floor, oddly chummy with the big boss. Until Byron proved himself, he wasn't assigned after hours on call. As near as he could tell, there weren't many after-hours calls anyway.

A most interesting cast of characters, there were three men and two women in the technical support group. Byron overheard one of the group's women refer to him as the old man—the not forty-yet old man. Starting as an outsider, the guy who replaced the legendary ghost of a guy who went out of his way to avoid work, Byron worked hard, kept his head down, and avoided relationships.

Declining Dan's, the lead provocateur, lunch invitations three times during his first week helped communicate he wanted to be left alone. He had no desire to make job friends—familiarity would lead to too many questions and potential inconsistencies in the answers. That is the thing about lies—you have to remember every one of them and each of their relatives. Byron was content with his arm's length bar friendships with Buster, even Gabby, and even at a distance Frosty. He figured if he ever wanted to get away from Gabby, he could go to the pool room and get hustled by Frosty.

Byron's contacts with the help desk associates were limited to occasional team meetings when Alfred announced such things as company policies, backup schedules, changes to the system or network, vacation or holiday schedules, and the unavoidable trips to the breakroom for coffee.

Being an outcast in the help desk unit suited him. He ignored them—all of them. It was perfect, Byron could focus on the job, not friendships, and his boss left him alone, and there were few questions to answer. He loved being an outsider, even the friction with Dan fit. He couldn't ask for a better unwitting ally to keep his relationships at arm's length.

When Byron entered the breakroom, Sheldon sat alone at the far end of the table wearing a long-sleeve blue shirt and skinny black tie, drinking a sixteen-ounce Coke. He was as buttoned-downed as anyone he ever met—an extreme nerd. He couldn't remember anyone in his high school or college so nerdy and whom he distrusted more.

There was something about Sheldon that drew Byron's attention. He thought his extreme nerdiness was an act—it takes a phony to know a phony, right. There was a twinkle of understanding of all the social innuendos flying around the breakroom table he claimed never to understand. It might be unfair to judge him so harshly, but if there was ever a candidate for a big-time hacker, Sheldon was his man.

Donna wore a white blouse; her long sleeves rolled up to her elbows, sitting next to Dan, the informal leader. He wasn't a bad-looking guy, pretty strait-laced with his military haircut and no sideburns, but his colorful shirts never coordinated with anything—striped or checked shirts with plaid pants, miss matching colors. Incongruently, he seemed desperate to be noticed but didn't take himself seriously and didn't want others to either. That was like wanting to be liked by acting hateful. He also often awkwardly suggested he was on the hunt for sexual exploits. Byron always wondered why he put on a man around town airs but behaved in ways that pushed women away.

Byron headed straight to the coffee machine, avoiding eye contact. While brewing a new pot of coffee, he surveyed the room. Dan was wearing the ugliest shirt he'd worn so far—palm trees on a silk field of pee yellow. He needed a woman in his life to help him with his wardrobe.

Marni entered wearing a low-cut sleeveless top, showing as much cleavage as she dared, and a tight short skirt. Dan's gaze followed her every step as she took a seat on the other side of Donna. She set her magazine on the table, reached in her purse for a file, and began to file her nails.

Byron turned back to brewing coffee, but out of the corner of his eye, he could see Dan folding a white sheet of paper into a paper airplane and fling it in his direction. It sailed past him and hit the wall and fell to the counter. He looked back to see Dan smiling smugly. Marni looked on over the top of her Glamour magazine. Donna seemed mesmerized, staring at her coffee cup.

Neither Donna nor Marni were hard to look at, Donna as soft and innocent as an old-fashioned schoolmarm, her hair pulled up in a bun, and Marni more like a pole dancer seductress. Marni put her magazine down. "Dan, how come you're still working here?"

"They haven't fired me yet," Dan retorted proudly.

Donna looked up from her coffee, "I thought you were going to quit?"

Dan ignored her and asked loud enough to be heard by everyone in the room, "You know what I want to know? I want to know how you got the name Army?"

Byron ignored the question and continued to watch the coffee pot fill up.

Dan pressed on. "So, how is it Army? How'd you get the name? Have you been in the Army?"

Taking a deep breath, Byron turned to meet Dan's gaze. With a tight smile, he answered, "Yeah, I was in the Army. Demolition. I blew things up. It was great…we didn't take shit from anyone. Everyone always figured in the end we had the biggest gun." Turning away, feeling satisfied, he couldn't resist peeking back to see the stunned expression on Dan's face.

Donna looked at Dan awkwardly, then Sheldon, who nervously fidgeted and ran his hands through his long wavy carrot-colored hair. The room went funeral silent as Marni and Donna exchanged glances and got up to leave. Byron filled his plastic mug and, as he walked out, looked back to Dan and stifled a smile.

When everyone arrived back in their cubicles, awaiting requests for help or Alfred handing out assignments, no one talked, just the sounds of clacking keyboards, air conditioning raining down, and the buzz of elevator hallway fluorescent lights. The overhead lights were off in the cubicle area, which created a cave-like atmosphere.

In the relative silence, Byron reflected how his day started and the strange break room encounter. It reminded him of the lessons he learned after college as he faced the real world in his job at Oreves, Inc. College fun and games, and all that college education, were mere speculations about what might lie ahead. Athletic and book smart, nothing could stop him. He recalled starting out brimming with youthful confidence and his dad's advice to make each day count because there were bumps in his road and no way to know how life would work out. He nodded appreciatively and ignored him, but now his advice resonated. Love can change a life. Cancer can too. And a boss like Valentin.

When he arrived to work that morning, he entered the elevator with Robert McDermott III, President, and CEO, of Seven Continents Financial Group, and as usual, never a hello, or even a nod. It reminded Byron he had a secret—he wasn't a worker peon. The joke was on McDermott. He smiled, knowing he knew many of the same people in the industry and could have easily been a vice president here.

Byron couldn't help but compare him to his old boss—Valentin. Both were the type of people who could run a company as massive and complicated as this. Only a select group of people would qualify, which explained the high salaries and exorbitant bonuses. He was definitely in the Valentin mold in more ways than one.

McDermott's elevator destination was the penthouse office suites. Byron hadn't set foot on the sixtieth floor yet but had to the fifty-ninth, so he had viewed the panoramic view of Lake Michigan and the Chicago skyline. Alfred was the only one from his department allowed to step on the hollowed white carpet.

Robert McDermott III was manicured and buffed, wearing an Armani suit, silk tie, and starched shirt. He could as easily have been on his way to a photoshoot for GQ magazine. The high life—he had movie-star good looks and gobs of money. Byron wondered if people like him ever maxed out and didn't need more money.

Alfred told him McDermott owned a villa in Italy, and his yacht was privately docked in Loretto on the Baja peninsula. He added, "That's not what I want. Not a villa, but a place on one of the islands. That's what I want." It seemed funny for a man in his position, of modest means, to have such lofty goals.

The last time he was on the elevator with McDermott, Byron was on his way to the 58th floor to fix a computer; he formed a lasting impression of the man. A young associate got on the elevator on the 33rd floor, dressed for success, in a dark suit and starched white shirt, ready to impress. He extended his hand to McDermott. "I've wanted to meet you, Mr. McDermott. I'm new but was on the Ruby Hong Kong team. That was a big deal." As he was talking, he kept his hand extended, waiting for McDermott to take it. He didn't. McDermott's unblinking steel blue eyes locked on the young man in a test of who would blink.

The young man got off on the thirty-eight floor. Byron never forgot how small he made him look. As the elevator doors shut, McDermott leaned over to the man next to him, a senior vice president, and whispered, "I wish we had a private elevator."

It must be the nature of power and riches that McDermott and Valentin seemed cut from the same cloth. Is there ever enough power and things to own for some people. Maybe it takes a tragic event to trigger a person's awakening, or more than one.

The keyboard chatter stopped abruptly, like the forest listening for advancing prey. Donna's soft voice interrupted the still, "So, how come Army never joins us? As near as Byron could tell, she was standing outside Dan's work area.

Dan quickly offered an opinion. "Maybe he just likes to be left alone, like he was picked on in high school." After a moment of silence, he continued, "Maybe he wore Army pants, and the kids made fun of him."

Byron smiled at Marni's response. "Ooh, I like a man in uniform."

Dan blurted out, "I thought you liked your men out of uniform."

For fifteen minutes, clacking keyboards were the only sounds to be heard. Alfred arrived and started talking to Sheldon, and the clicking sounds went silent again. When their conversation ended, the keyboards began to sing out again.

Fifteen minutes later, Donna moved out of her cubicle. Her voice easily distinguishable from Marni's, Donna's a fragrant warm breeze, and Marni's the first frost. "Do you know him? Army?" Donna asked.

"Not really," Dan answered.

"How'd do you think he got the name Army? That's a funny nickname. He's not like a bomber or something?"

"Nay, that's just talk."

"How do you know? You don't know him."

"Yeah, maybe he is."

Marni joined them. "You think he's got a girlfriend? You don't think he likes guys, do you?"

Dan laughed. "No way. I saw him checking you out. I think he has a girlfriend or had one anyway. Saw him looking at a picture of a woman. He keeps her picture in his desk drawer."

"How do you know? You go through his desk drawers?" Donna asked.

"Saw him pull it out once."

There was a long pause. Perhaps Donna and Marni didn't want to encourage Dan. But not easily thwarted whenever he had a captive audience, Dan said, "So, what's with the hairdo? He looks like a wannabe white Bob Marley."

Sick of the conversation, Byron wanted to tell them to shut up but instead tried a more diplomatic approach. Standing up, he looked over the top of the cubicle wall. Donna scurried toward her workstation like she was caught in the act and fleeing the scene.

"You know I'm right here, don't you?" Byron announced.

Dan stood up and looked over the top of his wall. "Hey Army, Donna wants to know if you ever had a girlfriend?"

"Dan, you're such a butt," Donna snarled. "Don't pay any attention to him, Army."

"Hey, what's the big deal? I'm curious. How about it, Army? You ever been in love? Did she dump you? Runoff with another man?" Dan jerked his head to watch Marni, in her short tight skirt, walk away. "I've been in love. I'm in love right now."

Chapter Seven

Byron used the slow times to search through the computer files to familiarize himself with the system architecture and the business. With his background, he was incurably curious. The company attracted globalists desiring to expand or break into the world economy, so who were their clients? Where were those companies located? The business was complicated, and it became his obsession to understand it.

Previously, he had heard of Seven Continents but was shocked to learn how big they were. It was five times the size of Oreves, Inc., much more extensive geographically—billions of dollars in assets. They operated in a different space.

For Byron, looking over financial reports was like reading a favorite novel. The numbers were flora and fauna of a National Geographic Forest scene. The account files, organized numbers, footnotes, and disclaimers told the story and revealed the report creators' unique styles. Byron quenched his thirst to understand the company by digging through the files—see the trees and wildlife. He enjoyed hiding out in his no-brainer job, with billions of dollars in accounts and financial information to entertain him.

For the last month, he kept seeing irregularities, like dots on his computer screen that couldn't be connected, unreconcilable bits and bytes nudging him to an obsession to make the numbers into a story. Perhaps it was a mysterious aliment stemming from his fall from grace. After a few weeks of going over the same files, he thought he was going crazy when he moved the cursor over specific fields became blurry rubbed out images like in news photos where innocent faces were blocked out. He knew technical that really couldn't happen. He thought there were hidden files but knew it didn't happen that way. Nonetheless, his imaginings pulled him in.

One quality of a successful investment banker is persistence, so he dug deeper, looking for ways to peek behind the curtain, connect lines of data to financial reports, even look at the source code. To the unknowing person, computer code was like reading a Russian version of Anna Karenina. Coding language, though, could be easier to understand than some human languages. Like deciphering a cuneiform language of symbols, letters and numbers might seem insurmountable; computer programming code was easy to use once learned. Computer life could be simple like that. If you know the correct keystroke, your computer performs all sorts of fascinating tricks. But unlike real life, in the world of computers, you can't get by just being close.

Byron spent too much time staring at the computer screen. At night numbers, letters, and characters scrolled through his mind. Something was eating at his subconscious, and it always brought him back to staring at the computer screen. What was it? He tried to shift his focus to relieve the pressure, but it often sent him back to his life with Sybie.

He had similar experiences in his investment banking career. Formerly, he scolded himself. Sometimes, when putting a deal together and unable to get a grip on it, when the deal's components could be right in front of him, puzzle pieces of different colors and shapes, he reverted to intuition. Subconsciously, working for the answer also felt like playing a game. Like a bulldog not letting go of a bone, he stared at the computer screen, like allowing the Ouija board to provide the hints. Then voilà, a simple discovery, then another, and another, and the last piece of the puzzle snapped into place.

Something was amiss. Byron enjoyed the sweet frustration of solving financial dilemmas, but now he didn't have the time or the resources to dig deeper, and he certainly couldn't ask anyone at Seven Continents. To complicate things, the suspicious accounts stretched across continents and in various currencies. He felt like he was trying to solve a murder, for which there was no murder weapon, no suspects, nobody—maybe no murder.

Byron's boring life prodded him to continue searching through the database on a safari to find errors, incompetence, conspiracies—conjure up mysteries to solve. Or he wondered if he was so wounded, he wanted to prove he was as capable as anyone on the 60th floor. He missed past business interactions and sometimes on the elevator with suited executives, in their starched shirts and sweet cologne, he wanted to extend his hand and say, "I'm Byron Kelly, with Oreves, Inc. Have we met before?"

Intuitively, by training and experience, there were answers—another way to read a report, a new piece of data, but also sometimes too many layers, too much information, too many dead ends. Dead ends. Hidden files? The lines between cause and effect can be blurry.

There are universal forces of right and wrong that prey on people who care, who listen passionately, are willing to be tortured to find the truth, patient overqualified people like Byron with nothing to do but service computers. He surrendered. Besides, spending his off-time nursing beers at Buster's in idle small talk talking about the weather, Cubs, Bears, eavesdropping on conversations of a bar filled with judgmental bastards dulled his mind, reduced his education and passion. Like a boiling frog, he felt like he was up to his neck in the slow death of intellect.

As he dressed for work, he gaped at his reflection. He resembled more a caveman than an investment banker. Byron's gaze narrowed, his mouth upturned slightly, indecisively; what was there to smile about? His thoughts bounced back and forth between the tragic story of Byron and the enigmatic illusion, Army. *Who am I?* His reflection barely recognizable. He was accustomed to a suit and white shirt image, not khakis and a flannel shirt, long ropes of knotty black hair, and a good start on a beard. He liked how the white man's dreadlocks cemented his image. He understood Donna's anxiety. He could pass for the neighborhood psycho.

Byron pondered how much time had passed since he ran away and how far he was from home, and how were his folks? In the heat of leaving, he never considered how much he'd miss them, how time would stretch out, his folks would get older, and the bridge home might become untravellable.

When Byron arrived at work, he immediately went back to the section of files he had been searching, still hunting for an explanation. At least one file didn't show up anywhere with no connection to another account or transaction, which meant it couldn't be on any financial statement. He kept searching to see if there were more. The most challenging aspect of the search was the mere tedium of going through lines of data—there wasn't any way to search otherwise, just time in between assignments and remembering where he left off.

Byron was in a fit. What was he expecting to find? There were no theories to guide him and very little success to keep him going. Still, he persisted. Perseverance. Sybie—his lost angel of perseverance. He pushed that aside.

In time he found more suspicious accounts and felt on the verge of a breakthrough. Each of the accounts had the same controlling password, but he couldn't tell who's password. Still, no operating theory, just a growing suspicion based on finding similar accounts, lost, alone, disconnected, not tied to anything, any human or entity. Someone surely knew of their existence. Somebody knew, an accountant, an auditor, but there wasn't a hint in the company financials to suggest a category or account, just a bunch of isolated files.

How could anyone find the mystery files when they were strung out randomly in thousands of lines of data, unattached to anything, hidden away in plain sight unless you knew what you were looking for or had a team of people and the time to go through all the files? If the accounts summaries passed all internal, state, and federal audits, why look further?

Byron confirmed the accounts did have money in them, American dollars. Were they lost files, forgotten, maybe they were deleted and in the wrong place, not together, though? When accounts are closed, they should be moved to a special place or archived as dead files. Were they dormant accounts? Could it be someone or several someones who didn't care about millions of dollars?

After checking the accounts over and over and yielding nothing, he captured a screenshot of the accounts and locations. He couldn't be caught printing off pages of account information, so he took his time. He could send a few copies at a time to the copier when no one was around, usually just before one o'clock when the early lunch crowd returned and was settling in, and the late lunchers weren't there. Byron started to carry a canvas messenger bag and each night took the screenshots with him. His bag was filled with magazines, and to avoid suspicion, he read them in the break room. It was a nice touch to fill them with military and biker magazines.

The only way to investigate further required dipping into the secure file of everyone's passwords, a large file he couldn't keep open very long and couldn't print. He hadn't determined if there was any special tracking of people entering that part of the system, but he assumed he was authorized. At least, he wasn't restricted or told otherwise. Anyone accessing this part of the system unauthorized would be fired on the spot. He couldn't know everyone in the company, but he knew who was on the 60th floor and in the accounting area. None of their passwords matched the passwords on the mysterious accounts. Byron's suspicions grew. Almost as if someone had whispered into his ear, he realized Robert McDermott III's name—Mr., keep the riff raft away, McDermott, was missing in the password control file.

Alfred respected his hard work and trusted him more than others in the department, so much he shared his dreams of retiring to some tropical island in the Caribbean. His dreams were different than Byron's simple wish to be exonerated and find his way back home, see his folks again, not live in Chicago, or trudge through the snow again. Byron thought they were kindred spirits because he was reliable and a loner who didn't take any guff from Dan. Who liked Dan anyway?

Respect earned Byron the right to be on the 60th floor but only when he accompanied Alfred to run programs and upgrade or repair computers. While servicing computers on the top floor, sometimes Alfred sat comfortably with McDermott's in his office in animated conversation. Obviously, McDermott didn't consider Alfred one of the riff-raff.

All the next week, Byron installed updates to the VPN, and McDermott's had to be completed before he returned from Indonesia. No one from his unit had ever been in McDermott's office, other than Alfred, and he was sitting in a dentist chair having two abscessed wisdom teeth extracted.

McDermott's office was palatial. Byron eased into his leopard-skinned high back executive chair and spun around toward the wall of glass and a panoramic pageant of sailboats and white cumulous clouds gathering on the horizon. He spun around and squeezed into the u-shaped glass-topped desk with polished chrome legs. In front of him were two opposing full-grain brown button-tufted sofas and a coffee table of glass and steel atop a 16[th]century wool and silk Brazilian rug.

Byron opened his desktop computer using the password Alfred gave him. The home screen was a fascinating picture of an African elephant holding a small lion cub in her trunk, the cub's mother walking casually beside him. The poignant image must have been photoshopped. It couldn't be real. Could it?

Feasting his gaze on the majesty of McDermott's office, he was awed by the array of gallery framed photographs that told a story of his travels around the world. It left Byron to wonder if it was a creative calling or maybe over the top ego, even possibly simply the rightful tribute to the excesses of success. He saw a Leica S2-P Camera that cost more than twenty thousand dollars on a table in the corner of the office, beside it an array of telephoto and wide-angle lenses. Kudos to his talent. Byron's grandmother always said, 'there was some good in the worst of us.' Even guys like him had some redeeming values.

Panning the room, he perused the photographic exhibit: The Grand Canyon, Glacier National Park, Mount Rushmore, an Egyptian pyramid, the Great Barrier Reef, several African safari pictures of a lion and a cheetah, a panda and her cub, a South American gorilla picture, an Antarctic ice cliff. There was a picture of him, with who might have been his wife, standing before the Eiffel Tower, but also a photo with a different woman standing before the Sydney Opera house. When did he find time to achieve all his success?

The password Alfred supplied easily allowed access into the mainframe computer but not into the secured financial section, which Byron found odd.

Byron couldn't resist poking around his desktop computer. He opened his file manager, and it looked just like everyone else's: pictures, documents, one labeled finance, which contained some file folders he assumed were personal expense folders for his yacht, and his Italian Villa, otherwise unrevealing. The mainframe was partitioned into a number of different drives. It was hard to believe McDermott didn't have a password to any of them. He closed the file manager and returned to the home page, where he noticed a protected password management system icon on his desktop screen.

While his computer updated, he pondered what he had learned. A hundred times, Byron surmised there was an explanation for the so-called mystery files. What was it? He couldn't recall seeing anything like it in all his training and education. Gaining access to McDermott's private password system was his best option to answer his curiosity. Whenever he saw the password icon on other computers, it allowed open access and depended on the primary password that opened the computer. It was hard to believe McDermott didn't have access to all the mainframe files, especially the financial ones. How could that be?

Curious, he attempted to open desk drawers and found they were locked. If he was anything like Byron, he wouldn't trust himself to always have a key to his desk drawers with him, so no doubt a key was hidden somewhere in the office. On the other hand, if he was like Byron, he wouldn't have locked the drawers. Some people think everybody wants to look in their desk drawers like they had stashes or secrets.

Several times McDermott's secretary peeked in. He could hear her coming, and he looked up from the computer screen and smiled. As soon as she shut the door, he rose and began to search the room for a desk key. Other than the furniture, the photo gallery suite also featured two tall, heavy African art sculptures, but the room's focus was wall photography. Thankfully, there wasn't a wall of books and shelves of memorabilia.

Byron moved around the office like a cat burglar, listening for hints someone was about to enter. He stopped in the center of the room and steadied his gaze around the office, asking where he would hide a key. A hidden key had to be easily accessible.

The framed photos were tightly secured to the wall. Tilting the two tall sculptures to their edges, he looked under the base. Nothing. He felt underneath both sofas and lifted the corners of each of the rugs. He began to sweat and returned to the desk and, as a last resort, picked up one of the faux leopard skin pillows. Unzipping each pillow and looking inside, he found a key in the third pillow.

His heart pounded against his chest as he quickly returned to the desk, unlocked a desk drawer, and found a leather-bound journal. Fascinating, there were several pages of numbers, which, in his experience, were bank account numbers. He didn't have time to jot down all of the numbers and began to panic. He fanned through the rest of the journal. On the back of the last page was a complicated eleven-digit series of numbers, letters, and symbols, which he jotted down.

Running out of time, he hastily clicked on the password manager icon and entered the eleven-digit series of numbers. He was in. He stuffed the password into his pocket, scanned the different programs, and found the files he wanted. McDermott controlled the mystery files. Quickly closing the book, he returned it to the drawer and locked it. When the computer completed the update, he hurriedly closed it and, on his way out of the office, returned the key to the pillow.

Byron returned to his cubicle, his heart still pounding. Quickly he checked to see if he could access the password management system with McDermott's password. The first account opened. The second one opened too, then closing it in a panic, he stared at the computer screen. There were numerous accounts scattered throughout the database. McDermott's password opened all of the suspicious accounts. Now he wondered if he had found all the accounts. Given the tedious process of going through so many lines of data, he wasn't going to look for more today.

Puzzled why he couldn't trace any of the mysterious accounts to an accountant activity, Byron still wondered if there could be an explanation. What were his options? He couldn't tell anyone he was going through the data and found some strange accounts and opened them using McDermott's password he obtained by breaking into his private desk. Who was he to question anything? He had gone from senior executive of a successful investment banking company to a man in hiding chasing conspiracies when he wasn't fixing computers and drinking beers at Buster's.

Chapter Eight

Late in the afternoon, as Byron prepared to leave for the day, a woman came to his cubicle and announced, "Mrs. P wants to see you in her office. Now." Without waiting for a response, she turned and left.

Human Resources was on the 33rd floor. When Byron entered the elevator, his first thought was to push the ground floor button and escape. He had broken through. McDermott was behind the mystery accounts. He reviewed the possibilities. Off to jail or fired, or would McDermott explain what he was seeing—then fire him. Standing alone on the elevator, his heart raced. Byron took a deep breath and went over the possibilities. He still had a copy of the recent screenshot of the file he opened using McDermott's password. Employees had to use an ID number to print from their computers, and maybe they wanted to know what he was printing. The file copies were in his messenger bag, and they could search it. No one but his assistant saw him in McDermott's office, and he was authorized to be there. Unless he had a camera in his office? He could have. Byron took another deep breath. He's the type of guy who would.

When Byron entered, a middle-aged woman greeted him. She had deep wrinkles that gave the appearance of a permanent scowl. The nameplate on her desk read Nancy Pescosolieo, Vice President Humans Resources, clarifying why they called her Mrs. P. As serious as a homeland security agent, she stated, "I understand you made a bomb threat."

Suppressing a smile, not wanting to suggest he didn't take her seriously. "Dan said that?

"That's not important. Did you?"

Byron wasn't sure how to refer to her, the more familiar Mrs. P or the impossible to pronounce, Mrs. Pescosolieo. "I wouldn't know how to light a firecracker. I did say something to him. It wasn't appropriate. I'm sorry."

"I was told you were a demolition expert in the Army. And you threatened him."

"I didn't, but sorry if anything I said upset him," he replied humbly. "He was making fun of my name, and I wanted to get him off my back. I was trying to be funny." As he was responding, his mind wandered. *So, is there a Mr. P? He must live in fear.*

"I've fired people for less," she said proudly.

"I hope you don't." Byron figured now was a good time to show a little contrition. "I like my job here."

"I talked to Alfred. He said you are good at your job and were always prompt. Said he could count on you to perform any task. Recommends you for more training."

As Byron waited for her to pass judgment, her assistant popped in. "Mrs. P., Mr. McDermott is back and wants to see Mr. Bendorf when he's finished here."

Mrs. P nodded to her assistant. "Well, Army, you best go see Mr. McDermott. When he says he wants to see someone, he means now. I guess we best find out what he wants."

As Byron entered the elevator, he leaned over and looked at his image in the polished chrome control panel. Loosening his dreadlocks and retying them in a tight ponytail, he tucked his shirt and straightened his collar. When the door opened on the 60th floor, he was immediately met by a woman, not his secretary, in her early thirties, wearing a short tight skirt and low-cut top. Her blond hair hung loosely over her shoulders.

She didn't ask his name and said, "Mr. McDermott wants to see you right away."

When Byron entered his office, McDermott was reading a financial report. He noticed they used the same poly binders for their financial reports as Oreves. Without offering his hand or inviting him to sit, Byron stood in front of his desk. *No doubt if I wasn't Army, he would have asked me to sit.* Standing at attention was a nice submissive touch anyway, so Byron stood stiffly like an Army private. McDermott studied his knotty long hairs and flannel shirt down to his scuffed casual shoes. No doubt he could just as easily fire him for his appearance.

Their gazes connected, and the silence added tension and curiosity until McDermott asked, and Byron's anxiety evaporated, "I understand you were in my office today. Did you find anything?"

Every once in a while, the old Byron Kelly sprang forth in surprising ways at the most unexpected times. No one knew the real him, not Gabby or Buster, and no one at Seven Continents. Standing at attention, he resisted the urge to announce he was Byron Kelly, not Army, and tell him he worked with far more accomplished people in his career, ones not nearly as transparent. Byron could see McDermott's reflection on his desktop and behind him a panoramic view of the city. What a weak question. He had worked with far more intimidating people, men and women, far more narcissistic, much greater egos. Byron felt he had the upper hand.

Was he paranoid? What were his insecurities? He knew he had been in his office, or he wouldn't ask. He didn't have anything but a weak, misguided misconception he could intimidate him, that Byron was some low life he could twist in knots. He wanted to laugh at the notion McDermott expected him to spill his guts like in some B-rated detective show.

Byron's answer came in an I don't give a damn voice, undetectable to a guy like McDermott who never experienced loss in his life, a man with the misguided super confidence of a king who thought he could get away with anything, who never made a mistake he couldn't cover-up. Like his grandmother said, 'Some people think they can talk their way out of anything.' She also said, 'those piss ant politicians can explain anything.' His curiosity grew along with his suspicion. Would an explanation of the mystery accounts make Byron out to be a fool or reveal one of the greatest frauds ever?

Grandma Kelly was a wise woman, wiser now, years after she was laid to rest. There was a lot of wisdom in older Americans, but nobody listened. Talking heads and politicians could explain anything. Where was the wisdom in that? His grandmother's wisdom came from knowing her neighbors, her church, and not relying on celebrities to tell her how to think.

Wisdom was also passed down from Byron's great grandfather, who immigrated from Hungary on a Canadian ship and settled in Monte Cristo, Washington. He staked his first land claim under the name Smith, but there were sixteen other men there named Smith, so he changed it to Kelly. His grandmother might have been the last resident of Monte Cristo, now a ghost town.

"Yes," was Byron's simple answer.

McDermott was momentarily speechless.

"Yes? Yes…you found something?"

"No. Yes, I was in your office."

McDermott suddenly seemed uncomfortably exposed. He realized the dumb question had exposed a flicker of weakness. Trying to regain the upper hand, he lashed out, "Nice haircut Army."

Byron wanted to laugh. Army. He knew his name, imagine that. The unrelenting boyhood bully wanted to come out and play—self-confident until someone punched him in the nose, and the sight of his own blood sent him running off to his mom.

McDermott, basking in his put down, continued, "It was reported as a security breach."

Byron shrugged his shoulders, confused. "I was updating the system. Alfred said anytime someone opens the system from your computer, it is reported as a security breach." *What an odd question. He is hiding something.*

"Oh yeah, that's right. Alfred is right?"

Byron answered humbly, thinking he played it perfectly. "Yes, sir."

Waving his hand dismissively, McDermott said, "You can go back to work."

As Byron turned to leave, he heard his voice again. "Army's your real name, right? I also heard you were threatening other employees. I could fire you for that."

Calmly, turning back, he answered, "That misunderstanding was cleared up. I hope I haven't given you any reason to do that."

How opportune. McDermott could get the last word and return to being in total control.

"I don't need a reason to fire you, but I could come up with nine. Hell, I could come up with ninety-nine reasons."

After a brief pause, McDermott waved for him to leave, and he quickly exited.

***

When Byron arrived at his apartment that misty evening, he emptied his messenger bag beside a neat stack of papers on the turquoise Formica topped kitchen table. Pad of paper and pen in hand, he sat, intending to clear his head; he began to write down what he knew, analyze it, and develop an action plan and see if any plan made sense. But as dusk descended and darkened the room, he sat staring at a blank sheet of paper with not even a doodle. Every thought died on the tip of his pen. Byron felt like a conspiracy theorist. Had life come to that—wallowing in obscurity, a false identity, a bottom-rung job, a dark bar in a windy city, no last name friends.

Grabbing a sweatshirt and an umbrella, he took off on a contemplative walk to Buster's. McDermott acted so secretive, so protective, guarded. Guilty people have the best reasons to be secretive. The forecast of rain and Lake Michigan wind signaled a chilly September night walk home.

It felt ridiculous to think the head man, the man who had it all, was stealing from the company or at least considering it. But there were no accounting principles to explain why the accounts were hiding in plain sight nestled in thousands of lines of data, unattached, unexplained, seemingly accessible to only the company president and CEO. Whose money was it if it wasn't tied to any financial report? Over twenty-six million dollars.

As he neared Buster's, it began to rain hard. The streets were crowded with people hurrying to find shelter. Byron popped open the umbrella and tilted it down to shield him from the driving rain, frequently peeking around the umbrella to make his way. With a block to go, he saw a woman up ahead, her back to him, her black shoulder-length hair shiny and stringy. Twice she turned slightly to the side so he could glimpse her face.

He rushed toward her, eager to get a closer look. She was the reincarnate image of Sybie. From behind, he heard a man's voice yell out. "Sybil! Sybil, wait up."

Turning to see who was yelling, then back to the woman, Byron saw her full face. Rushing toward her, he bumped into a man knocking his umbrella to the ground. After retrieving the umbrella, the man who was yelling passed him and continued toward the woman. When the man reached her, she smiled up at him, and they kissed and disappeared beneath his umbrella. The rain washed over Byron's head.

When Byron entered Buster's, Gabby was in her usual place, just like last night and every other night. Buster flipped a coaster onto the bar and set a draft Budweiser before him. "You okay? You look like you saw a ghost."

Reaching out for a napkin to wipe his forehead, he gulped down his beer and rubbed his temples. It took several more napkins to wipe the rain off his face.

Buster returned and filled his glass. "Goddamn Cubs. They lost again. A diehard Cubs fan, the one thing to be counted on, if Cubs were on WGN, they were on the television at Buster's. "Soriano struck out four times." Cub fans had higher than the usual high expectations this season with the hiring of Theo Epstein and the promise to break their 108-year World Series drought.

Just like that, Buster quickly sliced through his oppressed ruminations, and Byron smiled as Buster uncharacteristically raised his voice, "Damn them to hell. They've always been in love with the long ball. Hell, Kingman struck out all the time, then he'd slam a home run over Waveland Avenue off the building across the street, and they'd love him again. They need to trade Soriano."

Byron was now a Cubs fan. The Mainers were a memory, also loveable losers, a reminder of his past—the athlete, the executive, a different person from another life, a different part of the world. "There's always next year, right?" Byron asked.

"Yeah, we always have next year. But this year, we're awful."

As usual, when the after-work crowd thinned, Buster turned on the ten o'clock news. After reports of more south side shootings, angry politicians, seizing free air time to bolster their political prospects, made wild unkeepable promises no one would remember. Like the weatherman, no one remembers when sunny days are predicted that turn out wet and cold.

After a commercial break, changing to a lighter tone, a tan, handsome newsman and brunette newswoman, who looked like a vogue model, bantered back and forth as a picture of Bernie Madoff appeared, as nearly recognizable as Adolf Hitler.

The male anchorman began. "Bernie, as inmates call him, is once again in the news. It is estimated Bernie Madoff embezzled nearly thirty-six billion dollars and billions are still unaccounted for."

Buster paused and looked back to the television. "Look at that guy. Does he think it was worth it? I'm surprised someone hasn't put a bullet in him."

The male newsman continued. "Well, someone is making money on old Bernie. Entrepreneur John Vaccaro, who bought most of Bernie Madoff's wardrobe at an auction, has now released a line of IPAD covers made from his clothing."

Staring up to the television, Byron joined the conversation. "Fraud like that happens all the time. I've heard seven percent of company revenues nationally are lost to fraud. Can you imagine that, seven percent?" McDermott's image flashed before him. "He was an idiot. No, more than that, he was a narcissistic sociopathic idiot. Nobody said sociopaths had to be dumb, you know."

Gabby chimed in. "Wonder where all the money went?"

Buster looked to me for the answer. "What do you think? He still has some stashed away?"

"I wonder if we ever hear the whole story. I'm not sure follow-up stories are sensational enough to get air time. You don't always hear the whole story, and there's a lot of ways to hide money. A guy like that still might have angles. Maybe he has some money hidden away to bargain with. If not, maybe he wasn't that smart. He probably figures somehow he'll get out of prison, and there'll be a stash somewhere."

Byron held his glass out for another beer, another refill of already one too many. Buster filled his glass and began to rub the bar down. "Wonder what makes people think they can get away with big dollars like that?"

Responding quickly, "Because they do. It's a fact, as long as the economy's growing, schemes like this can go on working. The Enron scheme would still be in play if it weren't for an economic downturn. The same thing for Bernie, plus he got greedy, and it was too much money." Byron caught himself, feeling he was revealing too much about the financial world. "Maybe you gotta steal a lot at one time and plan to keep a little, or steal a little and get away with it all. It's like bank robbers. The odds of getting caught rise significantly each time out."

Gabby was grinning from ear to ear. "Oh well, they can't execute you for stealing money. Sometimes you just gotta do the time if you're caught. I'd go for it. Hey, Army, would you go for it if you thought you could get away with it?"

Buster was still thinking about what it would be like to get caught and whether it would be worth it. "And, if you make big donations to the President, you'll get a pardon, like Clinton gave that guy. In Chicago, you just gotta be a supporter of the mayor."

The last part of the discussion faded into the background as Byron stared into his beer, still pondering his day, what he discovered in McDermott's office—their conversation so revealing, the whole proposition so unbelievable, on top of the madness thinking he saw Sybie in the rain. As if coming out of a dream, Byron mumbled. "Well, there is an island somewhere where nobody knows your name or cares. Right?"

Looking up to Buster, he had a curious look on his face. "So, you'd take your chances?"

Laughing, he gripped his beer glass and drained it. "Take my chances? It's a matter of mitigating risks." Instantly Byron wished he could take back those words. It sounded like he was in a client meeting. It's hard not to be yourself. Awkwardly he tried to move on. "I figure the best way to beat the system, other than paying off the mayor, is to steal money from a thief. Not many corporate embezzlers start with a criminal record. They're just people who get caught up, then take one step down the stairway after another. You find an embezzler and steal from him; you got it made. Nobody believes the embezzler."

Buster shook his head as he took his glass and, with a nod, asked if he wanted another beer. Shaking his head, Buster added, "Why the hell does a guy need that much money anyway?"

"How about some new scenery? Like a beach somewhere warm and dry. A lot of guys who come into a pot of money would be outta here. Right?"

Gabby rejoined the conversation. "Money doesn't solve everything. Why does everyone think money's the answer?"

"Yeah, but a lot of people would trade this loud, smelly place for a beach somewhere? You gotta have money to do that." Looking over to Gabby. "Okay, If I gave you a million dollars, would you keep coming in here every night?

Gabby looked over to Buster. "You know he's right."

Buster looked away and, with a wave of his hand, responded dismissively. "I love it here. I'll die here." Buster was Chicago through and through. If he could be buried in Wrigley Field under home plate he would.

"Don't get me wrong, I like Chicago, but have you ever been to the islands?"

Buster responded defensively. "Nah, but there's nothing wrong with this place. I figure life's what you make it wherever you live. Buster laughed a loud belly laugh. "Man, you need to get yourself a woman and settle down."

Byron had had too many beers and began to think about the long walk back to his apartment. A woman, huh? He couldn't shake seeing that woman outside. *What a coincidence. Her name was Sybil. She looked so much like her.* "Nah, I don't need a woman. Never again. No, I think I need to get out of here." He pushed back from the bar. The room was spinning. Steadying himself, he reached into his pocket and pulled out a money clip, unfolded some bills, and set them on the bar. "That's it for me." After taking a few steps toward the door, he turned back. "I've gotta get out of here. I need a warmer climate. Need to get lost."

When he arrived at the exit, he heard Buster's voice. "Yeah, you're gonna get out of here, just like I'm gonna pitch for the Cubs next year. You're stuck here like the rest of us."

When he arrived at the door, he looked back. "You might wanna start warming up. The Cubs need pitchers."

Chapter Nine

The first time Byron was late for work, Alfred asked if everything was okay. He told him he had a plumbing problem. Glad he didn't ask today. Today he was late because he went to breakfast. Last night, he alternated between sitting at the kitchen table and his only comfortable chair trying to find a television channel to distract night worries; he hadn't eaten since lunch the day before, and too many beers soured his stomach. When he heard steps in the hallway early the next morning, he gave up trying to sleep.

What he learned the day before was troubling, and seeing McDermott close up confirmed power had corrupted him. Money, lots of it, unbridled authority, ego, and a lack of empathy was his profile. If you mix tuna, eggs, dill relish, and mayonnaise, you always get tuna salad. No doubt, he was always flawed, but wealth and power exaggerated his defects.

He plied on to those musings his conversations with Buster which revealed more of Byron's thinking than his brain had processed or at least informed. Byron's daily mantra had originally been to ignore the whole thing, go to work, do his job, and hope nobody ever discovered his true identity. He figured his best bet was to just do his job. As a young man, whenever he stuck his nose in other people's business, his grandmother always asked, 'Who made you your brother's keeper?' She also declared, 'it's better to give people the rope than to do the hanging.'

Again, the next night, Byron had more than his usual dose of Budweiser and, by the end of the evening, slurred his words. At first, he thought he was tired, but no doubt the alcohol was as much to blame and made for a deadly combination. He wasn't feeling friendly either. At one point, Frosty asked if he wanted to play a game of pool. The last time they played, Byron learned Frosty was a pool shark when he wanted to gamble on a game of nine-ball—pool sharks like nine-ball because it is a quick game and bets mount. When they played for money, Frosty's game found another gear. "You know Frosty," Byron said. "Someday, somebody's going to break your fingers. You ever worry about that?"

He had a puzzled look on his face but surely understood the implication. "Me?" he replied. "Why would anyone want to do that?"

Byron cut him off. "Save it. These Budweisers don't make me stupid. I'm not interested."

Frosty paused and looked away and, a few minutes later, without a word, slipped away into the back room.

Gabby looked on quietly, smiling a crooked smile that covered up missing teeth. "You eat dinner?"

He thought the question was odd. He swiveled around slowly, squinting to bring her face into focus. "I guess not."

"Let's order a pizza. My treat. You ever had Tony's pizza? Right next door."

Byron knew of Tony's; he walked past it every night but hadn't had their pizza. "Okay."

She disappeared briefly, and twenty minutes later, a large pepperoni pizza was on the bar between them. Byron pulled some money out and laid it on the bar, and motioned to her. "My treat," she repeated.

She handed him a napkin, and he took a piece. "Thanks." A nice gesture, her buying pizza, no doubt figuring he needed to eat, maybe because he had had too many beers or perhaps the sour mood he projected. A few minutes later, Byron asked her to take a piece to Frosty.

When she returned, she motioned to Buster to help himself. "What are we celebrating," he asked?

"Army is thinking about leaving town."

As if Byron wasn't sitting right there, Buster leaned on the bar and looked at Byron. "Army talk'n about leaving, huh?"

It was just a conversation. Days ago. And, at the time, he didn't mean it. *Did I sound so serious?* "It was just talk, but I'm thinking about it." Even as the answer left his lips, he realized plans were further along than he admitted.

Byron had a few more beers and stayed until after midnight. After the earlier conversation, goodnight seemed awkward and permanent, so he slipped out when the time was right. As he weaved his way to his apartment, he focused on one step at a time. *Don't do anything crazy.* A police car slowly passed by and watched him suspiciously, no doubt wondering if he was worth checking out.

Wandering home, trying to walk straight, accompanied by his past and now haunted by his future. The fall from town hero and successful banker was quick and painful. *I was the best quarterback. That was long ago, I need to stop thinking about the past, lost career, lost love, just failures, and the failed dreams of being the quarterback of Quarterback U too.* The Washington Huskies was one of the top producers of NFL quarterbacks. When he was young, they were one of the top football programs in the country. In his high school sophomore year, while he was setting records in his conference, the Washington Huskies were building toward a perfect 12-0 season and a national championship. *Is that all that's left? Old dashed dreams.*

For a time, high hopes obscured the truth. He was five foot ten inches tall stretched up on his toes, which he always did when his height was being measured. The truth was obvious to the eyes—he was a skinny 175-pound kid. Owning all the passing records of Work High School never added inches or pounds.

At about the same time Byron was coming to grips about the football future, an article in the Seattle Post Intelligencer featured the budding legend of Brock Huard and his record-setting number of touchdowns as a Puyallup Viking, a large high school in the Tacoma area. He was a strapping six foot four inches tall, weighing 220 pounds, and Gatorade National Player of the year. He was also a 4.0 student and the brother of the current Washington quarterback Damon. It was obvious Brock Huard was the Husky's future quarterback—not Byron.

Thankfully, the article was a reality check. If he hadn't seen the article and persisted with his boyhood dreams, it might have stayed with him for the rest of his life. Maybe, he would have played for some small school and ended up on a different career path.

Byron was almost to his apartment and still couldn't shake the notion he wanted to leave town but knew he couldn't go back west and become Byron Kelly again, arrested, facing a long court battle, risking humiliation, maybe jail, forever the man wearing the scarlet letter. Disappointing his parents, that too. More so, what he was thinking was far riskier and could have greater consequences—being Byron Kelley again the least of threats.

When he left the bar, he offered no explanation. They didn't know his past and had no idea about the last few days. Everything was moving so fast and beyond his grasp to understand, just blurry thoughts. Thinking back to Buster's, he never thought about it being a permanent goodbye, but somehow felt the decision was beyond his control. He told Buster the safest way to steal money was from a thief, not just any thief, certainly not a mafia-type. He had seen enough movies to know better. But stealing from a white-collar criminal was tantalizing.

What if the accounts turn out to be legitimate? Ignorance would be his defense and his embracement. Embarrassment? Wounded pride. What pride? He was a dreadlocked, bottom rung of the ladder employee named Army, who some think is a bomber. What's the pride in that?

But if he was right and nothing happened, he'd have millions of dollars. He will have won the lottery and disappeared. Gabby said, so what. What does a person do with all that money? Did he want to move to an island with a new identity—a clean-shaven man with money? He could buy a new wardrobe of island shirts, linen pants, and sandals and a fancy place on a beach and adopt a new name, Winchester Huneycutt, the third, live alone and take long walks on the beach—alone, eat fancy meals in restaurants—alone.

Gabby was right; money wouldn't make him happy, happiness so relative. But he would be happy to see McDermott become a cellmate with old Bernie.

***

For the next two weeks, Byron didn't go back to Buster's. He spent his evenings at home, setting plans in motion. Plan A or B, he knew the favored one, but when the time came, he would proceed based on the logic of the plan, odds of success, and select one or the other.

After the germ of an idea surfaced that night at Buster's to move to the islands and disappear, it became obvious any plan required him to leave the city. This place wasn't home anyway, just a hideout and a good one, but a man on the run needs to stay on the run.

Researching alternatives, forming an executable plan, creating an escape strategy, adding courage to each step with enough beers had taken over his life.

The first step was a new identity and a place to transfer what money he had, which was pretty much the same money he came with. Now that he was earning a living, he hadn't spent much money, and in fact, rent, beers at Buster's, and subway fare left the money in his account untouched.

If he took money out of the Seven Continents accounts, he needed a safe place to hide it under a new identity. There were numerous ways to hide money and create a new identity. No matter which country or bank he chose, there were layers of complexity and risk, and no doubt a good investigator could break through most schemes. He decided, at best, his plan was not permanent or even long-term, a mere step in the process.

The research and planning were exciting, reminiscent of his career putting big deals together. The first phase took time, like the first incline of a roller coaster, as he organized the options, accumulated information and options, pushed non-essential data to the side, and organized the information that would lead him in the most promising direction. With much of the information pushed to the side, it was easy to see a plan forming. Then at the top of the hill, he was released in a rush through the ups and downs and curves that tossed him from side to side. The ride ended in one last exhilarating plunge to the finish. This was like that—the biggest deal of his life, the stakes highest.

Byron needed a different offshore account under his new identity, untraceable back to his existing personal Cayman account, now in the name of Army Bendorf, and he wanted to avoid international banks that had branches in the United States who would be more likely to share information.

Offshore banks required some form of identification to determine the country of origin, and he didn't want to take the chance on trying to obtain a passport, at least a legal one. One way, which struck him as entirely unsafe, was to select a nominee in the offshore country where he wanted to bank. Finding a nominee was easy—they advertised. The nominee would handle everything in their name. No name, no references, no passport or ID were necessary. In the end, though, he couldn't shake the perception a nominee would be some low-life con man, maybe a disbarred attorney, promising he had helped hundreds of clients, claiming a spotless record—satisfied clients. He figured the nominee could provide references, but who could say they wouldn't be a cousin Vinny or aunt Natasha.

As he searched for a safe place to hide money, he considered safe places he could escape to. Long-standing beliefs and biases melted away as he investigated Panama, advertised as the country of abundant fish, trees, and butterflies. His memory of Panama called up the mug shot of the drug dictator, Manuel Noriega, who was driven from power when President Reagan invaded the country and returned constitutional rule. Now it was a desirable place to live, English speaking and American dollar currency. The average temperatures ranged from the mid-seventies to the high eighties—no hurricanes, ever. Millions of dollars could buy a beautiful place on the ocean and safety. No one would find him there.

Byron established a residency in Panama. He didn't have to go there or live there to accomplish it. It cost a little under ten thousand dollars. Panama was a friendly place to do business, so he incorporated an LLC corporation called Woodworks, a business to create teak wood products. Teak wood was a well know local common wood used in making furniture and shipbuilding. So common in Panama, it provided great cover for banking and passing through funds. He incorporated under the name Silas Kobak. He transferred all but a few thousand dollars from the Cayman bank account he set up when he left Seattle.

For banking and traveling domestically, the best option was a driver's license. A forged license would have to do, which turned out to be easy in Chicago. He obtained one in the name of Silas Kobak and Army Bendorf.

The offshore banks had a slew of fees, such as setup, transaction fees, and account maintenance fees, but there was competition, so he shopped around. Belize was a stable country with a lot of benefits. Belizean accounts were not subject to local taxes or exchange control restrictions, and he could choose from most major currencies, which might be necessary, and the exchange rate between Belize and the U.S. was two to one. The country was also known for upholding privacy, and they catered to their international clients—no local clients allowed. The final selling point was the interest rates, the country's low inflation, and strict local government regulations.

Since Byron told Buster he needed to get out of town, he hadn't been back for two weeks. The original plan today was to grab a bite to eat and go to Buster's one last time. Not knowing what would happen tomorrow, whether the accounts were monitored and what McDermott would do.

One of two things would happen when Seven Continents, or McDermott himself, discovered the accounts were empty. McDermott would pick himself off the floor, panic would spread up through his chest and redden his face, and he would either call the FBI or just be angry. Probably hire a private investigator then. If he didn't call the FBI, the mystery would be solved.

Like gnawing on a bone, in between self-doubts, he went over the options. One way of looking at things had him wearing prison stripes and the other in a bathing suit sipping pina Coladas. Byron Kelly feared the futility of it all, and Army didn't give a damn.

Either scenario was daunting. One option had him rich beyond his wildest dreams, the other inescapable return to being Byron Kelly. Under either option, it would be clear he was somehow involved in the caper. It was unavoidable when he didn't show up for work and disappeared. He would be accused of stupidity if he stuck around to be discovered. He had to leave and, as best he could, cover up any hints about what happened.

After work, he walked to the local Subway for a sandwich, and at the office supply store, he bought a jump drive to copy any pertinent files. He had hard copies but wanted a second set to cover his tracks as best he could. That night he downloaded a software program called Bleach Bit onto the jump drive. The software would remove all cache, cookies, shred files and wipe unallocated disk space off his office computer. He knew the mainframe files were backed up continuously and, in case of a natural disaster, the whole system duplicated in another state, so the company would always have a record. Still, he needed a real-time copy. Also, he wanted to delay things, give him time to escape and time to figure out the truth about those accounts.

Before going to sleep, he reviewed the plan. He would transfer the money from all of the accounts into his Panamanian business account, then immediately transfer a significant portion into his new Belize account. The accounts were opened under the new name Silas Kobak using a stolen social security number obtained by searching through the Seven Continents HR files. He considered several different employees whose social security number he could borrow. Typically, social security identities weren't verified. The purpose of the social security number is financial, so in the end, he decided on McDermott himself. He thought about Dan but in the end, hated to think it might benefit him using his number. McDermott wouldn't matter, especially if he was behind bars.

The minute Byron received confirmation the funds were transferred, he would wipe his computer's hard drive, barring any complications, just leave his desk and walk out the door. For that simple reason, it would be clear to McDermott he was one. When he didn't show up for work, they would consider him a prime suspect anyway. On the other hand, if he could stay until the end of the day, he might delay suspicion. His last thought before dozing off was, 'Will McDermott recall our conversation in his office? Bet it will piss him off.'

Chapter Ten

On an early Fall Day, a cold rain washed the dirt and grim off the city sidewalks. Umbrellas popped up and down, dodging and darting in and out of buildings. When Byron arrived at work, Dan was warming up his audience with accounts of driving in on the Eisenhower Expressway, how he barely avoided an accident, and how traffic backed up for hours behind him. He ended his monologue, directed at anyone who would listen to his scientific explanation of how the rain mixed with the oil and tire rubber to create treacherous road conditions, and his usual targets to blame, women, calling them idiots who didn't know any better. "Just wait until the first snow," he concluded. "I'll never get to work."

Marni had the last word. "Darn. Dan can't make it to work. What a shame."

The morning workload was one service call after another until the lunch hour started, and for one hour, Byron was alone. For the first fifteen minutes, he contemplated the game plan as a terrorizing flurry of numbers, letters, and symbols danced across his computer screen. Finally, he mustered the courage to proceed. As soon as he completed the process, he wanted to slip out of the office unnoticed.

Even as his confidence rode high, it would take time to discover what happened; the question remained how McDermott would react. His reaction was crucial. Whenever the missing funds were discovered, it wouldn't take long for McDermott to suspect him, call the FBI or not, but it should allow him enough time to be on the evening flight to St. Thomas. From Saint Thomas, he had the option of going to Panama or Belize under his new name Silas Kobak.

Dan and Marni were at lunch, and he could hear Donna talking on the phone. Byron slid his chair back out of his cubicle and looked to see if anybody was in the vicinity. Back in front of his computer, he pulled a list of account numbers from the bag. One by one, he transferred the funds from each account to his account in Panama. Fumbling his way nervously for thirty-three minutes to complete the transfer, it took longer than expected. Immediately he transferred a portion of the funds to his numbered account in Belize.

At 1:30 p.m., the help desk phone started ringing, and assignments were prioritized. Byron wanted to leave but was asked to team up with Donna on the first afternoon assignment. When they returned to their desks at 2:30 pm, Alfred requested Byron go to the 60th floor and fix a computer, the last place he wanted to go to.

This was only the fifth time he had been on the 60th floor and this time to help McDermott's secretary. The nameplate on her desk read Dorothy 'Dot' Tilly. He had to give McDermott a little credit; she was not a trophy secretary. Other factors must have ruled over the hiring decision. A square short, muscular woman in her fifties, about as friendly as McDermott. Smiling, he wondered if the hiring decision was for protection. One thing was clear, she was unhappy to see Byron. It was apparent last time he was there, she didn't like his looks, his hair, and how he dressed. She quickly described the problem and what the solution was, then left to get coffee.

As he waited for the system to execute commands, Byron feasted his gaze on the opulent surroundings—the Waterford Chrystal chandelier, wall-to-wall Indian wool carpeting, each private office door custom made of imported Costa Rican cocobolo wood, including the two executive washroom doors, which were off-limits to people like him who were instructed to use the bathrooms on their floors

Byron always thought the offices at Oreves were over the top, but this was to the moon. Valentin always said, "If you have a lot of money, who do you want to do business with, us…", waving his hands in the air to show off his private Taj Mahal, "or some investment banker in some strip mall?" Byron subscribed to the notion, it's usually more than one thing, and people preferred performance over opulence.

As he rebooted her system, Alfred emerged from McDermott's office and nodded. Ten minutes later, two men exited the elevator dressed in cheap black suits and white shirts, muted dark-colored ties, so similar in their attire it could have been their uniforms. They were accompanied by McDermott's secretary. Holding a cup of coffee, she walked past without a glance.

McDermott opened his office door and reached out his hand as if he expected them. "Glad you could come so quickly."

Both men reached into their pockets and opened a leather wallet, and flashed their credentials. "I'm FBI agent Barnes, and this is agent Galinski." Agent Barnes was a basketball-tall, thin, black man, and Agent Galinski, by contrast, was short, maybe five foot five inches—a grown man and a small boy.

Byron's heart raced. They weren't more than ten steps away. They entered his office and shut the door. He wanted to get up and walk away, but McDermott's squared-off assistant stood behind him watching the computer screen, anxious for the update to be completed. This was a major update and took longer than usual.

He could hear her breathing and shuffling back and forth impatiently. "Will this take much longer, she said impatiently.

Without taking his eyes off the screen, Byron answered, hoping to escape. "It might take a while. I can come back."

"Not on your life. I need to wait. You're not supposed…just get it done."

An eternally long fifteen minutes later, the agents emerged from his office and stopped just outside his door, not ten steps away.

The tall black agent said, "We will have a team of forensic accountants and IT experts here first thing in the morning. They'll be here a minimum of three days, maybe longer depending on what they find. They need a place to work—one of your conference rooms will do. A large one.

Full access to your system. No restrictions. Total cooperation."

Standing nearby and smiling, McDermott responded in a friendly voice, "Sure. But I need to check with legal counsel to be sure there aren't any concerns."

"You do what you need to do. But we need total access, and we will start interviewing people immediately to lay the foundation. Galinski here is a bit of a nerd, so he needs to talk to your IT guys—today. I'd like to talk to your HR chief."

Looking in Byron's direction over the top of his head, "Dot, take agent Galinski to Alfred's office…," then over to the black agent, "What was your name?"

"Barnes."

"Take agent Barnes to Misses P's office."

"Agent Galinski said, "Alfred is the IT chief?"

"No, but he will do."

Irritated, Agent Galinski responded. "No, please tell the HR chief to join my meeting with Alfred. I will talk to both of them."

"Just Alfred. He is the only one available. He'll get you anything you need."

The upgrade completed, Byron rose and moved to the elevators but remained still within earshot.

Galinski had more to say. "You said you already investigated the missing funds. The money can't just be misplaced? Right? You've already thoroughly evaluated this? I assume large sums are hard to steal? Over twenty million, huh? I guess you don't just misplace twenty million, right?"

Byron turned to listen for the answer. McDermott scowled. "We don't misplace funds."

Agent Galinski took a step forward, a pad and pen in hand. One more thing. It's a bit peculiar not to know who reported this or how it was discovered." Looking up from his notes and cocking his head, "So you have already thoroughly investigated this, and it's not just…"

McDermott's face turned red with anger. "It was anonymously reported by a loyal employee. And, yes, we just discovered it."

Agent Barnes had a puzzled look on his face. "That seems a bit odd. Why would a loyal employee report this anonymously?"

McDermott was ready with his answer. "I think someone wasn't authorized to be in that part of the system. I will make it clear there will be no repercussions, and I'm sure we'll learn who it was."

"Yeah. I think an employee would be proud to make such a finding."

McDermott smiled through clenched teeth. "I am sure they will be."

"We'll figure this out, and quickly." As Agent Barnes turned back to the elevator, he added, "We're good at this, and we always get our man. Or a woman."

The elevator doors opened. Out of the corner of his eye, Byron could see Agent Barnes and Galinski heading his way. He hurried into the elevator and selected his floor, avoiding eye contact and taking a deep anxious breath as the elevator doors closed.

Who was McDermott going to say reported this? An interesting telling dilemma. Was there really someone? The odds suddenly tilted toward the accounts being legitimate. Byron shrugged his shoulders. He was in a heap of trouble, and he needed to get out of there.

Byron strained to eavesdrop on Alfred's muffled conversation with Galinski until suddenly the conversation went silent. Byron held his breath, then suddenly Alfred startled him when he appeared behind him, "Army, come with me," he bellowed.

When they arrived at his office, Alfred introduced agent Galinski. "Someone anonymously reported missing funds to Mr. McDermott, but we don't know who. We need to determine which employees have access to those accounts.

Get me a list of all employees authorized to access that part of the system?"

Byron's heart raced as the agent's pinched gaze bore in on him like a bird of prey. He wondered if it was a technique to rattle him or he was trying to read his mind. Byron worried he would start asking questions about who he was, where he lived, did he have access to the system, did he know anything about some missing accounts. To avoid his stare, Byron gazed around the office and settled on the large poster of the Spanish Villa overlooking a white sand beach. Alfred's dream escape.

Byron nodded. "That shouldn't be too hard. I'll do that right now. You know there might be a thousand employees who have access?"

Agent Galinski answered. "It's a place to start."

Looking back to Alfred, "I was planning to leave a little early since I skipped lunch if that's okay. I'll do it before I go."

Alone at his work station, Byron quickly organized a list of all employees who could access that part of the system and sent it to Alfred, wondering if the FBI would notice McDermott's name missing from the list. He thought about adding a note but didn't, thinking it might invite questions. He left all IT employees off the list, thinking the omission would be understood as an easy oversight. In the following silence, he watched the clock and listened for unfamiliar sounds and anybody getting on or off the elevator. Whenever any of the team members spoke, he held his breath.

Midafternoon, an hour and a half before he normally left work, he couldn't stand waiting around. No doubt he would be a suspect when they determined he disappeared, hopefully not until tomorrow.

It was inevitable now; the plan in motion couldn't be stopped—the die was cast. At a minimum, when he stopped showing up for work, they would suspect him. If it was McDermott or someone in the company, even if the accounts were legitimate, he had to leave and let the FBI begin their investigation.

Byron's heart raced as he inserted the thumb drive, downloaded additional files, ran the Bleachbit program, and watched as it erased everything on his computer hard drive.

He strained to hear the hushed conversation between Donna and Marni. He could barely make out what Marni was saying. "Did you hear? There are FBI agents in McDermott's office?"

Donna seemed to be standing outside of her cubicle. "What's going on?"

"I don't know, but McDermott is really upset. You know how he's always checking me out. Well, I rode the elevator with him. Have you seen what I'm wearing today…"?

Dan interrupted, "I saw you. Ooh la la."

"You don't count, bug eyes. Anyway, you know how he's always checking us out. Looked like he was on his way to a funeral." Giggling, Marni continued, "Not even a peek."

"No one knows what is going on," Dan said, "FBI … something big…I heard somebody here might be a Russian spy."

Marni laughed. "I'll bet it's that old guy in accounting…you know, the guy with the thick glasses. The guy with the wig,"

Loud enough to be sure Byron heard, Dan said, "I'll bet old Army's a spy."

Holding his breath, the files disappeared at lightning speed. Byron knew a good forensic computer specialist still might be able to recover some of the files. The only way to be sure the private files were unreadable was to drill holes in the hard drive, which he couldn't do. He also maliciously deleted key mainframe files, knowing they were backed up and would take some time to restore, all more a diversion and a delay tactic. Soon his computer screen went blank, and it was time to leave.

Byron pushed back and surveyed his desktop. For good measure, unsure of the FBI's immediate capabilities, knowing he was going to be suspected anyway, he unscrewed the computer case and poured a half bottle of Coke over the motherboard. The urban legend corrosive effect of a Coke might just add another layer of the coverup. He took a deep breath. His hands were shaking. As casually as he could, he proceeded to the elevator and found no one in the hallway.

When the elevator door opened, the two FBI agents were standing there, cold-faced like they were waiting for him. Moving to the back of the elevator across from them, he felt their gaze bore in. He steeled himself against Agent Galinsky's penetrating glare, his mind probably thumbing through most wanted bulletins, or maybe a practiced truth test.

Agent Galinski broke the silence halfway to the first floor. "You still here? Thought you were leaving early."

"Yeah, I was…er, I am," Byron answered hesitantly.

As he broke away from Galinski's stare, he noticed his gaze shifted to his messenger bag. The bag suddenly felt heavy, weighed down with the malicious jump drive and the additional printed pages. Byron counted down each passing floor. They stopped on the third floor. There was no one there.

Agent Barnes continued to study Byron from head to toe—his flannel shirt, long natty hair, bird hunting jacket, and the messenger bag. His gaze stopped on the messenger bag.

Sensing he wanted to ask a question, Byron looked down at the bag and said, "Also, my lunch bag." He retrieved an apple from the bag and bit into it. Mustered courage, and with the anxiety and coolness of a dive bomber, Byron continued chomping on his apple. "Busy day." Looking back to Galinski for confirmation, he added, "Didn't get time to eat."

Byron got off on the first floor, and the agents continued to the garage level. Outside, he began to walk westward on Randolph Street, resisting the urge to break out running. It was a clear, warm, late October afternoon; the sun reflected high off the steel monoliths at his shoulders, darkening the crowded sidewalks.

The scheduled flight to St. Thomas departed at 8:40 p.m., easily enough time to get home, pack a bag, and grab the rest of the papers. He had planned to take the train to his apartment but leaving early and not knowing the schedule, he hailed the first cab.

The cab driver was a middle-aged man; a cigarette dangled from his lips as he watched him through the rearview mirror, smiling, awaiting instructions. His name posted was Tariq Batwal, and judging by the small flag hanging from one of the air vents, he was from Pakistan. Byron gave cross streets in Evanston then sat up, ready to give him more instructions for the fastest way out of the loop, but the cabby looked away and sped off before he could add, "I need to get there in a hurry."

He smiled and began to weave in and out of traffic, honking at cars in front of him. Ten blocks later, on the Kennedy Expressway heading north, he continued weaving in and out of the traffic, onto the shoulder, and at one point exiting and shooting through the overpass intersection, down the on-ramp, rejoining the Kennedy traffic, bypassing probably a hundred cars.

Nothing said criminal on the run more than dodging in and out of Chicago traffic. Holding onto the armrest, Byron called out, "I am not in that much of a hurry. You can slow down."

Tariq smiled and shrugged his shoulders indifferently. Byron felt like a man on the run—wanted in two states. Regret swept over him and stuck in his throat. Without warning, the cab exited the freeway and began to travel on surface streets. Byron thought better about questioning him, sensing he was in the category of Chicago navigational genius.

When they were close to his apartment, Byron asked him to pull over. Ahead, he saw a three-story run-down ivy-covered brick home. Leaning over the seat and pointing, "You can let me out there. That brick one on your right. Tipping him generously, he waited for the cab to pull away then walked a half-block back to his apartment.

Byron planned to pack a bag and take the train to the airport. He sat his suitcase and messenger bag at the front door and shuffled over to the easy chair, and sat, preferring to wait in the apartment rather than at the airport.

Chapter Eleven

Random thoughts flashed before him. Always in his first thoughts were Sybie, his folks, the fall from grace, and wondering how much further he could fall. At dusk, he walked back into the kitchen and drank a glass of water, and out the window saw a black sedan pull up two buildings away, looking ominously like an unmarked police car.

Agent Barnes exited the car and moved around to the passenger side. He appeared to be waiting for something, maybe his partner on the phone, maybe local police. Had they already discovered Byron had vandalized his computer or traced activity to his workstation, worse did they already know he took the money?

Darting to the door, he retrieved the messenger bag and luggage, then, thinking it too conspicuous carrying luggage, tossed it aside and raced for the rear stairwell. Once outside, he ran up the alley. Pausing at the end of the alley, looked around, trying to decide where to go, he saw an Evanston police cruiser enter two streets away.

Ducking behind some bushes beside the front porch of a large three-story house, he watched the cruiser crawl in his direction and pass by. When the police car reached the far end, it turned and moved slowly back, shining the spotlight into the back yards, garages, and shrubs along the way. Behind Byron, the lattice surrounding the porch was loose, and he pulled it back and crawled underneath. The ground was wet and cold.

The police cruiser crept forward like a hunched lion parting high grass, looking for prey. When he reached Byron's location, a spotlight swiveled around and slowly illuminated the area, forcing him further back. The police officer opened the car door and began to talk on his radio.

"567, I'm in the alley, over."

"910, hold your position. The suspect is believed to be on foot, over."

"567, copy. I have secured the alley. Will hold my position. Over."

"Copy that."

The policeman stood beside his car for several minutes, then turned and walked back up the alley, shinning his flashlight in the back yards and shrubs. As he walked to his cruiser, swinging the flashlight side to side, Byron saw his airline ticket had slipped from the front pocket of his bag and was lying on the ground next to the bushes. When the policeman looked away, he pushed the lattice back and retrieved it. Rolling away from the opening, something moved next to him. A cat screeched and darted through the opening. Byron jumped. Clenching his teeth and holding his breath, his heart thundered like a thousand hoofs in a stampede.

The beam of the policeman's flashlight flared out toward the cat. "Fucking cat," the policeman exclaimed. He chased after it, kicking wildly, yelling out, "Get out of here, you fucking cat."

Rolling onto his back and closing his eyes, shivering in the cold, damp muck, with only the light from the streetlight, Byron watched and listened. For the next several hours, the cruiser pulled away and, a few minutes later, returned to the same spot. He could hear intermittent muffled radio conversations and the faint sound of a television from the house above him.

This went on until after two in the morning when his eyelids drooped as he fought off sleep in the trembling cold. No matter what, when morning came, Byron had to find a way out of the area. As daylight was breaking, at least two hours passed since the police cruiser returned—maybe a shift change, or another call, or they had given up searching.

When the sun came up, Byron saw the dirt floor that had been his bed and peeked through the lattice to watch an old couple walking their dog and several cars pass by. On foot and covered with dried mud, his escape options were limited. There were no signs of police nearby, but no doubt they were watching the apartment. He couldn't stop shivering—no matter what, he couldn't spend another night under the porch. Luck would have to be on his side.

Mid-morning, the front door opened above him, and he heard footsteps and clanking sounds moving toward the front steps. Byron watched an old man, aided by a walker, shuffle slowly, cautiously, to a cab waiting at the curb.

Unable to stand another minute under the porch, it was a good time to escape. If he could get to the gas station two blocks away, he could use the restroom and clean up as best he could. He recalled the restrooms were on the outside and accessible to use without being seen. Pushing aside the lattice and crawling to freedom, a feeling of relief then dread hit when he spied a police cruiser at the stop sign a block and a half away.

When the police cruiser turned on to the street, Byron hurried up the porch steps to the front door. In its day, the house was one of the more expensive homes on the block, but now rundown, the siding and front porch were badly in need of paint. He rang the doorbell and waited, glancing over his shoulder to watch the police cruiser creep toward him. Anxious, he hoped someone would answer, and he could quickly talk his way inside. Then what was he going to do? Trapped, each escape idea felt to be only the next step, nothing beyond that. There seemed to be no way out. Resignation to his fate was taking over.

He rang the doorbell again and knocked loudly. He would ask to use the phone. His car broke down. Nobody in their right mind would let him in, especially given his appearance. It was a long shot. He practiced his lines as he listened for someone to come to the door. He could fake an injury, being in great pain, and say he needed to call his wife to come and get him. He could say he lived close by but didn't think he could make it.

The police cruiser at the end of the street was crawling his way. He tried the door and found it unlocked. He entered, then turned back and watched the police cruiser pass, savoring his momentary freedom. Surveying the room, he listened for sounds. The silence was stifling but safe.

"Anyone home?" In a louder voice, "Hello. Anyone home?"

Byron was alone. The heavy mahogany front door, with smoked side panels, opened to a long hallway, stairs to the left, and a dark living room to the right with mahogany plantation shutters on four large windows facing the porch. At one time a magnificent home, but now it was old and lonely.

The furniture appeared to be expensive but was covered with sheets. The floors were tongue and groove oak. A deserted, broken umbrella leaned against a dust-coated entryway console. House keys were hanging on a peg near the door. He gazed back, out the front door to the empty street.

Byron walked toward the back of the house, past the dining room, into the kitchen. Opening a cupboard for a glass and deciding against it, he turned the faucet on and let the water run cold, then cupped his hands and drank generously. He wiped the sink dry with a stained and ragged dish towel lying on the counter.

A spare bedroom next to the kitchen appeared to be where the old man slept. The bed was unmade. There was a recliner beside the bed and a television mounted on the wall opposite it. The furnace came on and startled him. Still shivering, he stood in front of the register rubbing his hands, listening for sounds.

Moving back to the front room, he stood before the window, watched, and listened. Only five cars passed in the last half hour, so he cautiously ventured out to the front porch and was surprised to see the police cruiser still parked a block away.

Back inside, Byron sat on one of the sheet-covered chairs in the living room and considered his options, which were few. It seemed apparent the old man lived alone, and there was no way to know when he would return. He would have to leave soon, and his best option was to use the back door and retreat up the alley. At the same time, he had no plans to make a run for it and was prepared to just turn himself in if confronted. Cooperation was important, and he wasn't a stupid TV criminal who thought he could outrun the law. What was he going to do—steal a car, kidnap a hostage? He smiled for the first time in what seemed like days.

Standing at the foot of the stairs, listening, watching out the window, he waited, ready to make a quick exit. What stories was the house telling him? An old man lived here alone and by appearance, really old and unable to get around very well. There wasn't much in the way of memorabilia or pictures to tell his story. Nothing on the walls and one picture leaning against the stairs, a college graduation picture of a young woman. He noticed the walls leading up the stairway were faded and discolored, except where pictures had been hanging.

Byron decided to quickly explore the upstairs. There were three bedrooms on the second floor, including a master bedroom, with a bathroom and another hallway bathroom and a door leading to the third floor—an attic. None of the bedrooms were being used. One looked like stepping back in time to when a young woman lived there.

Leaning against the hallway wall were several framed pictures that told a better story—long ago family pictures, two of golfers posing after a round of golf, one of a man shaking hands with Arnold Palmer, a gold-framed picture of a beautiful woman that had yellowed and faded. He picked up a studio family photo of a husband, wife, and teenage daughter—likely the old man with his wife and daughter? What happened to them?

When he decided to return to the main floor, he heard a clanking sound outside. When Byron arrived on the ground floor, he could see the old man struggling to climb the ramp beside the steps.

Byron didn't have time to escape out the back of the house, so he ducked into the front closet, instantly aware of his mistake—the old man was wearing a coat. Byron watched through the slightly ajar closet door. The old man struggled to remove his coat and, after several frustrating attempts to wrangle the coat off while bracing himself on the walker, pulled it off and angrily threw it to the floor outside the closet.

No reason to panic; the old man didn't spend any time in the living room and turned toward the kitchen and back bedroom and into the bathroom. Byron could leave when it was safe.

A few minutes later, the old man clanked toward him and stopped at the foot of the stairs. For a couple of minutes, he heard only the sound of the old man's heavy breathing. He watched as he picked up the framed picture leaning against the stairs. He was older than he originally thought, his full head of white hair uncombed and straggly, his long, thin face wrinkled and hollow—maybe in his eighties but frail, sick—very sick. His forearms, once strong and athletic, now were gaunt, loose skinned; his blue-veined forearms looked like a highway roadmap.

Finally, as the old man set the picture down, he stumbled forward and braced himself against the stair baluster. Red-faced and breathing heavily—inches away, only the width of a door separated them. In the stifling hot closet, Byron felt panicky. He tried to hold his breath to stay quiet. A bead of sweat trickled down his face as he watched the old man struggle, terrified he might collapse, forcing him out of hiding. He had to remain calm.

After a few minutes, the old man collected himself and began to walk away. Clank, step, clank, step. When it was safe, Byron went to the front door and was startled to see the police cruiser slowly approaching and stopping in front of the house. Retreating to the safety of the second floor, pausing, he withdrew to the safety of the attic to wait until nightfall.

The dim light of a lost day filtered into the attic. Yesterday he lived on the edge, unknowingly minutes away from his last day of freedom. No one could ever know the real Byron again. From his viewpoint, he couldn't see much of the attic—a large unfinished room with a plywood floor and open rafters cluttered with a lifetime collection of items and stories awaiting a day of visitation and new life. On closer inspection, he saw the house ductwork was preinstalled for the day when someone finished it into a bedroom. In the far corner, plumbing for a bathroom was installed and stubbed off.

Exhausted from shivering through the night laying on the cold damp dirt under a porch, the fear of being caught, and the pressure of not knowing what to do—an unfamiliar feeling, great turned to bad, then to worse—how can a life fall so fast, so far? Yesterday, he had plans, and today he was trapped in a hot attic. He curled up on the floor next to a storage trunk and closed his eyes, longing for fifteen minutes of warmth and security.

Byron didn't come back to life until the early morning sun burst through the oversized floor-to-ceiling shadeless double windows at the end of the room. He slept like he was dead and awoke, not knowing where he was. Looking around, he felt he had awakened in the middle of a rummage sale—racks of hanging clothes, scattered women's flats and high heels and men's dress shoes, several pairs of scuffed weathered, wrinkled white leather golf shoes. There were three large chests and two columns of neatly stacked moving boxes and tubs, old newspapers and magazines, old comforters, blankets, and pillows. Curious anyone canned in this metropolitan area, he couldn't explain boxes of canning jars. It suggested a more rural background—probably they were from somewhere else.

Two sets of old golf clubs leaned against the wall aside an open box of old pots and pans. Whoever lived here didn't throw much away. It reminded Byron of his folks. *How were they doing?* He was in such a panic when he left; he never considered how hard it would be to stay in touch. No doubt his extended absence worried them.

Dad could fix anything from his collection of spare parts, nuts, bolts, and duct tape. He never replaced anything unless it was broken beyond repair, couldn't be fixed with duct tape, or had a hole in it. If dad found a screw, nut, bolt, or washer lying in the road, he'd pick it up and put it in his pocket, and add it to his collection.

The sound of a flushing toilet interrupted his exploration. Moving to one of the registers, he listened to the sound of running water, and a few seconds later, clank, clank, clank, then later kitchen sounds, the faint opening and closing of the refrigerator, the toaster popping up, and more clanking sounds. Later, he heard the sound of a blaring television through a register across the room, so loud Byron could have been in the same room. The old man was back in bed, the only room where there was a television.

He found comfort in the late Fall sunny morning and the warmth and momentary security of the attic. Byron moved to the window facing the street and sat on a trunk, and watched the vacant street below. There were no signs of police. Across the street, outside a well-maintained older home, two kids' bicycles leaned against the front steps. There was no reason to leave his newfound safety today. Given the old man's age and the loud TV, he could leave anytime.

Byron read that a person could live for days without eating but only 100 hours without water depending on conditions. Four days—he could do that but wouldn't want to try. He could manage a couple of days if he had to. He figured the longer he stayed, the safer his exit. Right now, he had to pee. Looking back to canning jars, it occurred to him he had his own bathroom right there in the attic.

He began to go through a stack of magazines and newspapers, occasionally dozing off to the sound of an unknown old detective movie or western. This one sounded like a Bogart movie. It was hard to tell if he watched all those movies, one after another, and so loud, or was he sleeping. Either way, he was hard of hearing.

In the afternoon, the wind came up and blew away the sunny day. He made a chair using women's dresses, old blankets, and pillows. His gaze was drawn to a stack of Life magazines arranged by year. A family of readers or at least collectors lived here. He wouldn't be bored biding his time. A note was paper-clipped to one of the magazines, a Look Magazine cover of a rooster. The note read, 'Rare?' He determined there was no 'Life logo' on the cover. There were two others without logos, one for the assassination of President John Kennedy and the other when the cover was solid green to commemorate Earth Day. The collection of magazines started in the year 1936 with a photo of Fort Peck Dam, in Montana, and the last in October of 1996, a commemorative sixty years issue. The first issue cost ten cents.

***

The television went silent at ten o'clock, and in the middle of the night, Byron was awakened when it came on again. He dozed off until another burst of sunlight woke him. He moved back to sit in front of the oversized windows and the warm sunlight.

Perched on an old trunk watching the street below, he began to read old magazines and newspapers to the accompaniment of unintelligible movie sounds. The January 1994 issue of Life magazine featured stories about killer weather storms and why nature was so mad. Inside the magazine was a newspaper clipping from the Chicago Sun-Times with a note in a woman's handwriting, 'Big news.' The newspaper clipping reported on a National Weather Service story they had uncovered an error at all the reporting stations of half a degree every day for the past ten years.

In the background, he could hear the news coming on the television and scampered to the far register and strained to hear. When he put his ear to the register, he heard the tail end of a report. 'And the FBI says this man, Army Bendorf, is still in the area. If anyone has any information, please contact them at the number shown here."

The television channel switched to a western, *Rio Bravo*.

Byron identified the distinctive voice of John Wayne, "All right, quit. Nobody's trying to stop you. If you want to quit, quit. Go on back to the bottle, get drunk. One thing, though. Somebody throws a dollar in the spittoon, don't expect me to do something about it. Just get down on your knees and go after it.

He recognized the next voice as Dean Martin, "I'm sorry."

"Sorry, don't get it done, Dude."

Byron remembered John Wayne's character, Chance, punched Dude in the scene.

Chapter Twelve

When Byron awoke the next day, he was light-headed and needed to get out of the attic and drink some water. He figured it was Sunday. There was a second-floor bathroom he could easily get to. He could wait for the old man to use the bathroom, and when he flushed his toilet, Byron could fill up some jars and also empty the jars that served as his commode at the same time.

He knew the old man was sleeping, so he waited for the opportunity as he watched the street below. It was still sunny but colder. Two boys were playing catch across the street wearing coats, stocking caps, and gloves. It bought back memories. When he was young, he loved playing catch with his friends. Every time he threw a tight spiral to a teammate or friend, he got a twinge of satisfaction.

Byron eased forward when the ball rolled out into the street, and one of the boys ran after it. A car approached from the west, directly into the sun. It was easy to see the ball, the car, and the kid could arrive at the same spot simultaneously. He clenched his jaw and braced himself. There was nothing he could do but watch. The driver screeched on his brakes and skidded to a stop just in time.

The driver stormed out of the car, shaking his fists at the boys. Byron couldn't make out what was said, but they were angry words. The boys retreated toward their house as the man continued to yell at them.

The boy's mother stormed off the porch and stood in the middle of the yard, her arms folded defiantly, and began to yell at the man, so loudly he could hear every expletive. The man shook his head and returned to his car. As he drove away, she continued yelling and raised her middle finger in the air to punctuate the whole exchange. How the world had changed. Byron's mom would have thanked the man and dragged him in the house on his heels, crying, and he wouldn't be able to sit down for a week.

Two hours later, he slipped down to the second-floor bathroom and waited. While waiting, Byron was aghast, seeing his hardly recognizable reflection in the mirror. He had forgotten how long his hair was and how ratty. He looked like a white Rastafarian, unshaven and still caked with dirt. His clothes looked like he had been crawling around on the ground. Who was Army Bendorf? Where did Byron Kelly go? Or, was he Silas Kobak?

The shower hadn't been used for a while, soap caked on the shower door, and mold around the drain reminded him of Seattle moss. He opened the bathroom closet and saw it was stocked with towels and washcloths, a pack of disposable razors, band-aids, unopened bars of soap and toilet paper, and an unopened box of Tampons. The medicine cabinet contained a bottle of aspirin, a nearly depleted tube of toothpaste, an old toothbrush, a half-full bottle of Tylenol, deodorant, Band-Aids, hand crème, nail clippers, and shaving cream.

He heard the old man clanking toward the bathroom. Byron waited. Poised over the sink, he held one of the canning jars beneath the faucet. The second he heard the sound of the main floor toilet flushing, he began to fill as many jars as he could. At the same time, with his foot, he flushed the toilet. He held his breath and listened. As soon as he heard him clanking his way back to his bedroom, he returned to the attic.

When the old man switched the channel to news, Byron crawled over to the register he determined was best for hearing the television. The local news followed the national news: more shootings on the south side and an update on out-of-control gang-related fatalities.

A male newsperson reported. "According to statistics released this week by the FBI, Chicago is on the way to becoming the nation's murder capital. We will soon exceed 500 murders and pass New York and Los Angeles in murders. Chicago police Superintendent Garry McCarthy vowed to fight the perception the city is the murder capital and reported the rate of murders in the city is going down." Next, Governor, Pat Quinn, promised the state was doing everything it could to help Chicago.

Following a commercial break, a male news anchor reported, "News 4 is at the scene of one of the greatest bank heists in Chicago history, over twenty-five million dollars. Jim."

News reporter Jim Snyder began reporting. "I am standing in the lobby of Seven Continents Financial Group. The FBI is no closer to solving this crime, and President and CEO Robert McDermott has not provided a statement and declined to be interviewed. The FBI is hunting for this man. His name is Army Bendorf, an employee who has now vanished. There are no clues as to his whereabouts. The FBI is seeking the public's help in tracking him down. The FBI has opened a tip line and is asking the public to call if they have any information. An unnamed source has revealed he was previously an Army demolition expert and may be dangerous."

Byron rolled onto his side and closed his eyes.

A female news anchor spoke next. "No, closer Jim. I guess that explains how he got his name Army? Do we know anything about him, where he's from, his personal life?"

The news reporter responded. "The FBI hasn't released any details about the man shown here. They believe he is still in the area."

***

Byron rolled onto his back and stared into the open rafters. He retrieved the picture of Sybie from his bag as the sound of the television faded away.

On their way back from Banff, they drove along in silence. All the warm vibrations of a week in Banff slowly cooled with the passing of each milepost. Drip, drip, drip, the mood changed. As the periods of silence increased, Byron called up the image of Sybie's twinkling blue eyes and silky black hair popping out from beneath the white comforter, framing a blooming rose smile, the Gray Jays on

107

the deck singing out the new day, the magnificence of Three Sister's peak on the horizon.

The silence and brief exchanges twisted his thinking as they passed through Coeur d'Alene, Idaho, and crossed the Washington State border. The silence between them raised doubts; the time they spent together was real. *Wasn't it? Nothing could change that, right, everything so good, so perfect?* They made love like every time was the first—memorable, sacred moments when they were one, inseparable, in love. Nothing like that could be phony. Byron admonished himself to give the relationship time, not to rush her, give her time to trust it was real, to understand how deeply he cared. Something held her back, though, and she was worth figuring it out.

She finally broke the silence. "There is something I have to tell you,"

Byron turned the radio off and looked at her. Only the hum of the tires weaving through last winter's studded tire ruts that had carved up highway 95 could be heard. Sybie sat stiffly, staring to the top of the next hill through the bug-splattered windshield, "Before I left for Banff, I had a biopsy of my lymph nodes."

Byron braced himself.

"I should have told you. I should have, but it was such a special time, and I was with you. I didn't want to destroy my dream."

"What are you saying?"

Taking a deep breath and looking out the side window, she continued, "Let me tell you about me. The real me. My disability was more than just a crippled girl with a wandering eye. When I was a baby, I was diagnosed with the nail-patella syndrome, NPS, which is a rare genetic disorder. My form of the disability was milder than most, but that's like saying a little pregnant. It affected both knees but more my right knee. My knee caps were more like pebbles. Corrective surgery, growing older, and corrective glasses did wonders. I'd like to think my persistence and physical therapy aided my progress.

"When I was just a blob in my mother's womb, the doctors discovered my calcium was not developing normally. It also meant my bones were not developing properly. Worse yet, it meant my genetic codes could be all mixed up, and there could be other surprises lurking as I grew older. When genetic codes are missing or go off on their own, it's anybody's guess what else might be amiss.

"I was left with a painful leg brace and having to go through life wondering, living from one doctor checkup to another." The blood drained from her face as she tried to swallow her words, words she hadn't spoken but had been on her mind since right before the trip. "Right before we met at the grand opening, my doctor said there was something wrong and then more tests. I have more tests this week."

Byron tightened his smile and tried to lighten the horrible news. "Okay, we'll get some tests and see what happens. We'll deal with tomorrow, then someday. Right?"

Sybie's Queen Anne one-bedroom apartment was several miles south of his and an easier commute to the downtown area. When they arrived, Byron wondered if she would invite him in. He loved her place; it was so her. She described it as a studio apartment, but it was more like an art studio. If invited, should he go, should he stay, did he want to? He was relieved when she didn't invite him in. Bad news made him tired. He felt he just had the wind knocked out of him.

The next day he was off to work, and she to the clinic for some more blood tests and a visit to her doctor. They exchanged several text messages after she left the doctor's office and several more throughout the day, about nothing in particular—it felt like a brother staying in touch with a sister. She said the doctor's visit went fine, then from the hospital, she was undergoing further tests. They scheduled dinner Friday night, and she would know more then. Her final text read, "We will always have Banff. You call me Sybie, and I'll find a name for you."

They decided to go to their favorite out-of-the-way white linen candlelight Italian restaurant. Byron asked for their special table in the back. Two tables away, a young couple ordered a bottle of Champagne, their gazes locked in a tantalizing embrace, clinking their glasses in a toast to their first anniversary. Feeling they were being watched, they turned and smiled.

Hearing her report on her doctor visits crushed their romantic mood. Byron listened attentively, expecting an all-clear given her texts. Dispassionately, like reporting on a shopping extravaganza, she described her visit with the doctor. "The doctor was such a nice person, so caring, so understanding," she said. Reviewing her history and all the tests for the third time, he began to feel she was building up to something. Finally, she said, "Good news, cancer hasn't spread to my other kidney."

Byron's mouth dropped open. *Did she say cancer?* "Good news?"

Coolly, Sybie continued. "I have thought all along there would come a day when there would be a problem with the tumor they found in my kidney. It has taken over, and I need to have surgery."

"Hold it," Byron interrupted. "I never knew your kidney had cancer."

Looking away sheepishly. "I knew about cancer before the trip but didn't know enough to say more. I didn't want to get into it and ruin the moment. Byron, I hope you understand," she pleaded. "I didn't know how it was going to turn out and thought the best."

"Sure. I want to know everything. Always."

"I knew there was some kind of tumor, but I didn't know how big a deal it was. I was shocked. I wasn't in pain, and the symptoms were so vague. I guess with kidneys, you can have cancer, and before you know it, suddenly it's stage-four."

"Stage four?" Reaching across the table and taking her hand in his, he continued, "Sweetheart, this is a lot to take in. You're taking this all so well."

Fighting back the tears, Sybie answered. "Not really. But I faced the devastating news a long time ago. I always knew this could happen. That's why I told you we couldn't marry."

"That was just talk. Getting married is a separate discussion, for another day. We need to deal with…what surgery? When?"

"It's called a radical nephrectomy. They take one of my kidneys out. Toss it away. Good riddance. The other one is fine, and there's a good chance it hasn't spread there. It seems the bad kidney didn't develop fully, and my good one has been doing most of the work anyway."

Sighing audibly, hoping it wasn't too obvious, Byron folded his hands and rested them under his chin. "You said, cancer? Did you say stage four?"

For the first time, he could see she was losing her grip as sadness swept over her, and a tear bubbled up in her eye and trickled down her cheek. She dabbed it with her napkin. "Yes, and yes. I think this whole thing is going to be harder for me with you in my life."

"With me by your side, every step of the way, harder? Not easy, I understand but better. This changes nothing about how I feel about us. Not even about marriage. Someday, we'll get married; just you wait and see."

***

They removed her diseased kidney the week after they returned from Banff. The surgery went well, and two weeks later, she had her first appointment with her oncologist at the Ruth Asarch Cancer Center (RAAC). Ruth, the namesake benefactor, great-granddaughter of a timber tycoon dating back to the 1800s, doubled the family fortune with shrewd investments in emerging tech stocks. She died of ovarian cancer.

Byron insisted on accompanying Sybie on the first visit to the cancer doctor after surgery. She agreed to his being there after some negotiating. He assumed she wanted to shield him, hear the news alone, like a bad report was worse in front of him, more dramatic. It's hard to tell what she was thinking, but he insisted, and she relented. After the first visit, she was more agreeable.

Doctor Charles Payne, her oncologist, looked to be Sybie's age, seemingly too young to be a touted super-specialist. A tall, thin, angular man with short-cropped hair, wearing a white shirt and a bright paisley tie, soft blue eyes that by training or sincerity connected with his patients like he appreciated every word—he said there were no dumb questions, "I have all the time in the world." Certificates on the wall were from Johns Hopkins University and Georgetown University along with a plaque entitled Top Doc, ten years running.

"I'm sure glad Sybil invited you," he said as he shook Byron's hand. "No one should see a guy like me alone." He led Sybie through a series of questions about her family history, more for Byron's benefit, noting her parents both died of cancer and she had no siblings.

"Removal of your kidney will not affect your life," he started. "Some people are born with only one, and you'll be fine with one. Your remaining kidney is healthy and cancer-free."

He didn't sugarcoat the fact the removed kidney was at stage IV cancer and had metastasized to her lymph nodes. They would monitor her closely to detect any spreading of the disease to the lungs, bones, liver, or brain. If that happens, we will deal with it." Trying to add a lighter touch, he added, "At this stage, we are like hunter-killers. We will hunt down any cancerous villains and kill them."

He outlined a four-week course of radiation treatments, explaining the radiation doesn't kill all the cancer cells right away. "It takes days or weeks before the cancer cells are damaged enough and die. Then, the cancer cells keep dying for weeks or months after the therapy ends. We push the radiation in fast and flush it out."

When her radiation treatments ended, she resumed her Pilates classes and daily workouts as if nothing had happened. Byron proudly watched her resume her life as if nothing happened, like if anyone could beat cancer, she could. The toughest person he ever met, he joked she should become an MFA fighter. She was that tough. He was reminded every time he went into the Sound Tower, where her commissioned sculpture, 'Perseverance,' dominated the atrium.

***

The next morning from the dusky, gloomy attic, he saw the streets were busier, obviously a workday for most people. He hadn't seen a police car for three days or maybe four. Byron began the day rummaging through the boxes and tubs. He had a twinge of regret invading the homeowner's privacy, going through their private stuff but he guessed it no worse than living in his attic without the old man knowing. With growing curiosity about his host, he hunted through their collectibles. The old man's name was Henry Steele and his wife, Margorie. In their wedding pictures, he appeared to be several years older than her.

There was a crystal appreciation trophy for Henry's years as the President of the Bryn Mawr Country Club and a framed studio photo of him as a younger man. He was a good golfer judging by the three hole-in-one certificates and a stack of pictures of him with friends. There were two sets of golf clubs stashed in the corner, a set of Tommy Armour Silver Scot copper-faced irons and persimmon woods, and a set of ladies Callaway Gems, which looked like they were never used. He pulled one of the persimmon drivers out of the bag and gripped it like he was teeing off on one of those frequent rainy Northwest golf days. Digging into the golf bag pockets, he found it chocked full of new Titleist balata golf balls.

Henry served as a sergeant in the infantry, a foot soldier. When he left the Army, he attended Northwestern University on the GI bill, which led to a sales career at Baxter Travenol, a Chicago company, and helped them grow into a multi-billion-dollar business employing over 10,000 people in Chicago.

That night the house filled with the sounds of Monday night football. The San Francisco 49ers were beating the Arizona Cardinals, and at halftime, Henry started suffering through the channels. Byron laid on the floor next to the register and rested his head on an old musty pillow, half-listening and dozing off. He recognized the sound of an old western movie—*Hondo*.

Byron heard a Mexican man's voice,

"Oh, so you steal the money. All right, we trade with you then. You give us the money, or we shoot the woman."

He remembered the scene. A Mexican man was holding a woman hostage and was looking up the hill to Hondo, who was played by Paul Neuman.

"All right then. Shoot her," he said.

The Mexican man continued,

"The nice little soft woman you don't care if we shoot her?"

Hondo responded. "She means nothing to me."

Byron dozed again and woke up when he turned the television off, well after midnight. He saw no good outcome from being stuck in the attic—or starving to death, captured, or turning himself in.

Chapter Thirteen

When the next morning arrived, he woke to a growling stomach. What seemed easy to do intellectually, fasting a few days, was becoming more challenging than he thought and pushed him to consider options. His growing confidence in living in the attic, frequent trips to the second-floor bathroom, the predictability of Henry's bedroom visits, television, and sleeping habits added to the notion he could sneak into the kitchen.

The past few days, the sounds of western movies and shows, clanking, flushing, popping toaster, opening and closing the refrigerator door or cabinets, were predictable. When Henry went to the kitchen for a bite to eat at lunchtime, Byron planned to wait one hour then sneak into the kitchen, knowing the old man was hard of hearing and would doze off after lunch to the sounds of loud television.

Byron moved to the far register, which was best for listening to the kitchen sounds. At lunchtime, he heard the opening and closing of a cabinet door, the clanging of a pot, then clanking his way across the kitchen to the refrigerator. He must have been sitting at the kitchen table when the phone rang. The phone rang several times a day, which he either ignored or didn't hear. It rang several times before Byron heard him clang across the floor to answer it.

"Hello." Henry answered the phone in a loud voice, then again louder, "Hello. Who is this?"

"The hospital? No? The hospice?" In a louder voice, he said, "Doctor Woods? Who is this?"

There was a brief silence before he heard Henry again. "Yes, I can hear you. You don't have to yell. Yeah. I know I wasn't there. Yeah, and I said I wasn't coming."

After a silence, no doubt the old man was listening. "I know all that. Not going to let you poison me again. I told you guys."

For two minutes, he spoke in a softer voice, and Byron strained to hear. Then his voice boomed through the house. "Goddamnit, okay! I don't care. Sure… I'll drive myself."

After more silence, "That's a joke. Yes, I'll call if I'm not coming. You'll pick me up. Thursday. 6:30 am. Of course, I'll be here. Where am I going to go? You tell Doctor Woods this is the last time I'll let him poison me."

Two hours later, the television blared an infomercial about vitamins. The old man was asleep, and Byron's stomach was still growling.

With the caution and stealth of a jewel thief, Byron crept down the attic stairs. If caught on this mission to the kitchen, he would escape out the front door, so he took his messenger bag. He recalled some of the steps creaked, so he carefully stepped on the outsides of the stairs. He dropped off mason jars in the second-floor bathroom for strategic use of the sink and toilet before he returned to the attic.

When Byron arrived on the main floor, he saw unopened mail lying on the floor in front of the front door mail slot. He crept toward the kitchen. The old man was a snorer.

Surveying the kitchen, he saw the sink was full of dirty dishes, bread crumbs scattered around the countertop, and a ragged, stained dishcloth hung on the cabinet knob. His wallet was on the counter. He peeked inside. He kept a good amount of cash in his wallet. The clock said it was two o'clock.

He opened the refrigerator with the hope he could select something the old man wouldn't miss. He took the cap off a half-gallon of milk and found it spoiled. There were two have full jars of pickles, dill, and sweet. He opened the dill pickles and picked one. The first thing he had eaten in days, the salty, briny, dilly flavor burst over his taste buds.

There were cheese and sliced meats in one of the drawers. He set a package of moldy cheese on the counter along with one slice of ham and bologna. In the vegetable drawer, he found a rotten cucumber and wilted carrots and took two of the firmer ones and placed them on the napkins, then took the third one. The old man wasn't going to eat them. Using a wood-handled corroded paring knife, he cut away the mold on the cheese and stuffed the moldy pieces down the garbage disposal but didn't turn it on.

He stopped to listen for Henry's snoring before continuing.

The only thing in the freezer was a full tray of ice cubes.

There were two loaves of bread in one of the cabinets, one white and the other wheat. He pulled two slices from the middle of the moldy wheat loaf, examined them carefully, and cut away some of the crust.

He picked a few crackers from several boxes and set them on the napkin. From a box of Saltines, he took a full waxed paper packet. There was an opened jar of peanut butter, and using the paring knife, scooped some onto what could have been an S & H Green Stamps plastic saucer. He'd never miss one saucer. After cleaning the knife, he laid it back on the counter. From a can of mixed nuts and a pack of raisins—he took a handful.

One cabinet was filled with snack foods. The old man liked cookies. Byron picked a few cookies from several packages of Oreos, Vanilla Wafers, and Lorna Doons. He felt safe in taking a handful of potato chips and Virginia nuts. He loaded the trove of food into a plastic sack he found beneath the sink.

Byron remembered seeing batteries in one of the drawers and took two AAAs and two DDs, for a flashlight and cheap clock he found in the attic. There was some adhesive tape in the upstairs bathroom he could use to label the mason jars to keep track of the ones he peed in, so he took a ballpoint pen from a lifetime collection of cheap ones.

When Byron arrived in the second-floor bathroom, he panicked when he realized he had left his bag in the kitchen. He hurried back down the stairs and stopped and listened to the silence—no snoring. He froze, unsure what to do. Beads of perspiration appeared on his forehead. In the silence, the only sound was his breathing and the ticking of a gold-plated mantel clock above the fireplace. A few minutes later, he heard him clanking his way toward the bathroom, and when safe, Byron darted into the kitchen and rushed back up the stairs, with no regard to the sounds he might be making. The next sound he heard was of him clanking toward the kitchen.

***

Wednesday, Byron awoke in the dark early morning to a snow globe scene of large puffy snowflakes seesawing to the ground, uncharacteristic in the Windy City. The large fluffy snowflakes reminded him of windless days in the Cascades when he could hear the snowflakes floating around him. Looking out, it was easy to forget what caused him to be stuck in the attic of a stranger's house. His feelings were conflicted. Secure for now, he knew he couldn't stay much longer and was frightened at the thought of escaping into the cold and accumulating snow.

Sitting on his perch atop the trunk in front of the tall double windows, watching the street below, he contemplated everything he had learned. The bright light of a full moon marked the pattern of the double window panes on the rafters. The reflection off of the snow-covered streets and lawns gave a midday appearance.

Pondering his dilemma—a man on the run, hiding in an attic like a cornered wounded animal, with another wounded animal, an old man he couldn't help, revived the realization he couldn't stay here much longer even though the FBI was still searching for him—he could hear the howling of hounds.

He hadn't heard the old man use the bathroom yet, so he went to the second floor and waited. When he arrived, he heard him rummaging through the kitchen. He seemed to be looking for something, leaving Byron to wonder if he had done something to alarm him.

Byron's concerns evaporated when he heard him on the telephone. "I need some groceries delivered? This is Henry Steele…I have an account…speak up…that's the one."

He began to read a list of groceries into the phone. "Soup, Campbell's…chicken noodle and Cream of Chicken…three of each…one can of pork and beans…sliced turkey and ham, white bread, two loaves, dozen eggs, milk." He hesitated before he continued, "Size? I don't care. Two of those little pizzas…Totitos, Toninos, whatever."

After hanging up, he made another call. "This is Henry Steele, again. I just ordered some groceries...add a package of butterscotch hard candy to the order."

Mid-morning, sitting on the trunk, staring at the snow-covered street, Byron thumbed through a stack of letters with one eye on the street below.

One of the letters read,

Maj, I love you. You're the love of my life. I'm so sorry. I know I'm working too hard and don't spend enough time with you. Ok, and sometimes playing too hard. When I'm at work, I miss you terribly, and when I'm at home, I feel like I should be at work. We will get through this. Tough times.

Your ever-loving husband, Henry

P.S. Let's run away.

He pulled out a thick stack of rubber-banded letters addressed to Barbara Ryan in Coeur d'Alene, Idaho. As he thumbed through them, he saw most had 'Return to Sender,' written on the envelope; one said 'DELIVERY REFUSED." He assumed the mail was to his daughter.

He opened one of the letters and read it.

Babs,

I know you hate me. I hope it is not forever. I know you blame me for your mom's death. I don't know what I did? I couldn't live with myself if that were true, I loved her so much. And now losing my daughter too, is too much to bear. Please answer my calls. Please call me.

Pop

Byron hadn't noticed there were fresh car tracks in the snow-covered street and a black Crown Victoria parked across the street. Not ten minutes later, two men dressed in black coats, the two FBI agents he met on the elevator and also at his apartment, emerged from the house across the street and walked to the car. Before they got in the car, they talked over the roof and turned in unison back to the old man's house. They began walking his way. If Henry answered the door, he wanted to hear the conversation, so Byron made his way back to the second floor, doubting they would search the house, but if they did, resigned to his fate.

At first, he thought Henry wouldn't hear the doorbell over the loud television. No doubt the FBI agents could hear the television, so they persisted, pressing on the doorbell repeatedly until the television went silent and Henry clanked his way to the door.

Henry opened the door and gruffly said, "What do you want?"

"I'm FBI agent Barnes. And this is agent Galinski." Holding out a photo, "We're looking for this man."

"What did he do? Looks like a mugger." Henry stated.

"We don't think he's dangerous. But we think he could still be in the area. Do you live here alone? Have you seen this man," agent Barnes asked?

"What'd you say?"

Agent Galinski, in a loud voice, said, "He said, have you seen this man?"

"Yes."

The two agents exchanged glances. "You have seen this man," Agent Galinski asked?

"No."

Agent Barnes said, "Here. Take my card. If you see anybody who looks like this man, would you call us?

There were new footsteps on the porch, and a muffled conversation as somebody entered the house.

Below, Byron saw a young man carrying an armload of grocery sacks into the kitchen."

Next, he heard footsteps of the agents leaving, the door closing, and Henry clanking toward the kitchen.

The grocery delivery boy, wearing the nametag Rocco, wore jeans that rode so low on his hips they appeared to hang impossibly below his waist. His black hair was pulled straight back over his head and tied in a long straggly ponytail. "You live here alone?" He asked.

Tell him its none of his business. Byron wanted to scream out, Tell him you live with a retired cop.

The boy's question was loud enough to be heard, but Henry ignored it. Maybe he nodded; Byron couldn't see. He heard the rustling of sacks.

A few minutes later, Henry asked, "Can you take this out to the garbage can as you leave?"

The boy answered rudely, "I ain't your boy. You take out your own garbage."

Henry must not have heard him because he repeated his request.

There were footsteps, and he saw the boy leaving the kitchen, mumbling, "What are you deaf? Me, take your garbage out?"

"Here," Henry exclaimed loudly, "I'll pay you."

"Oh boy. You're deaf and dumb."

Creeping back up to the attic to watch the boy leave, the bitter taste of what he just witnessed fresh in his mouth, irritated at how anyone could treat someone so rudely, especially someone as frail as Henry. Alarm bells were sounding. *I'll bet if Henry's wallet was still on the counter, it's gone.*

∗∗∗

A second kid leaned against the passenger door of an old gray Nissan smoking a cigarette, waiting for Rocco. He was the same age, shorter, and porky; his sandy hair was long too and pulled back into a ponytail. Rocco lit a cigarette and joined his friend, leaning against the car.

121

"Paydirt. We struck gold, man." Looking back at the house, smiling, "That guy's loaded and old as dirt. Can't hear a thing. He must have 500 dollars just laying around."

The fat kid followed Rocco's gaze back to the house. "We gonna rob him?"

"Rob him. Hell yeah."

"Now?"

Looking back to his friend, "In broad daylight? Tubby. Are you nuts? I just made a delivery. You don't think they would suspect me? This weekend."

"Oh yeah. We just going to break in?"

"Nah. We are gonna just walk in and take his money. Simple?"

"Jimmy, the locks?"

Rocco held out a set of keys. "Grabbed his keys as I was leaving. I'm telling you this guy's so old he can't hear and can't walk."

***

Byron watched the boy's conversation from the attic window. He couldn't hear them but was alarmed by their glances back to the house. As the boys drove away, he felt more trapped than ever. He sat back and waited to hear Henry return to the kitchen. The quiet was broken by the sudden outcry. "God damned kid."

Minutes passed in silence. Byron held his breath and listened. Not a sound. Creeping down the stairs, he stopped on the bottom step of the attic and sat in the open door. He waited in the oppressive silence, assuming the boy had lifted his wallet.

Finally, Henry broke the silence. "Goddamn it. Sons a bitches kid. This is great. I'm going to be one of those guys they find dead on the floor a week later."

Byron peeked around the corner to see him sprawled out on the floor in the entryway. He waited helplessly, feeling there was nothing he could do. Was there? He couldn't leave him there on the floor, either. *Come on, get up.* Not a sound. He waited.

It must have been fifteen minutes later when he heard the sound of his walker scraping across the floor. "Goddamn it. I have to get up. I can't just lay here." Byron heard more scrapping and huffing and puffing. "God Damnit." A few minutes later, he heard clanking and the front door open.

Where was he going? Daring to peek around the corner again, the front door was open, and the garbage bag was sitting on the front porch right where the kid left it.

Byron crept to the ground floor and, from a distance, watched out the open front door. He could see Henry struggling to carry the garbage sack to the can. Standing there, shaking his head, he hoped the situation resolved itself without his help. *I don't have a choice. Do I?* Time crawled. The last hour was heart-wrenching.

Ever since Byron arrived in Chicago, running from the law, and life, creating a new one, he'd had the frights, off-kilter in every step he took, like being in a foreign country speaking a different language. His small-town upbringing counted as a good thing but at odds with the extremes of Chicago. In his little town of Work, Washington, there were no strangers, now, everybody was a stranger. Sometimes, when he walked to the subway, he stepped over homeless beggars passed out on the sidewalk. When he grew up, anybody would have helped the man to his feet. Here, you step over them. The city had a split personality, the dirty old and the shiny new, the bustling and broke, monuments to prosperity, and the murder capital of the country.

Watching Henry struggle to perform the simple task of taking the garbage out, crawling around on the floor like a wounded animal, told another story—old people who do not have someone in their life, well they die. That's what they do. When the old man finally negotiated the last step to the porch, the last leg of his mission, Byron retreated up the stairs to the second floor and waited. His heart ached, wanting so badly to help.

Safely back in the attic, he installed the batteries in the old alarm clock and flashlight, fluffed up his bed, and laid down and waited, listing to every sound, signs that Henry was okay.

Tonight, the quiet of the house was unnerving. No doubt Henry was troubled and exhausted. Who wouldn't be? He heard him rise only once during the night, and not too much later turn on the television, and didn't hear him again until morning.

As Byron understood it, he was supposed to go to the hospital the day after tomorrow for some kind of treatment. Making himself comfortable on the floor next to the register, he settled in for a day of old-time television westerns. In the afternoon, the old man watched one John Wayne western after another. Byron couldn't recall seeing the movie he had on, but the distinctive voice of the John Wayne, Duke, was easy to recognize. He was speaking to his daughter.

"There's something I ought to tell you. I guess now is as good a time as any. You're gonna have every young buck west of the Mississippi trying to marry you. Mostly, cause you're a handsome filly but partly because I own everything in this country from here to there. And, they'll think you're gonna inherit it. Well, you're not…But, the real reason Becky, is because I love you, and I want you and some young man to have what I had. Cuz all the gold in the United States Treasury and all the harp music in heaven can't equal what happens between a man and a woman with all that growing together.

Byron looked over to the picture of Henry's daughter lying at the top of the stack of photos. What did Henry do to her? Why did she hate him so?

The sound of the television went silent earlier than usual, and Byron moved back to his bed of dresses. Unable to get comfortable, his wide-eyed sleeplessness made him more sensitive to the nocturnal happenings—there was a critter living with him. His flashlight beam sought out the scratching sounds of a fearless mouse attempting to steal his stash of stolen food. He threw one of Henry's old golf hats and ran him off, laid back, and starred up to the rafters dimly lit by the streetlights. *I've got to get out of here.*

Chapter Fourteen

The next morning, there were no television sounds, just the clanking sounds to and from the bedroom, running water, and flushing toilet, and then to the living room and a half-hour of silence.

At 6:40 am, a Sisters of Mercy van pulled up to the curb, and the driver, an older man, walked to the door. Next, the doorbell rang, and the door opened, followed by muffled conversations and clanking sounds across the front porch. The clanking stopped as the driver hurried to the van and retrieved a wheelchair.

As the driver rolled Henry onto the liftgate, he looked back to the front door, then suddenly up to the attic window and made eye contact with Byron. Byron immediately stepped back into the darkness but continued to watch.

As the driver pushed him into the van, he asked, "That your son?"

Henry didn't hear him, so he repeated the question louder, looking back to the attic window, "Your son? That your son?"

Henry held his hand up to his ear to hear better. "Yeah. Not too bad."

The driver secured him, retracted the lift, and slid the door shut; he commented, "Good to have help, huh."

Henry answered, "Yeah. Could be."

***

Byron was excited to get out of the attic. First, he washed his jars in the second-floor bathroom and used the toilet. When he saw his image in the mirror, he was reminded how long and scraggily his beard was. He hadn't had a haircut since he left Seattle and couldn't remember the last time he shaved, before the interview with Seven Continents, he guessed. His sleepless eyes, red and sunken, resembled a street bum that would scare Henry to death had he opened the closet door or if he helped him with the young hoodlum delivery boy.

Next, he headed to the kitchen to forage for food. Henry wouldn't miss a couple of slices of meat or two slices of bread. He ate the sandwich as he tested out his new freedom and surveyed the ground floor.

The living room was intended for entertainment comfort, meant to be admired and complimented. He pulled the sheet off one of the two matching leather club chairs. Seated, he surveyed the room and finished his sandwich. A long sofa and two opposing chairs encircled a blue medallion Turkish area rug and a molasses-colored oval coffee table. On the table was a book entitled *The World's Top 100 Greatest Golf Courses.* There were two end tables with matching terracotta lamps. On both sides of the old Chicago brick fireplace were built-in floor-to-ceiling dark stained bookcases.

After he finished the sandwich, he walked to the bookshelves. Among the items on the shelves were matching nineteenth-century brass Italian candlesticks, a crystal antique serving bowl, two tarnished silver teapots, and a collection of pipes and an old humidor devoid of cigars. Among the books were two leather-bound first edition books, *The Complete Works of Ralph Waldo Emerson,* standing between two old world globe bookends, and a full set of Encyclopedia Britannica, outdated and obsolete.

He next went to Henry's bedroom. It smelled of urine and unwashed clothes, his bed unmade, and there was a crumpled pile of clothes on the recliner next to the bed. He thought about turning the television on but was uncomfortable staying there. He returned to the second-floor bathroom and filled the mason jars.

Looking at his disgusting image in the mirror again, then back at the shower—*Could I? Should I?* Opening the bathroom closet, he paused, saw there were towels, and several tubes of toothpaste samples, floss, and several unopened packages of toothbrushes, an unopened packet of disposable razors, and a rusted can of shaving cream. He tested it. It worked.

Back to the kitchen, he retrieved scissors. In the kitchen, he saw the number for Sisters of Mercy Hospital and picked up the phone. "Please connect me to the nurse's station on the Oncology floor." When a nurse answered, Byron asked, "I am trying to reach Henry Steele...yes, that's him...I'm not sure what room he is in or how to call him directly."

The floor nurse responded, "He won't be able to take any calls...maybe later this afternoon or tonight."

"Yes, I assumed that. I can try tomorrow." Byron jotted down the number she gave him and thanked her.

Once he confirmed the old man wasn't coming back today, he breathed a sigh of relief. Back in the upstairs bathroom, he peeled off his shirt and pants, and underwear, then wrapped the towel around his waist and went to the first-floor laundry. His clothes reeked, filthy from rolling around on the ground and sleeping in an attic. On his way, he peeked into Henry's bedroom. It might be brave to wash his clothes, but he shouldn't come home to a smelly bed. He threw all of it in the washer.

Back in the upstairs bathroom, Byron brushed his teeth. His teeth and mouth were dry and filmy. How many days had passed since he last brushed them? He weighed his options. Draping a towel over the sink, he cut away as much of his beard as he could with the scissors, lathered up, and began the painful, tedious process of shaving. When finished, his nicked-up face was dotted with dabs of toilet paper to stop the bleeding.

Next, he began to cut away at his hair. It looked worse when finished, much worse, and with no way to straighten it to make himself presentable, he lathered up his head and began to shave it. When finished, his head matched his face with islands of red dots of toilet paper. He looked closely at the razor for rust, wondering if he should worry about getting lockjaw. He then took a long, hot, soapy shower.

When done, he cleaned the bathroom like it was a murder scene.

Satisfied, he returned to the main floor and waited in the living room for the laundry to finish. The room was musty and dark, shut off from light and outside air for months. He pulled one of the Emerson books off the shelf—volume one. He recalled one of his professors saying Emerson, the sage of Concord, was one of the great thinkers of his day, in many ways ahead of his time.

Engrossed in reading Emerson, he hoped for enlightenment—the unveiling of a hidden truth about how he got here, a free man imprisoned in the attic of a dying old man, condemned, waiting for the unknown to tap him on the shoulder and reveal what to do. Instead, he read about fate and love. One passage triggered a memory: 'Love is like wildflowers; It's often found in the most unlikely places.'

The passage reminded him of Sybie's wildflower watercolor paintings, the one inspired by the Wordsworth poem, a most treasured memory but a reminder it was in the suitcase he left behind when he fled. Never to be seen again.

***

Love is like wildflowers. That simple phrase from the poem sent his memories whirling back to his time with Sybie.

Byron recalled, after kidney surgery, Sybie moved in and gave up her apartment with the great view of the Space Needle. His condo, well north of hers in Magnolia, was near Discovery Park, a 534-acre park on the shores of Puget Sound. From the private deck of his three-bedroom condo, he had a spectacular view of Salmon Bay and the Olympic Mountains. She loved the spacious open spaces, hardwood floor, with a large half circular sofa stationed in front of a large gas fireplace.

They made the extra bedroom into an art studio, which before long leaked into the living area. He didn't care. He loved watching her paint, the serious expression on her face breaking out in a crooked smile as she tilted her head and dabbed at her paintings.

For the next year, he did more business for Oreves than anyone ever had. His boundless energy for work no doubt rooted in gratefulness for every day and having Sybie in his life. What better way to celebrate life than by excelling in his career? He went for weeks working 100 hours a week, sometimes four in the morning until ten at night, and every other precious remaining moment was with her. They grabbed onto the tail of a comet and loved like it was the last time they would be together.

Byron admitted to a certain hubris to his success. He stayed in shape, didn't drink, never missed a haircut, which bordered on a military-style, and always dressed for the occasion—often a statement black suit or a black Tommy Bahama silk shirt. He was born for the job. He had a high aptitude for numbers. Balance sheets were like realism paintings to Sybie. Company financials that didn't make sense, no matter the bottom line, he rejected. He turned back more deals than he put together.

As important as the numbers were to a deal, the secret ingredient was his genuine regard for people, at least the ones who deserved it. People, not products, not dollars, were the prime ingredient of success. People can destroy good products and spend money needlessly. He could be pretty confrontational with the guys in the industry who would do anything to get ahead, step on anyone, make any deal, the ones who hurt people. He became the guy in the magazine and newspaper photos alongside top executives at unveilings or mergers in major cities around the country.

Whenever Sybie could get away from her job, she traveled with him. In a year that rivaled the best of their lives, they saw the musical Grease on Broadway and celebrated Saint Pat's Day, along the green-dyed Chicago east river— but didn't drink the green beer. On a windy day, they swayed to the top of the St Louis arch. They dined on a Mississippi riverboat in Memphis and danced the two-step in the Losers Bar and Grill on Music Row in Nashville, Tennessee.

Byron liked Chicago best and even became a Cubs fan. Sybie liked Chicago, too. They were perfectly fit Cubs fans, the consummate underdog, believing there was always next year and the best was ahead.

They hadn't talked about marriage again, but her words were always on his mind—*How will you feel in five or ten years? Will you regret not having a family?* Byron accepted the future they were creating but always wondered. He reassured Sybie, "Their relationship of commitment held more meaning than a parchment marriage certificate." Choosing every day to be with the woman he loved was the true commitment when leaving a marriage was as easy as packing a bag.

He suspected the marriage question was never far off for either of them. They were trapped in the best days of their lives after the worst, neither of them brave enough to bring marriage up again. Neither wanted to lose something few people experienced. It was okay to be trapped as the snare tightened around them, so tight the only escape was if it broke. Byron also knew she was worried about him— feeling he might feel trapped. He would have understood it if he came home and found she had moved out and left a note.

Friday night, another Viva la Italia dinner night, but also a special occasion—her birthday. Giovanni Ricci, the proprietor, was a short, round, horseshoe-shaped balding man in his early sixties. He immigrated from the Basilicata region of Italy with his parents, which explained his thick accent. As a boy, he learned to cook in his parents' St. Louis restaurant in the Hill District. He offered more than good food—and no other restaurant offered a table side Caesar salad –he dished out large doses of good feelings.

Over dinner, they discussed her latest interior design project, and he told stories about Valentin, not the threatening ones, mostly his thoughts about the Splash project, a great idea that faced insurmountable odds competing against Facebook and their treasure chest of a billion subscribers.

Last year they celebrated being cancer-free. Now, they celebrated her birthday and life itself—living like dying was their silent mantra. During dinner, Sybie reflected the past year was the best of her life. She said that about the Banff trip as well. Byron knew she wasn't just talking about being cancer-free.

When they finished dinner, Giovanni brought them a cake and lit a single candle. In his typically animated fashion, his arms and hands waved about as he talked, his head bobbed up and down from side to side. "For my beautiful angel. I made this special for you and frosted it with love," he said as he set it before them. Before he walked away, he led, singing happy birthday and everyone nearby joined in. She blew out the candles and said she couldn't tell him her wish because it might not come true.

Byron had something else on his mind, and hearing her talk about the best years of her life seemed like a good time to bring up marriage. "I'm so proud of you. It's time we think about our future, get a house."

Sybie responded in a soothing sympathetic voice. "I told you before, marrying you is a beautiful thought. I don't know what to say, but..."

He braced for what she might say. The loving enigma gave her a good life so far, but deep beneath the surface lived lingering doubts. Byron always admired her watercolors but found them more complicated than they appeared. He saw her in her art. She called it expressionism—sunny days, often in fields of flowers with the sad faces of little girls and old people without faces.

She avoided talking about marriage, but all the time living together hadn't revealed any concerns, at least that he could tell. In many ways, he was a perfect husband. They cooked together, puttered around the kitchen, and he didn't leave his clothes lying around, did his own laundry.

"I love the thought of you being my hubby." Sybie looked away, then down at her folded hands resting on the table. In the uncomfortable silence, Giovanni seated a couple at the table next to us, lit the candle, filled their water glasses, and placed menus in front of them as he described the specials. When he left, in a hushed tone, Sybie finished, "Oh Byron, I don't know what to say."

"If you are against it, we can keep living like we are. Couples who live together in such a committed fashion can be more married than one with a piece of paper."

After dinner, Giovanni stopped and picked up the bills Bryon laid in the tray with the check and asked if there was anything else. He seemed to sense they were in a deep conversation, so he turned and left quickly without saying anything.

"Being married to you, taking your name, would be wonderful, but I'm not sure we should. "I don't want to have a baby, and I know you do."

"Of course, I'd like to have kids…but…"

In a caring and sympathetic tone, she exclaimed, "Oh, Byron, I hate to disappoint you. If we marry five or ten years from now when we are an old married couple, you might have regrets. Nobody knows how they will feel five or ten years if there is… Our friends would be raising families, and we'd be the awkward couple no one wanted to run around with." Sighing deeply, she added, "Byron, you know there's a fifty percent chance our offspring could have the same genetic deficiencies I have. My parents both died of cancer when they were young. I can't bring a baby into the word and take that chance."

Lost in a rush of thoughts, a feeling of hopelessness overwhelmed him, not just the dead-end discussion of marriage, but reality, overwhelming, stifling, inescapable reality left no space for dreams. Just the truth.

She began to tremble. "Byron, I am so sorry. I shouldn't have let things go this far. This is so unfair to you. You need to be honest with yourself and think this over." Her eyes were glassy as she fought back the tears. "You'd be crazy to marry me. I would understand if we ended this tonight."

Byron wanted to leap across the table and hold her, tell her everything was going to be okay, but she could be right. It was time to leave the restaurant. They couldn't continue the conversation here. He already felt customers sneaking peeks in their direction. Sliding his chair back to leave, he searched for words and kept coming back to deep feelings that blocked anything he wanted to say. "Yep, you're right about one thing, I'm crazy. Crazy for you.

When they returned from their last trip to Chicago, Sybie was scheduled for her annual blood test, x-rays, and check-up with her doctor. Summer had ended early, and it was already raining. Byron insisted on being there.

When Doctor Payne entered the room, he moved differently and took his seat in a harrumph. Still, he smiled and said it was good to see them again, no doubt a reference to seeing us together but portending bad news.

"I don't have as good a news as I usually do. We found a spot on your lungs."

Byron usually knew what to say, but there were no experiences to draw on. Doctor Payne continued, "We can't know much at this stage without a biopsy. I can get that scheduled right away." Sybie's blood drained from her face as she slouched down in her chair.

The biopsy was scheduled the next day, and the news couldn't have been worse. The cancer they thought disappeared from her body had popped up in her lungs. They always knew there was a chance it could spread from her kidneys to other organs. Now it had.

Lung surgery was scheduled to remove the cancerous spot or, maybe if needed, a lobectomy to remove part of her lung. The surgeon discovered cancer had already taken over her lung, and, in a four-hour pneumonectomy, her entire lung was removed. When they left the hospital, she looked small, feeble, slumped down, her head hung low.

Life changed in a rush, long grass days forgotten, a lifetime away, the rainy season back and pressing down. They still had Banff, but even that memory felt faded and tarnished. The first two weeks following surgery, her five times a day pain medication produced a zombie existence. Byron didn't go to work and watched helplessly, mesmerized by the image of her with half-open eyes, slurring her words unintelligibly.

One day, as they were lying in bed together, she began to cry uncontrollably. He had never seen anyone cry as hard. Weak and drugged, tragedy had a tight grip on her. He held her close and waited. "Byron," her syrupy thoughts rolled around her mouth before they reached the end of her tongue. "Byron," she said again. "I'm so sorry." Her tears gushed forth, and her shoulders shook. "I should have told you. I should have told you. I should have," she repeated.

He pulled back far enough to see her face and squinted while trying to make meaning of what she was saying. "You couldn't have anything to be sorry for. This is me. Byron. I'm here. I'll get you through this."

"No. I should have told you. Shouldn't have kept the secret."

He knew the whole ordeal was torturous, but she felt she hurt him somehow. It couldn't be true. Not Sybie. They couldn't have been more married. He understood she felt guilty he was a victim of her tragedies—he had a choice, and she didn't. Either way, she felt badly—married or kind of married. He understood her dilemma. Their dilemma. And he didn't want to talk about it, the only solution unacceptable, too painful. They could fight through whatever they faced.

Suddenly her tears dried up, and she forced her eyes wide. "No. You don't understand. I knew before I went into the hospital. I didn't tell you. I didn't tell anyone. I should have. My life is bad enough without lying to you. Always lying. Lying to myself."

Byron let out a deep sigh, unsure what she was talking about.

"I was pregnant before I went to the hospital. A month ago. I knew it, and I didn't tell you. I didn't tell the doctors, but then in the hospital, I miscarried."

Her shoulders were shaking again, uncontrollably. She grabbed her chest, doubled over in pain. More tears gushed forward. Her nasal cannula fell to the side, and she ripped it away.

Byron pulled the nasal cannula back into place.

"How did that happen? We were careful."

"I know when it happened. It was in Chicago, the day we went to the top of the John Hancock building. We were on top of the world. I didn't care. I didn't care about anything. I felt so alive, in a cloud, on top of the world. That night when we made love, it felt like we were making life. Love...it was the life we were making." Through her tears, she repeated, "I miscarried in the hospital. I'm so sorry."

Pulling her close, he whispered, "It doesn't matter." She closed her eyes and relaxed. "It doesn't matter. Sybie, I love you; that's all that matters."

When she went to sleep, he moved to the covered patio and looked into the misty gray, so thick, he couldn't see yesterday, today, or tomorrow. The moss growing on the railing swelled in the moist air. He was in a place he'd never been before, never imagining life could ever get like this. He had never seen anybody go through anything as dire, so pitiful, so painful. *Is she going to die?*

In the days that followed, Byron helped her dress and undress, helped her to the bathroom and sat her up in a chair in the living area, and coaxed her to eat. He told her there were kisses on each bite of food he fed her. The incision was so painful she stayed in her pajamas all day and couldn't wear a bra. She said it helped when they took hot showers. Now daily activities were reminders of dying, not living. He pushed those thoughts aside.

Umbrella days added to their hopelessness, and her despair was contagious and grew like the cancerous causes of it. She didn't know how he felt. Not really. How could she know? There weren't words, no novelist to do his talking, just the beating of his heart.

After a while, she stopped taking her pain medication, was no longer dependent on oxygen, and gradually her appetite returned. Still, sleep remained elusive, and he insisted on being awake with her when she couldn't sleep. He returned to work but, to Valentin's dismay, more in a supervisory role so he could stay in town, always in contact with Marcy, his assistant, and available to the other partners and associates.

Byron's old routine was to be the first one in the office; now, when he did go in, it wasn't until mid-morning. He always took pride in his appearance, right down to his short-cropped every two-week haircut. Now his hair covered his ears, parted to one side. Always disciplined to promptly return phone calls, even if just to acknowledge he received them, now pink message slips accumulated in a neat stack prioritized by his assistant. Everyone in the office knew how sick Sybie was, and behind his back, judgments were being made about the severity of her illness, and based on his appearance, why he hadn't taken on any new clients.

When he wasn't tending to Sybie, he spent his time reviewing the work of junior partners and, when requested, consulted with them, studied domestic and international financial markets, stocks and bonds, and worldwide money markets, regulatory rulings, court decisions, the maneuverings of congress and trends in business, especially the tech industry, which was his specialty.

Clients he usually dealt with he passed along to other senior partners. When Valentin called to meet with him, he gave him vague excuses and promised to have his assistant work out a time they could meet. He told Marcy under no circumstances to schedule a meeting with him. She felt the same way about Valentin, and besides, she grieved for Sybie

Following her post-operative recovery, she underwent a much more aggressive series of radiation treatments. This time the radiation treatments took her to a new low; nausea zapped her appetite, her strength, and even caused a loss of hair. Accentuating the mood, day after day, gray early night falls and late mornings, tender tears of rain clung to everything, and tragedy clung to them like mist. It was difficult to believe the sun would ever come out again.

She was back to wearing pajamas all day. When she began to lose her hair, she went to Byron, crying, holding strands of her black tresses in her hand. "I want it gone," she cried out.

"I want it gone, too," he whispered.

She pushed back and held out a handful of black hairs. "I want this gone." I want it all gone." Reluctantly, Byron sat her at the dining room table, a towel draped over her shoulders, and using electric shears, began to buzz the long silky ebony strands and drop them to the floor. Then lathering her head with shaving creme, using a safety razor, he shaved her head bald. Amused of how he fumbled his way through the process, she smiled weakly.

If he was restructuring a business, he would know what to do or would figure it out, but this was life, at its worst, coming after the best. Life was known to be cruel, but until this happened, it happened to other people. He always knew the potential of her disease, but it wasn't going to happen to her. To them. Never. Life was too good—how could it not be like that forever?

One single moment in Doctor Payne's office changed their life forever—"We found a spot on your lungs," he said. A spot? It sounded so innocent, a spot, a bomb. Not cutting his hair for two months, Byron's long hair combed behind his ears; he even thought about shaving his head in solidarity. The same thoughts over and over were like humming the same sad song, unable to get it out of his head—it became his theme music.

When awake, they snuggled on the sofa under a lightweight Kashmir soft blanket and watched old Turner Classic movies—sappy love stories matching their mood.

"Funny thing," she said. "Sometimes, I wish we had never met, but I'm not sure how I could have gone through this without you. I couldn't ask for a better hubby."

She had voiced the same concerns in different ways, but he especially loved to hear her call him hubby. "I like that. I call you Sybie, and you call me Hubby."

The year ended starkly opposed to the way it started as she gained some strength and began to pop out of her malaise. Radiation therapy finally concluded, and Sybie regained her strength and pajama days ended. Short walks to the corner progressed to strolls along the Discovery Park trail to a local coffee shop and dinner at their favorite restaurant.

Customarily, in good times, they dined Friday nights at Viva La Italia. Tonight, Byron made the reservation, and Sybie put on makeup and a dress just like old times. Giovanni greeted them warmly, pausing to consider her pixie hairstyle, hugged Byron and kissed Sybie on the lips like family, and seated them at their regular table in the back. "You are more beautiful than ever. I missed you guys." No doubt he knew more than he let on. He saw her recovering from kidney surgery, and it was obvious how sick she was then, and now he sensed it was worse. He never said anything except went out of his way to fawn over her. "I have missed you," he repeated.

Sybie smiled at the attention, no doubt pleased with the supposed anonymity of her situation. She confided she was afraid people would treat her like she was contagious.

"Let me make you a special dinner. I will bring wine."

Byron waved him off. "No wine tonight." Looking over to Sybie for approval, he added, "We love your special dinners."

Giovanni turned his gaze skyward and finger kissed the air. "Eccellente. Makes my heart joyful to cook special for you." Looking at Sybie, "You are my favorite girl. I'm in love," then back to Byron, "Does that make you jealous?"

"Not at all. Every man is in love with her…and she's all mine."

Sybie blushed and folded the napkin in her lap.

"Today, I slow cook tender veal shanks, braised in white wine. I serve with fresh vegetables and a gremolata, a condiment made with lemon zest, garlic, and parsley. Today, when I saw you were coming, I made Tiramisu. I know how you like it. A special night, you will meet Tony, my nephew. He is working here now. I hope he will take over someday. Tony. My Grandfather came from Italy. His name was Tony, too. You know why we Italians are called Tony?"

Pausing, Sybie and Bryans exchanged glances. Neither could tell if he was joking.

Giovanni continued, "Serious. When my grandfather came to this country, they stamped 'To N.Y' on his arm. Tony." Bunching his ten fingers together and lifting them to his mouth, he touched his lips and released his hands. "Oh, itza so nice to have you here. This is a special night."

Unknown at the time, it was the last of the good times, five steps higher than all the days of misery, a delusion of bright high sky promises of better days ahead.

Chapter Fifteen

Byron dozed off on the living room chair and awoke to a growling stomach. In the kitchen, he found an old phone book and ordered two large pizzas and two sixty-four-ounce bottles of Diet Coke. When the laundry was done, he dressed and made Henry's bed.

Moving back to the safety and solitude of the attic, he continued to investigate the Steeles. Still, he wondered what happened to his wife, Margorie, and Barbara's estrangement from him.

There were only a few boxes he hadn't been through, one filled with the usual array of Christmas decorations, including a few personalized, commemorative, and sporting bulbs, the Illini, DePaul University, shiny Cubs, and Bears ones. He twirled a Las Vegas ornament, wondering and hoping they didn't get married there.

He went to the box of photo albums and found their wedding album. They were married in a church. The photo albums told a story of a happy marriage and a daughter with an idyllic upbringing. So, what happened? The love letters suggested they had a good marriage, but a stack of returned letters from Barbara revealed a deep divide between father and daughter. It appeared she lived here when she was in college; her second-floor room looked like a college girl still lived there. She attended DePaul University right here in Chicago. Whatever happened must have happened suddenly.

When the pizza arrived, he paid with cash and moved back to the safety of the attic. It didn't take long to feel bloated with pizza and Coke. He figured it safe to temporarily store the left-over pizza in his refrigerator. He planned to take the pizza boxes out to the alley late in the night and stick them in a neighbor's trash can.

His curiosity grew as he pulled the last of the returned letters from his daughter out of the stack. His handwriting was unmistakable but jittery and frail, a major change from the earlier letters. The envelope was postmarked six months ago.

Dear Babs,

This is my last letter. I don't expect you will read this one either, and you've made it clear you want nothing from me, and especially my money.

What happened to your mother was the worst thing that ever happened in my life. Your life. She was troubled. I wasn't a perfect father or husband but her soul will never rest if we leave things this way. No doubt her soul is anguishing even now, she loved us both so much.

I hope you will call and come and see me this last time.

Pops

The one thing in the attic he hadn't looked through was their financial papers. He felt they were too personal, but then all his prying was personal. Good at unraveling stories by reading financials, he rationalized he would never get to know any of them, so what difference did it make. He sat before a stack of containers labeled, 'Financial Records,' going back many years. Like most people, they saved financial records as required by the IRS but forgot them.

The records showed Henry enjoyed a lot of success in his career, a veteran of the Army, a good golfer, and socially active. Marjorie, his second wife, was ten years younger. The common thread was his year after year financial success, documented by the increase in earnings over time, his investments, and that Marjorie was troubled. There was very little information on Barbara. She married while in college and divorced a short time later. After the divorce, she moved out of state right away.

As he dug deeper into the records, he could see Marjorie's mental health expenses were growing year after year. Viewing her life through a financial lens revealed a life slowly spinning out of control. After a suicide attempt, she was diagnosed as bipolar when Barbara was a very young girl.

He saw a folder in one of the boxes labeled in feminine handwriting—*Maj's Mind*. In it, he found a plethora of loose papers, notes, and typed pages of rambling thoughts on her life—a journal of sorts. At times her life seemed full, celebratory, boundlessly loving—she loved Henry, and he loved her. At times her journal read like a Romeo and Juliet affair. She had high praise for her father, who was alive then, writing about his bravery, and how much he had to endure, how sad his life was, how unfair. Nothing hinted at the reasons for the estrangement from his daughter, Barbara.

Her writings at times were giddy, funny stories, jokes she heard, and hilarious stories about Henry and how he doted on Barbara. But Marjorie had a dark side—tortured by demons she couldn't share with Henry and especially Babs. In her dark moods, she wrote, 'Babs has nothing to look forward to. A life of worry and never knowing. I could never tell her. Sometimes it's okay to hide the truth. Henry doesn't agree but promised to keep our secret. Swore an oath.'

There were several brochures in the folder about depression and bipolar disorders. According to the literature, bipolar people live a life of unpredictable mood swings, days on end, even months—high states of euphoria and exhilaration and crashing to the earth. It was like riding a roller coaster of invincibility, loving yourself at times, shifting suddenly to states of anxiety and feelings of worthlessness. Commonly, it was easy to mistake the condition for everyday depression. Suicide was not unusual.

Byron pulled a vacation picture of Henry and Marjorie out of the stack of pictures and propped it up against one of the containers. They were such a nice-looking couple, so happy right to the end. Oddly, there was no death certificate in the official family papers, so he couldn't determine when she died but had the impression Barbara was a grownup woman when it happened.

Why wouldn't she speak to her father? Looking down at the picture, everything he had seen in the attic pointed to a loving family and love for both Mother and Father, and nothing suggested he did anything to warrant a lifetime of rejection. What was it?

Sitting on the trunk in the attic the next morning, after a breakfast of cold pizza and diet Coke, he called the hospital to check on Henry. Calling the main number, he asked for the oncology floor nurses station, knowing they wouldn't give out information to just anybody he needed a good story.

"I'm calling for Henry Steele. He's a bit hard of hearing, so I doubt I'll learn much from him. Can you tell me how he's doing and when he is going to be discharged?"

She asked if I was a friend or family member.

"I'm a neighbor. I've watched the house. We had an attempted break-in the other day, and I'm going to be away, so was wondering when he would be coming home?"

She told me he'd be released after lunch and added, "He needs a caretaker but refuses."

"I'm not a caretaker. I'm just a friend…It sounds like him…yeah, I'll talk to him about getting help…Thanks."

It wasn't until after lunchtime when Henry returned. Byron was sitting on the trunk when the hospital van pulled up. The driver wheeled him out of the van and up to the house. Henry was slumped over with his head down.

Moving to the second-floor landing, Byron listened as the driver wheeled him back to the bedroom and helped him to bed. Henry said he was going to be all right, and the driver left. The rest of the day was silent, with no television and no clanking to the bathroom or kitchen.

Just before midnight, Byron awakened to the sound of clanking. For fifteen minutes, the sound of retching filled the house, then silence. A half-hour later, he was heaving again. Then a period of silence.

Byron snuck down to the second floor and listened. An hour later, he heard Henry cry out. "Goddamn it. Where in the hell are you? You are cruel and uncaring. If you care, you'll take me right this minute. Loving God, humph."

A few minutes later, there was more retching, and then his voice crying out again, "Why? Why can't you hear me? I can't go on."

For an hour on the second-floor landing, Byron listened, hoping he'd recover and brooding over the dilemma.

Well past midnight, a car pulled up in front of the house. Being on the second floor didn't allow him to see outside but provided a clear view of the ground floor. Minutes later, there were footsteps on the porch and two flashlights shined through the smoked glass door side panels. Someone had a key and they gained quick access to the house. Two flashlight beams moved around the room and shined in open drawers and cabinets.

Sitting on the second floor provided a perfect observation point to view the bouncing flashlight beams and hear their whispered conversation. The other day he felt so helpless, so conflicted, as he watched Henry struggle to get to his feet, worrying he might die right before his eyes. The feeling of helplessness was back but now mixed with anger.

The two boys were easily recognizable, Rocco, the skinny taller one, and the one called Tubby, the shorter fat one. Rocco whispered, "It's in the kitchen. You look around here, and I'll go get it. If the old man shows up, I'll take care of him."

As one boy searched the living room, the other made his way to the back of the house. A few minutes later, Byron heard Rocco gasp. Tubby rushed to him and, in unison, directed their lights into the bathroom. Tubby whispered, "Do you think he's dead?"

"I don't know. This is creepy. Let's get out of here," Rocco whispered. Rocco backed down the hallway and shined his flashlight into the kitchen, "His wallet was right there on the counter. It's gone." Quickly he rummaged through drawers and cabinets and rushed back into the hallway where Tubby was waiting. "It's not here. Let's go."

They backed away slowly. When they reached the foot of the stairs, they were startled by a creaking sound on the stairs behind them. Tubby exclaimed loudly. "What was that?"

Byron was fuming mad, still furious at the way the boy treated Henry the other day, now doubly so that they were trying to rob him, compounded by all the time he spent holed up in the attic and how far his life had tumbled. Rushing down the last flight of stairs, missing the last step, he went flying and landed against Rocco, slamming him against the wall. Grabbing him by the throat, he pressed his head against the wall. Shinning the flashlight into his face, Rocco's eyes were wide with terror.

Tubby flung the front door open and dashed outside.

Employing his best imitation of Clint Eastwood, Byron said, "You're dumber looking close-up. I was so hoping you'd come back. I was planning to shoot you in the knee cap and call the cops. Leave you something permanent to remember this night by." Still holding him by the throat, Byron pushed him toward the open door and out onto the porch. When they arrived at the top of the stairs, he pushed him hard. "You're welcome back anytime. You hear me. Love to see you here again. Next time, you're dead."

Byron watched him crawl across the snow-covered yard and scramble to his feet and race to the car, and jump in the passenger side. Standing in the open doorway, the cold winter air slapping his face, he watched them spin the car tires, trying to escape.

When he arrived at the main floor bathroom, he found Henry lying on the floor in a fetal position in front of the toilet. He was as white as the bathroom floor; his breathing was shallow and raspy. Byron sat on the floor a few feet away, watching and wondering what to do. He couldn't leave him there. *Should I call in an emergency? I have to do something.* A half-hour passed, and Henry hadn't moved.

With nothing but compassion to guide him, Byron picked him up like a small child and carried him to his bed. He never stirred. Byron sat in the recliner next to the bed and waited. When the sun came up, he moved to the living room.

Mid-morning, he went to check on him and found him asleep, lying on his back, his mouth open. He decided to wake him. In the night, he made a decision. It was time to leave the attic forever, call in an emergency for Henry, if necessary, ready to take his chances. His new look, old clothes of Henry's, a Bryn Mar golf hat, gloves, and winter coat renewed his confidence he could make it to a bus station and escape far away from Chicago.

In the bathroom, he retrieved a glass of water and a wet washcloth. Gently rubbing his forehead with a cold, wet washcloth, Henry slowly opened his eyes and looked off into the room, then to Byron, trying to focus on his face and make sense of where he was, what was happening, who was the man with the shiny head. He laid his head back on the pillow and closed his eyes.

"You had a rough night. You need to drink something."

After the old man took a drink, he labored to ask, "Who are you?"

"My name is Byron. It felt good to say that. I came here to check on you. The door was unlocked."

Confused, he asked again, "Why are you here?"

"I'm from the hospital."

Henry went silent, pondering the situation, his eyes open, wide and clear, his thoughts spinning around, working their way into a question. "Hospice?" Mustering as much energy as he could, he barked, "I told you guys I didn't want any help. I was clear about that. Get the hell out of here. I'll call the cops and have you arrested for breaking and entering."

Byron responded calmly, "Okay. I got it. I was just checking in. Byron moved back to the doorway. Before I leave, would you eat something? A little soup? Some juice? Then I'll leave you alone."

"I don't want anything."

Smiling, hoping to keep the conversation light and nonthreatening, Byron pressed on. "You on a hunger strike?" Easing his way out of the room. Trying to stay engaged, he asked, "Are you sure? You might be a little weak. Help you get your strength back." Pausing and taking one step toward him. "You sure?"

The television control on the nightstand was not within easy reach. "Here, let me get the television control for you. How about I turn it on?"

Henry didn't answer but looked up to the television.

Byron turned the television on and searched through the channels, and looked to Henry for a reaction as to what he wanted to watch. He stopped on a Gunsmoke rerun and looked over for approval."

Byron left and went to the kitchen, hoping Henry's empty stomach wouldn't resist the smell of chicken soup. Henry was still awake and watching television when he returned. He pulled up a chair from the dining room to his bedside and offered him a spoon full of cream of chicken soup. "My mother always told me chicken broth would cure anything. This is the best I could do."

He sipped the soup and pushed Byron's hand away.

"What can I get you?"

Henry turned away. When he looked back, Byron offered him another spoon full of soup.

"How about my life back? Not more life, just to do some things over."

"I wish I could help you there."

"Nah, nobody can do that…just old man talk. What I want is for this to be over. I am sick of being an old man. I want to be goddamned left alone. That means you."

Byron offered another sip of soup. "Well, all things come to an end. But now is not the time. You need to eat."

When Henry wouldn't eat anymore, he rose.

"Before you go, there is one thing you can do. Help me into the bathroom."

Pulling the covers back, he helped Henry roll over to the edge of the bed. Byron moved his walker bedside and helped him into the bathroom. When they returned, Byron asked, "Mind if I come back later, maybe fix you some dinner?"

With a wave of his hand, Henry dismissed him. He didn't say no.

After helping Henry back into bed, Byron moved to the living room, then not wanting him to know, he stayed he returned to the attic. Unsure what to do, as concerned about the old man as his own situation. How satisfying to do something special for someone, different when not for a friend or a loved one, exposing at the core who he was as a man, who he was supposed to be. Thinking back, he recalled a quote from the Emerson book, 'Nobody can bring you peace but yourself.'

Byron thought about his mom and dad and the good fortune to have a loving and stable upbringing. Everything came from them. No matter what was ahead, nothing could steal away the warmth he felt for them; at this moment, his essence laid bare. Some decisions are literally about life and death, and people cast aside lesser important things in life, even overrule major decisions. Henry, no doubt, felt the same appreciation; life was worth it until striped of joy, all hope, any future. Had Byron arrived at the point in his life where there was nothing left to be joyful for? Without having anything to look forward to, what is there? Not living is a lot like dying. What could he do for Henry? Could he leave him and just let him die?

Chapter Sixteen

Byron wasn't trained for this, but most humans know how to care. If only Henry allowed it and didn't keep pushing him away. *At some point, I have to leave no matter what, right?.*

Not a sound from downstairs all night. Byron peeked in, and he seemed to be sleeping. The next morning, he decided to give it another try. When the television came on, he scrambled eggs and toast, hoping to tickle hunger pangs to overcome his obstinance.

Byron startled him when he entered his room carrying a tray. He was awake, staring at the television. "I brought you something to eat."

Pausing, looking at the tray of food, and then to Byron, he weighed anger against eating. Propping him up in bed with some pillows was harder than expected, worried he might hurt him in his frail condition. Byron sat beside him.

"Where'd you come from. I told you I was done with you guys."

"It's my job."

"Even when people don't want help?"

It saddened Byron to think he didn't want any help, but he admired it a little too. "Yep, sometimes even when they don't want help."

"You got yourself one hell of a job. I could call the cops."

"You could." Smiling, Byron added, "What are you going to say…that you didn't like my scrambled eggs. This job's not so bad. Most people I work for appreciate me. Besides, I get to be the boss in this job."

"You'll never be my boss," Henry said obstinately. "I'm better. You need to leave me alone."

He had a bit more energy today and maybe could eat, possibly feed himself, and Byron didn't want to argue with him. It troubled him he hadn't seen him get out of bed yet. Fifteen minutes later, when he returned, he had eaten all the eggs and half the toast?" He motioned for Byron to take the tray. "I'd take some coffee, and then you can go."

"Why do you insist on running me out of here. You don't think you can use a little help?"

"I didn't invite you here."

Byron tried to bluff him. "I can get somebody else to come in."

"Nah. I don't want any help. I know what I'm doing."

"And, what is that?"

"I'm an old man, beyond my years. I'm going to die. You live. You die. Why prolong my misery? Why delay the inevitable?"

"I get it. But you don't have to suffer along the way."

"Suffer? What the hell do you know about suffering?"

Instantly he thought about Sybie but knew it wasn't appropriate to argue equivalency. Why argue at all? "I understand."

"You understand, do you? How? Have you ever had every bone in your body hurt when you simply try to roll onto your side, and you can't do a simple thing like that? You know how the doctors ask you to rate your pain on a one to ten scale? What do you do when the enjoyment of life is zero? You die. When you can't pee when you want, but can when you don't. Sometimes I lay here with my eyes closed and think I'm still young until I open them and try to move—I'm already dead. When I lay here and daydream of my better days, I'm at peace. But, when I am wrestling with people like you trying to get me to do things I don't want to do, I suffer. So, what would you choose? I've got nothing to live for. That's not pity. I just don't. I have a daughter, the only one left in my world, and she hates me. Nope, you don't understand. So, get the hell out of here."

Knowing his relationship with his daughter was strained, she was on his mind, probably all the time. Byron feigned surprise. "I'm sorry to hear that." Picking up the tray, he started to leave when the old man said. "You can make me a cup of coffee before you leave. Black and strong."

When Byron returned with his coffee, Henry had a pained expression on his face. When he moved beside him and reached out to comfort him, he flinched. "Bed's wet, huh?" So what? Let's change it. Then I'll leave."

Henry looked away.

"Come on; it's not a big deal. I'll help you to the chair. You can watch television and drink your coffee."

Byron thumbed through the television channels and paused on a news channel but, not wanting to take the chance his mug shot would appear, hurriedly changed it. He stopped on an episode of 'Young and the Restless,' and looked over to him and smiled.

Henry twisted his face up and said, "Don't you dare."

Byron settled on a western channel, Grit, then went to the chest of drawers and found fresh underwear, pajamas, and t-shirt, helped him change, and moved him to the chair. Henry may have had help changing his clothes before, but maybe not a man, a total stranger, and Byron never helped a man change his underwear and pajamas, and the moment turned awkward for both of them. No words were exchanged until finally, the silence was broken. "You're not from hospice, are you," he asked?

"What makes you think that?

After a few minutes of silence, he said, "You're some kind of angel, aren't you? You just show up one day, and you're still here, despite my efforts to run you off. I had a bad time a couple of nights ago and ended up in bed. I dreamed someone carried me in bed. Did you do that?"

Byron chuckled and turned to him. "No one ever called me an angel…been called a devil. No, I'm no angel." Bundling up the sheets, pillowcases, and blanket and leaving the room, he heard him call out, "I still don't want your help."

After breakfast, Byron sat in the living room to avoid conversation and began reading an old book he found in the attic—*The Grapes of Wrath*.

In the afternoon, he coaxed Henry to drink some water. Leaning in, he held the glass out to him. "You have to stay hydrated."

"Why? Am I gonna die if I don't?"

"Yeah, you'll die. Me too. But you don't have to die of thirst."

He took a long drink and broke out in a smile. He had a good sense of humor, and maybe his bark was worse than his bite.

Henry narrowed his focus on the stranger forcing his way into his life. "You have a mom and dad?"

"Yep. Mom and Dad live out west."

"Hope you stay in touch with them. Everybody says time moves so fast. Well, it does. And, you can't get back one pitiless, indifferent, unforgiving minute. It doesn't go in the bank, and you can tack it on to the end of your life." His eyes were growing heavy, and he was about to drift off. "Not even one second," he mumbled.

As he prepared a cold-cut sandwich and a bowl of chicken noodle soup, Byron reflected on his situation, satisfied he was doing the right thing, not the easy one.

Henry wasn't hungry and wanted to talk. "It's not so easy to know what's important at the time. I wasn't mean or anything. Just worked all the time. I didn't think she was sick, and then she died. I mean, she didn't have any bones sticking out, wasn't crippled, had a good heart, no cancer, didn't drink…not like me. I just couldn't believe it. Then Babs was so upset with me…moved far away and, in time, refused to talk to me."

"Babs is your daughter?

"Barbara."

Henry turned his head to the side and closed his eyes. Byron sighed and shook his head. Yesterday, Henry seemed to accept his presence and, at times, alert. Still, he was living in his attic, and he didn't know it. *What happened to his wife?* He wanted to hear the whole story. What caused his daughter to never speak to him? Would he tell him?

Henry slept most of the day. Byron stayed close by, hoping for more conversation. Searching for answers, he fought off images of Sybie, their bittersweet wedding, and the tragedy of it all. The room was growing dark as the afternoon sun shifted to the other side of the house, another day drawing to a close, of not many more for Henry. Young men, Byron's age, didn't dwell on thoughts of dying. Maybe when you are old like Henry, near the finish line, thoughts about the end were unwelcomed companions.

Byron held the glass of water for Henry to take a drink. Henry was weak today; it was hard to keep his head up, and he slurred his words. "Didn't work out, huh?"

Byron wasn't sure what he was referring to unless he could read his mind. He didn't answer. Henry's attention span was short anyway, and he knew it wouldn't be long until he drifted off. After he fell asleep, Byron watched for a while, wondering about Henry's life's twists and turns.

Byron fell asleep in the chair, and when Henry stirred in the morning, he turned the television on the news, ready to switch the channel, and watched for a report on the Seven Continents investigation. There was none.

At 8 o'clock, he opened the blinds. The dim light of an early winter day crept in like morning tide. Henry had a pained expression on his face.

"You okay?" Byron asked.

"I'm not Goddamn okay. You know I told you I didn't want any help. I don't need you." Feel good days and bad days, Byon thought. Before he could say anything, Henry added, "No. I don't want anything to eat."

There was no reason to argue. "Can I help you to the bathroom?"

Henry heard him and considered his response. After a long pause, he answered, "I suppose so."

After helping him to the bathroom and back in bed, Byron paused to see if he wanted anything else. Today, he seemed less able to help himself with even small tasks. There would come a time he wouldn't be able to make it to the bathroom on his own, and he needed to be more vigilant. He was so cantankerous he wasn't sure how to ask him if he wanted his teeth brushed, face washed, or a change in clothes. Also, there must be medications he was supposed to take, but he couldn't find any.

The next morning Byron spent most of his time in the living room reading a book and listening while Henry slept. At noontime, he checked on him and found him still asleep. Worried, he checked on him again at 2 p.m. When he entered the room, the old man was wide awake and seemed to be waiting for him to show. He clearly had something on his mind, but first, he helped him to the bathroom. When they returned, Byron stood beside the chair and waited.

"I wasn't perfect, but I loved them," Henry stated forcefully. Byron knew he was talking about his wife and daughter and seemed to be in a funk, no doubt wrestling with issues. "Hell of a thing. You think you're a good man, good husband, good father, and your world still goes to Hell. Losing your wife and daughter at the same time tears your world apart, and you start questioning yourself. I worked hard. Played a lot of golf. Cards. Drank a little, well, more than a little.

"God, we used to have fun. For twenty-five years, the same guys. We got too old to play golf, so we started playing cards, pitch mostly, but then the dying started. First Nate, then Marty, and then Jim. Now they're gone. Hell, they're all gone…I'm it. The last man. I used to joke Jim would outlive us all; he was so damn healthy. Halfway through a round of golf, he always pulled an apple out of his golf bag. He died of pancreatic cancer, the first of our group to go. It was so sudden. But I was a good husband. Father. A damn good one."

"I saw your daughter's picture. She's a beautiful woman."

"Looks like her mom. Spitting image." A tear formed in his eye. "She's dead wrong. She doesn't understand. Maj made me promise not to tell anyone."

There was more to the story, but he was quickly running out of gas. What he had to say seemed important, like a family secret, maybe a dark secret. Henry shook his head to sluff off the memory. "I could have done better, I guess. Not better in business. I was good at my job, and the better I was, the more addicted I became. Jobs can steal your soul, just like drugs. Hell, when you're in the hunt all the time, bagging game is the only thing. And then all you have is a dead game in your bag. And dead is dead, and that's it. And when the hunt is over, you look around; you're all alone."

Henry looked so sad, so lost. All the talk recalling painful memories, stuck in a time years ago when his wife died and daughter left, isolated and refusing to go anywhere, talk to anyone, wore him out, and he began to slur his words.

After a long pause, Byron said. "You should rest. We'll talk again. It's starting to snow. I'll hang out here for a while. If it's okay, I'll just crash on the couch."

"Suit yourself. There are beds upstairs if you want."

It must be the way it is, being old, dying, up times and down times, memories, and mounting regrets. By the time he left the room, his eyes were closed.

For dinner, Byron cooked him some eggs and toast, which he seemed to like. He wasn't very talkative, and when he left, he was watching an old Audie Murphy western. Byron spent the evening in the living room so he could look in on him periodically. He thought about sleeping in one of the second-floor bedrooms but decided to stay close by.

For the most part, Henry was quiet during the night, and when he did check on him, he was fidgety and needed to go to the bathroom. He doubted he could make it on his own ever again.

Throughout the sleepless night, Henry turned the television on and off and finally found a couple of hours of sleep in the late morning. When he awoke the morning, the routine was the same—he didn't want to talk and didn't want breakfast. He just wanted to be left alone.

Just like yesterday, it wasn't until mid-afternoon that he wanted Byron's company. "I wish you'd eat something. How about a malt? I ordered some ice cream. I make the best malts…nice and thick."

His eyes lit up. "Malt? I might try it."

"Rest, I'll be right back."

"Rest? For what? Am I going on a trip?"

Byron smiled back at him as he left the room. When he returned, he was in a talkative mood, happy he was there; of course, that came from feeling better.

As he drank the malt, they watched the news together. Nervous, there might be a news report on the so-called heist, and there might be another mug shot, Byron decided the old man couldn't hear and wouldn't connect the picture of Army to him—there weren't any pictures of him bald anyway.

Henry was uncomfortable and antsy; no doubt his old bones ached from lying in bed all day. When Byron asked if the doctor prescribed anything, he responded angrily. "I ain't taking any of those Goddamned pain pills. I flushed 'em. They made me feel worse. I don't want anything." He paused and, as an afterthought, added, "As I told you before, my life back. That's what I want."

"So, your daughter is upset because… her mother died?" Byron knew a bit more about his story than he let on.

"She blames me for her mother's death. They had a special relationship, her mom and her. I thought Babs and I did too, but theirs was over the top. They were clones."

"I saw pictures of them. They could have been sisters."

"We were okay until she went off to college…till that thing happened to her mom."

Byron waited for him to continue. When he didn't, he looked over to see his eyes were red, and he was fighting back the tears, searching for the right words.

"You okay?" Byron asked

"She killed herself." Henry poured it out, fighting to talk through his tears. "Right here in our bedroom upstairs. I never slept in there again. She hung herself. Who does that?

I thought she was doing so well. Babs still doesn't know what happened; she was away at college. We hid it from her. She knew she had bouts of depression, but not to do this. Maj made me promise not to tell her. Oh, not just the suicide, but the other."

"The other?" There was a story he was dying to tell. "Barbara doesn't know?"

Tears gushed forth uncontrollably. "Maj was so worried Babs would find out."

Byron handed him a tissue and laid his hand on his arm. Henry's shoulders shuddered uncontrollably as he tried to finish the story. "I promised not to tell Babs. We argued about it. I thought she should know. So, what would you do?"

Byron worried he might choke on his tears, leaned in, and placed his hand on his shoulder to calm him.

"Break my promise to my wife, knowing how important it was to her, or tell Babs? I knew how important it was to Maj. Really, what would you do?"

Confused, Byron asked, "I'm not sure what her secret was?"

"Secrets. Goddamned secrets. I am tortured by family secrets. We argued about it. When Babs came home from college, we had a small graveside ceremony. No one knew how she died. I never told anyone else. Not her friends. Especially not her friends. Not Babs. She thinks it was an accidental overdose. Maj was so ashamed. She hated her disease. She felt like less a woman."

Searching for the right words to form sentences, bracing himself, desperate to let it all out, he finally said, "They call it…" Taking a deep breath, "They call it bipolar. You know, like at times, she was on the north pole, and next she was the south pole. What a confusing life…She was so normal."

Shaking his head, wiping his eyes with the back of his hand, he continued. "I know Babs didn't understand. Most of the time, her mom was the life of the party…She…that's…was often just fine…scared in ways nobody could understand. I was always on guard when she was down, then all of a sudden, she was so bubbly… I'd say…that's my Maj, and breathe a sigh of relief. After she was diagnosed, her medications smoothed out her highs and lows. But she would get to thinking she didn't need her meds. I always thought she missed the highs. The highs were like cocaine."

"She didn't want Babs to know she was bipolar?"

"Maj always told me she wished she had cancer—not just that…her mother committed suicide, too. And, her aunt."

There it was. The bombshell. Byron couldn't have guessed where the story was leading. It was starting to become clear. He was suffering under the weight of all these secrets and the pressure of estrangement from his daughter. All those years. And now he was taking the secrets to his grave. Out of honor. Loyalty. His wife's unintentional dying wish left him alone, without the only person left who could care.

Henry's eyes were closed as he continued to weep softly. "She just wanted to be like everybody else and didn't want Babs always wondering if she had the disease, worry it would claim her like it did her. Like the rest of her family. She didn't want her always looking over her shoulder every time she was sad. Everybody in the family guarded her secrets. How could I not honor her wishes?"

His expression turned angry. "Babs grandmother and her sister both. She doesn't know about that either. Her aunt put her head in the oven, and her grandmother…you just can't believe it…doused her car with gasoline and lit it on fire. Nobody understands the bipolar disease. But the biggest secret of all was how I've had to hide the whole thing."

Henry's words slowed and were coming hard, his eyes glazed over. "We were going out to dinner at our favorite restaurant. That's the way it worked. Maybe she didn't take her medications; I didn't know." Henry began to cry again, inconsolably. Byron placed his hand on his shoulder again and pulled the covers up under his chin. His shoulders shuddered. "When I came home, I found her…"

The brochures Byron found in the attic described the highs and lows. Would he do the same—keep the secret at the expense of his relationship with his daughter?

Two people loving each other so much, demanding secrets, keeping secrets—life and death secrets. One demanding secrets of the other, all the while keeping her own secret. A secret so important to her she died for it and ruined lives.

Henry's eyes closed. Byron wondered if he had more to say and was too tired. "I know how much you loved her. How much you loved Barbara. I'm so sorry. I wish… what can I do for you?"

Without opening his eyes, he said, "I told you…" Pausing for several minutes, Byron thought he might be going to sleep. When he opened his eyes, he mumbled, barely intelligibly, "Ever married?"

"I was once. It didn't last long."

Byron watched and waited. When Henry fell asleep, it was still snowing, so much so that he went to the unattached garage out back by the alley and shoveled off a path to the porch and front sidewalk. It felt good to be out sweating in the cold air. The hard work felt like freedom, all the while he was haunted by the revelations about the family secrets.

Chapter Seventeen

That night sleep was elusive. Byron couldn't shake how tormented the old man was, how he felt the weight of those secrets for a long time. Every day Barbara wouldn't talk to him compounded his misery. It was clear what he wanted. He wouldn't give up hope until his last breath. Byron knew what it was like to lose the love of his life. *I never gave up hope Sybie would survive—right to the end.*

***

Sybie's mom said the quarterback didn't date girls like her, but dreams do come true. When she commissioned the 'Perseverance' sculpture, she knew exactly what she wanted, and the artist captured her feelings. She refused to be Tic Toc.

For Byron, he was her hometown hero, the financial wizard, the fastest to the top in an industry of silver hairs. The upshot of being the youngest to make full partner had the potential for wealth, the riches of a small farm town. But it wasn't what drove him.

Being a full partner at Oreves, Inc., at any age, under the annoying, ineffectual, ruthless leadership of Victor Deroche made the achievement even more astonishing. Success and wealth could feed his lifestyle, but the empty feelings were filled by Sybie. Maybe it was the definition of chemistry.

Valentin's insecurity stemmed from the truth he never earned a dime in his life, even in his lofty position. He thought his attempts to control senior partners, who were geniuses in their craft, somehow made him as smart, or like he was contributing. And for his money and power, it didn't help that he thought he could say and do anything he wanted.

As a partner at Oreves, Byron felt he earned some freedoms unavailable to the analysts and support staff. He saw nothing wrong with passing along the business to junior associates, opportunities he usually pursued. He limited his travel, knowing all along it upset Valentin, but everything seemed to upset him anyway. Byron always thought success granted him the confidence he could ignore him.

Byron remembered Monday afternoon of Sybie's birthday. Marcy, his assistant, said Valentin wanted to see him right then. In her usual dry manner, she joked, "He probably wants to give you some pointers."

Marcy, a platinum blond who liked to wear tight knee-length straight skirts, was as fiercely loyal to Byron as he was to her. She knew everything that went on in the company, about every employee, especially Valentin, even personal matters. She graduated from Eastern Washington University in Cheney, Washington. She was brilliant beyond what her job required, and he often wondered why she didn't field greater opportunities. When he asked her, she never gave him a straight answer and usually evaded personal questions with her caustic sense of humor.

When Valentin demanded he come to his office, it sounded like he was being called to the principal's office, or in this case, the palace as it was known. When he arrived, Valentin leaped to his feet and met Byron halfway. If it were not for the cashmere carpeting and wool textured wallpaper, his cavernous office might have produced an echo.

Surprisingly, he shook Byron's hand with his trademark wet rag grip, just as he did with every man he met. The Valentin fish grip, sometimes several times a day, even hours apart, felt more like a special business code that signified he belonged to the club. He always dressed to the nines in an Armani suit, white starched shirt, silk tie, mirror polished black shoes, shiny cuff links, and was the only man Byron knew who wore a diamond-studded tie clip.

Byron took his hand. It felt like he had just applied hand lotion or had just run it through his black oily hair combed back over the top of his head. He smiled through perfect white teeth. A man unrecognizable to himself—his cologne was cigarette smoke.

Byron took a deep breath. He knew what Valentin wanted to talk about, and it was going to be frustrating and painful—worse than shaking his oily hand and stinky breath. He wanted to talk about the Splash project, a new social media platform to compete with Facebook. If successful, they would be a billion-dollar company. Byron knew, as usual, Valentin was seeing stars.

"What's up with Splash?" Valentin asked as they were shaking hands.

Byron knew the Splash deal inside and out and also what Valentin was after. He wasn't going to make it easy for him. A double major in the computer sciences and finance gave Byron confidence in the technology deals, but in this case, the deal was flawed more because of the owner's lack of business acumen and, more importantly, their lack of trust—a prime ingredient any deal depended on.

The tip-off, in the beginning, was the owner's unrealistic notions about the value of creation. They felt they were worth 90% of any deal. Ninety percent. They had no respect for the risk of investors, in fact, held outright disdain. They felt investors were greedy and would never agree money and risk could have a larger voice in deals than creative genius. It was just money they proffered.

More than once, Byron explained money people had options and could pick and choose who they dealt with, usually products further along and more tested. They had a lot of options. No one would work with owners who didn't appreciate the risk. Byron's admonitions offended them.

Byron did everything he could to educate them and told them even an invention like the light bulb wouldn't be lighting our homes without capital and management working together. They debated for two weeks in a ridiculous chicken and egg argument. In the end, he ran out of patience and asked what they wanted. They countered with a series of options, each one as ridiculous as the other, and Byron wasn't going to embarrass himself or the company to take them seriously.

While Byron might be a young man, but had already seen his share of wanna bees like the owners of Splash. It would be hard to convert Facebook subscriptions to a new social media alternative, even their growing number of users who hated it—so-called friends. The subscription base needed to move to Splash in mass. A deep pocket angel investor, not an investment banker, was needed or alignment with someone in the industry who wanted their technology. There was also the problem of the emerging threat of regulations. No matter what, Valentin saw it as the next billion-dollar deal.

Finally, Byron advised the Splash owners they needed to find another company to represent them. They eventually softened their positions, although he didn't feel they bought in.

Valentin didn't trust anyone, just like the Splash owners didn't, but somehow believed meddling made deals better. And Byron couldn't tell Valentin that he had told the Splash owners to find a different company to work with.

Smiling, Valentin began to grill Byron, knowing but not caring; he knew very little about Splash or what they needed from Oreves. "Why aren't you going to Silicon Valley to meet with the Splash guys."

Valentin didn't even know where the meeting was or the names of either of the principals. Returning his smile and standing his ground. "Val, I don't need to." Byron never knew if calling him Val irritated him, but he thought it might.

"You should go. It's important."

"No."

"Why not?"

"It's Sybie's birthday. I wouldn't miss her birthday for anything. Not for a million dollars. More like not for a billion dollars."

Byron could see how uncomfortable he was when he began to fidget and took a half step back, still facing him. Valentin smiled through gritted teeth.

It was late afternoon, and Byron planned to leave early and buy flowers for Sybie on the way home, so he bailed Valentin out, not wanting to prolong the meeting. "Rollo's got it." Rollo was one of the more seasoned junior associates. "He's really good. He has established rapport with the principals. He is more familiar with them and the deal than I am. And he knows I am available and will go over whatever comes out of the meeting. He knows enough not to stray. On top of that, it's not that important of a meeting, and if you want something to worry about, I'd worry more that somebody will steal Rollo away from the company."

Valentin was steaming mad. No matter what Byron said, he wouldn't like it, but he knew better than to stray too far, as much as anything, to not prolong the discussion. No doubt he would have more to say later, or someday, especially if the deal bogged down, he'd blame it on the missed meeting with Splash. No doubt about it.

There was no arguing the details of this deal, any deal for that matter. No, he had tried that before. "You know a lot about this deal, do you?"

"I know enough," Valentin responded defensively.

"Enough? About what, the technology field?"

"Of course not. Don't toy with me."

"I'm not. They haven't even had a successful beta test yet. I think they are too early. If we can nudge them in the right direction, we might be able to help them."

"Whatever. You need to get the deal done now. And, you need to handle it."

"Don't count too much on that. Not with these guys. Besides, others are entering the space, in fact, companies heavily capitalized, and further along."

"All the more urgency to keep this moving along."

"Val. You need to know more about this before we talk any more. I'll have Rollo come by and go through this in detail with you. When the time comes…if it does…I am sure you don't want a bad deal made."

"I know enough already."

"Great. Okay. If we do a deal, watch them burn through the first stage of financing like a hot knife through butter. Why don't you go introduce yourself? Have Rollo brief you and then go and meet with the principals." Byron knew it would be a disaster. Senior leadership always kept him away from clients, knowing he could screw things up. Right then, he didn't care. If Valentin got involved, he'd save the company a lot of trouble.

Byron felt blood rushing to his head as he clenched his fist. This was Sybie's birthday, and there was nothing more important. He turned his back and walked away, knowing it would irritate him. It felt like he was turning his back on a man holding a gun, believing he wouldn't shoot but knowing he could.

***

Stubbornly, he didn't make the trip as Valentin demanded, but he did pay more attention and sent reports to Valentin. Byron's financial value to the company had ruled over personal battles with Valentin until recently when he learned Valentin was undercutting his standing with the other partners, partners who had been covering for him.

Byron was infuriated Valentin would undercut him because he was devoting his attention to Sybie. It bothered Byron he missed her last visit to the doctor—the first one he missed in two years. In between his trips to California, he spent as much time as possible with her—frequent summer walks on the Discovery Park trails, sampled their way through Pike Place Market, and toured the waterfront Olympic Sculpture Park for the umpteenth time. When he asked about her last doctor visit, she evaded him and said everything was okay.

He noticed on their outings she didn't have as much stamina, their walks cut short, the trail was always uphill to her. She had lost her appetite, looked pale and thinner, gaunt like she was losing weight again. He hated to sneak around, but he easily gained access to her digital calendar to learn she had been to the doctor again without telling him and even had some more tests. One of his college majors was computer science, and he knew his way around a computer and the internet. He didn't want to accuse her of not sharing

165

with him, that would have been worse, but he had to know what was going on.

On the way back from a short Sunday evening stroll, Byron asked, once again, what was going on. He knew she was shielding bad news. As loving as their relationship was, it was a bit dysfunctional the way they worried about each other.

They walked on until she was out of breath and asked if they could stop and sit on one of the trail benches. After a moment of silence, she said, "The doctor says it is back."

He knew what she meant "Okay, we need to get after it."

"No. I told the doctor no. Byron." Bravely looking into his eyes, she continued, "It has gone too far. It's too aggressive."

Stunned, he watched her and listened to the determination of Miss Perseverance, no sadness, no hint of tears. She was probably all cried out. She was protecting him; maybe she had been for a long time. Shaking his head, his mind raced for a positive response. "What did your doctor say?"

"It's gone too far. That's what he said…"

Byon interrupted, I need to talk to him."

Shaking her head, she continued, "they said they could try some experimental drugs. I'm not doing that."

Byron wanted to tell her they should never give in, that they could beat anything together? Facing a new kind of determination, words failed him. There was so much finality in her declarations he wanted to scream. "Oh, Sybie…" Pulling her close like he always did when words failed, when he wanted to comfort her when he needed her to comfort him, panic seized him and choked any words. She was so brave—he was a wimp compared to her. She knew all along he was allowing dreams to control him. "What are we going to do?"

Only a few people were in the park at dinner time. They stopped talking when a man walking his golden retriever stopped not too far from them, and an older man and a woman holding hands passed by and smiled. He imagined they had been in love for a long time.

It was the end of a summer day, and the sun was low in the sky. Gazing at the older couple, Sybie said. "How sweet,"

"What are we going to do?" Byron asked.

 I guess we know what I'm going to do."

His eyes moistened, then a flood of tears gushed forth as he melted into her arms. "It's always us," he muffled onto her shoulder. "Remember, I'm your hubby. In name only, but twice as strong, no matter what." Pushing back and wiping tears on his sleeve. "So now, what is your objection to getting married?"

Byron and Sybie always communicated best in the way they held hands, clinging to each other like there was no tomorrow, gazing into each other's eyes as their souls embraced. He loved that she called him hubby. She knew they were as good as married.

"What's the point," she asked?

"The point is I love you. What better way can I tell you that? Let's make it official. Anybody would say we are married already."

"Well, I certainly would be proud to carry your last name."

"Then, why not?'

"Why not? Because you know I'm going to die. That's why not."

Byron hadn't uttered the words, accepted the surety of it like she had. He focused all his energy searching the internet to learn about scientific breakthroughs. Every day something new, plenty of miracles, but off shore and without credible sources. "There could be a breakthrough tomorrow. We can't give up." How frustrating to think breakthroughs were happening all the time, and most doctors wouldn't learn about them until they saw a report on the local news. The lucky patient who happens to live in the right place and be available at the right time. "Medicine is changing every day." He could hear the panic in his voice. His words were coming out in a rush. "We'll face this together… science…that won't stop me. Why let that stop us? I want us to be us."

Calmly, sympathetically, she responded, "I couldn't do that to you. And, I can't chase after miracles."

"Why? Why not? You used to say because we couldn't have a family. Now, children are out of the question. No longer a factor."

"It wouldn't be fair.

"Fair to whom? You? Me? It's not fair for you to go through this alone. Not fair that I can't marry the woman I love, who I know loves me. The whole thing is not fair. We are trapped in not fair, and you know it."

Sybie broke down and began to cry, and they held each other. Through her tears, she said, "This is hard. Crazy."

"Hard. Yes, it's hard. In every way, it's hard. Nothing easy about it. Hard for you to go through this alone…for me to not be there. That would be hard. I am way over my head, and I might be crazy. Yes, but it's crazy about you. I'm in this fight. Don't leave me out of it. Talk about fairness?" Byron stopped and looked startled. "No, not alone. Never. Either way, you'll never be alone." Holding his hand in the air as if weighing the options, "Over here, with me by your side or over here with a man who loves you, till death do us part, Mrs. Kelly?"

Committed to doing it right, a week later, Byron got down on one knee and proposed to her with a ring. He wasn't going for memories. He simply wanted to express his love and make every day special.

He remembered there was a historic one-room church in Work, a twenty by forty-foot wood structure with a forty-foot-high steeple with a cross. Every morning as a little boy, he walked by the church and watched the years crackle the white paint, volunteer trees spring up and mark time, weeds grow out of the wood steps. His mom told him stories about a local lumberjack who built the church for his wife, who was dying of consumption. When finished, he invited everyone, any time of the day, any day of the week, to come and pray for his wife. There were varying stories as to whether the prayers saved his wife, but the sentiment wasn't lost on the citizenry, and for the longest time, it attracted people as far away as Oregon, Montana, and Idaho to offer prayers, celebrate new life, get married, beg for forgiveness, seek a miracle.

On a whim, Byron's learned the Grange Society had purchased the church from the county and eventually planned to make it into a meeting place. He offered to pay for the church to be painted and cleaned up in preparation for a miracle wedding.

***

Byron no longer tried to keep up with business. He referred everything back to Marcy, and she passed messages on to the other partners. He stayed on the Splash deal, more than anything, to not desert Rollo, who badly wanted it to come together. Byron still thought it would eventually end up with an angel investor. He even privately tipped off a few investors who might be interested.

The next big deal Valentin wanted him to take was the upstart Sunnyside project, but he avoided taking it over. He laid low and tried to be advisory. Given his state of mind, it wasn't fair to the company and other partners. Sunnyside had developed, but not yet patented, a key technical component for self-driving cars. A great product, and the timing couldn't have been better. The original capital investment was relatively minimal, but in time infusion of a large amount of new capital would be needed, and the deal would take months of development.

Right before the wedding, Valentin began to send Byron emails and made several attempts to call. His voice mails were threatening, "I'm sick of trying to track you down. You better call me back within the hour." He didn't. Marcy said Valentin was on a rampage and had torn into Lisa, a junior partner who was working on the account. He demanded Marcy contact Byron and make him come to the office. He learned from Marcy the meeting wasn't about Sunnyside. Splash had dropped them. Byron couldn't face him.

Byron and Valentin's disagreements were private for the most part. At the same time, Byron knew personal feelings shouldn't mix with business, and not inviting him to the wedding would be a blow to his fragile ego. He wasn't naive enough to think Valentin was powerless, though. He was the owner. He had all the cards.

Chapter Eighteen

When Henry fell asleep, it was still snowing, so much so that Byron again shoveled a path to the garage, the porch, and the sidewalk. It felt invigorating to be out in the cold air, exercising half-starved muscles, sweating—the hard work felt like freedom.

The days were inching toward the earthly end of Henry's life—not so much how but when his life would end. Christmas came and went—the second Christmas of Byron's life that passed without celebration. Neighborhood houses, apartments, and condos were decorated for Christmas as the bitter cold staked its permanent claim on the dark December days, just like the snow and ice claimed the streets.

Henry had his ups and downs, every step up followed by two steps down. He would die in his own house, as he wished, but without seeing his daughter, and Byron would have to call officials and Barbara to announce his death and explain himself.

More than once, Byron thought it was time to leave, run away again. The old man wanted to die without help, and Byron worried he wouldn't know what to do when it got complicated. Maybe he should call his doctor, try harder to get him real help. He prepared to talk to Henry, push him a little, explain he wasn't qualified, maybe come clean he wasn't hospice. If he told him he was on the run, no doubt Henry would stubbornly tell him to get the hell out of his house. He would call the police—but die getting to the phone. Byron tried to shake off such thinking. Dying decisions must be easier for the dying.

When Byron went to Henry, hoping to broach sensitive topics, he found him in a talkative mood. Every day was different. Always he entered his room hesitantly, expecting the worse. Finding him upbeat relieved his uneasiness; the timing couldn't be better. "Where you from?" He asked before Byron could sit.

"Out west, a small town east of Seattle, called Work."

"Never heard of it. Is that close to Babs?"

"It's on the other side of the mountain from where I'm from. She lives in a place that catches all the weather from Seattle and turns it into the rain, snow, and cloudy days. Where I'm from got darkness from the other side, and we gave them weather in return. I've only passed through Coeur d'Alene—it's a beautiful place. A lot of rich Californians are moving there. Someone told me the Tahoe billionaires are driving the millionaires out and moving to Coeur d'Alene."

"What was it like there? Where you lived."

"Small Townsville, where everybody knows everybody. My great-great-grandparents were from a little town east of there, Monte Cristo, now a ghost town. A mining town in its day, then timber. My great-great-grandfather changed his name to Kelly because there were too many Smiths."

Byron told him his plans to play football in college and dispassionate stories about shattered boyhood football dreams, the esprit de corps of teammates and tight spirals, and winning games. "When I blew my knee out, life veered off in a whole new direction." It felt good to talk about himself—the real Byron Kelly, but he didn't share anything about his academic or career achievements.

How simple, youth, worrying about what to wear, grades, decisions about where to go and what to do with friends—friends scattered around the country now. Byron softened his voice and smiled reflectively. "Out of the blue, manhood stole all the fun." Snapping his fingers, "Just like that. It's like jumping off the Sauk River railway bridge into the summer glacier runoff." He circled around stories about Sybie, but the memories were never far away.

Henry reciprocated with stories about his youth. He grew up in the age of honesty when free was free; lies were lies, and truth, truth, and deception had consequences. Byron liked how Henry said it. "It was a time when you get what you see. Less pretending to be something else. Now evil has been pushed to the shadows, just as potent but unseen. People were more honest back then; at least everyone understood the consequences of lying. Even criminals lived by a code. Today, politicians make a sport of lying, and nobody cares."

Looking out over the top of the television, Henry's memories jumped around like popping corn, "I was born and raised in Rockford, Illinois, just west of here. We were poor. Real poor, not like today's poor. Now everybody is rich. Even poor people are rich. Everybody has a cell phone, colored TV, and a car or two. We had soup and sticks to play with and fish with. My father made furniture. People couldn't afford furniture, so a lot of guys got laid off in the depression. He took a big cut in pay but always said at least he had a job.

"Momma was so frugal; she used to say, 'Use it up, wear it out, make do or go without.' She patched everything; sometimes, my britches were more patches than pants. She was a beekeeper and sold honey. We used to chew the honeycomb like it was gum. I got my selling skills from her. When I earned a penny or found one, I spent it on candy, but if I ever got a dime, I saved it. Once I found a brand-new shiny dime and thought it was the most precious thing ever. I saved it like it was found treasure. Don't know what happened to that dime," he said reflectively.

The energetic side of Henry surprised him. Watching him, he traced the deep lines in his face that curved downward to form a permanent scowl. *How could I desert this man?* Those scowl lines could turn upward and form a smile, too, when he talked about his mama. "She had a rain barrel for washing and cleaning. She was the cleanest woman I ever met. She always said, 'Not having money doesn't mean we have to be dirty.'

"We didn't have much to entertain ourselves with. During the depression, the movie theaters closed down except one, and we couldn't afford that anyway. Miniature golf courses popped up everywhere, and board games were popular. Billy Parker had a monopoly game we used to play for hours."

All the talking and reminiscing eventually wore him down, and suddenly, like the flipping of a light switch, he rolled his head to the side and closed his eyes. He slept all afternoon, ate a half bowl of soup at dinner time, then fell back asleep.

Seeing Henry so alert earlier, he hated to see him give up, so Byron decided to call the doctor. In the kitchen next to the phone, he found the number for Doctor Woods.

Taking a deep breath, he asked for the nurse. When she came on, Byron explained, "I've been looking in on Henry Steele…"

She interrupted and told him he refused any follow-up visits; said he was done with doctors and hospitals." Before he could respond, she interjected, "I know Doctor Woods wants to talk to you. Henry's a rock star here. Can you hold? As soon as he comes out of the exam room, I'll grab him."

When the doctor came on the phone several minutes later, Byron recited what he had rehearsed and hadn't been able to say to the nurse. "I'm not having any luck. He refuses any follow-up, any care at all. He's a stubborn man."

The doctor laughed, "That's Henry. How's he doing?"

"Up and down, more down. He isn't eating much. But there are times I think he's going to get out of bed and start dancing. He seems resigned to die at home. Adamant. He wants that. He won't even talk about seeing you."

Byron's tension released when the doctor accepted his explanation and didn't press him for more personal background. "I love Henry. He's one of the last salt-of-the-earth men. A precious relic. Don't tell him I called him that."

"He doesn't think the chemo works."

"We don't know either if he won't come in," Doctor Woods added.

"I don't think he will."

"I'm torn," the doctor responded. "I want to do more for him, and if he cooperates, there might be more. I respect him, though. He told me he wasn't going to go whimpering to his grave. 'Die like a man,' he said. 'Not going to die, puking into the toilet with an IV line in my arm, begging for a miracle.'" Doctor Woods went off the usual script. "At his age, his condition, he's right. It's not the worst place to die. Home."

The question Byron avoided finally came when he asked, family or friend? He explained he was a long-time neighbor—guess it made him a friend, and he had been looking in on him for years when nobody else was, helping him out with chores.

"Sounds like you might be all he has right now. I know about his daughter. If you are in it to the end, here are some things you should know." Byron could hear the nurse in the background telling him his next patient was in exam three. "His skin will become cooler; keep him warm. He'll sleep more…"

Byron interrupted and told him he was already sleeping a lot.

"He may become constipated and incontinent. He might refuse to eat or drink. Don't force him. It only makes him more uncomfortable. When his breathing shifts to raspy, long deep breaths, it might be all you can do is talk to him, soothe him. He will hear you."

The doctor stopped talking and waited for Byron to acknowledge, more to determine he was on board with the tasks ahead. "Okay, one more thing. He has heart failure and should be taking a prescription I ordered. I will renew it. Make him take it. Also, I'll prescribe something for his anxiety and confusion. Make him take these. I will review his chart and renew essential prescriptions. Tell the nurse which pharmacy you want to use. The best thing you can do is get him into Hospice. If he refuses, are you okay with all this?"

Byron wanted to say, how the hell do I know, or hell no. "I can't let him lie here and die alone."

"Don't hesitate to call me. Day or night. He's a special guy. Good luck." Without waiting for a response, he hung up.

Later, he called the nurse and instructed her where to send the prescriptions, and called the pharmacy for delivery instructions.

All night Byron fretted over the challenges he faced. If he wasn't committed before, he was now. He also had to contact Barbara and hear for himself she didn't care enough to come and see him. No matter what she felt, what kind of person would not want to be respectful, do what they would for a stranger. Afraid of what he was being asked to do, not by the doctor, but his heart, and almost as scary, he had to encourage him to accept hospice, fearful Henry would react, shut him out.

The next afternoon, he was alert and in a good mood, so Byron ventured, "I talked to your doctor."

"Okay." He said, squinting his eyes, knowing there was more and deciding how to react.

Byron hoped he valued their brief time together. "Doctor Woods said he couldn't evaluate whether the chemo was working without you seeing him."

As firmly as his weak voice could muster, he burst out, hoarsely, "I'm not going. Not going. Why would I go? I'll never go through that again. I'm too old. Those doctors are just smart piecework assembly line workers—one patient at a time; the more pieces get processed, the more they make. It isn't logical. So, I go to the doctor, and he says you are better, you're gonna live a long time, maybe another month. Or maybe they say you're not doing well. I already know that." With a mischievous grin, he continued, "I told Doc Woods that, and you know what he said, nothing. He smiled and didn't respond. I think he knows."

He drew a breath and reverted to a softer voice. "Look, there comes a time we all face, and this is my special time. I've been heading this way all my life. Right? I'm dying. It's my time. Let me die with dignity."

Byron's eyes moistened. He wasn't allowed to cry, not in front of him. He had to hold back. "I respect that. I hope I'll look at it that way when it's my time. But, Henry, there are people more qualified than me to help you through this."

Henry had a puzzled look on his face. "I don't want no Goddamned stranger coming in here. Do you hear me? Make that my dying wish if you want."

Having bravely taken the next step with Henry and his face mashed up against the next one, was he capable of climbing up to the next one? Maybe not, but he made it a dying wish. Damn him. He's so stubborn. Is there anything worse than screwing up a person's dying? How could he refuse him?

"Well, Henry, I guess it's me and you. But don't be dying on me right away. We have more to talk about."

He had been up for a while, so Byron searched the television for something to watch, probably something to sleep by. He stopped at a Bonanza episode. Later, when he checked on him, he was half awake watching the news. There was nothing new nationally; severe weather out east, a mild front expected in Chicago. He wondered if he was gone for a year if the news would be any different. So much of the news sounded the same, local murders, grandstanding politicians, all the same.

Toward the end of the news, there was a segment of news that updated old stories, called Sixty Second Update. A blond female gave quick updates on several stories, one about the Houdini bandit. Byron's disappearance had become a regular story on the Seven Continents heist—the Houdini bandit they called him.

"Police are still looking for this man. They are doubling their efforts in the area to find him." A picture of Army flashed on the screen. Quickly looking over to Henry, his eyes were closed. "He disappeared with 23,956.00 million dollars, and the FBI can't find him." Byron was startled to hear that number. It wasn't what he transferred to the offshore bank. He transferred more money. A lot more. The female newsperson continued. "He has been spotted in Miami, Florida, Des Moines, Iowa, and in as far away as Hawaii. The FBI believes he is still in the Chicago area and is doubling efforts to find him. They are asking for the public's help." The tip line number was superimposed across Army's Rastafarian image.

***

When Byron snuck into his room at 2:00 am to check on him, the hallway light revealed he was awake, starring into the dark. The television was turned off; it was more just background noise anyway. He pulled the chair up to the bed and, in the dim light, asked how he was doing. He had a pained expression. The Doctor said he would grow more restless and agitated, unable to get comfortable, so Byron watched for that.

Henry wanted to sit up. Leaning close, Byron pulled Henry's arms around his neck and wrapped them around his back. His muscles had atrophied; he was bony and fragile so repositioning him felt like lifting dead weight. He gently inched him up to the propped-up pillows, all the while worrying he might hurt him.

Henry sighed. "I keep thinking it was all my fault. Bipolar—yeah, but what could I have done?"

"No, don't go there. Nobody knows. You can't know. It does no good to think that way. Who in the hell is perfect anyway? I'd bet my house she didn't feel that way. If I had a house."

"Maybe I worked too hard. I made a good living. Got money in the bank, but what good is that. Can't spend it, and Babs doesn't want it. There was this guy at the club who lived in this big beautiful home, swimming pool, tennis courts, and home theater. Threw the best parties. He had a summer home and a ski chalet, too. But he was the most unhappy guy I ever met and drank himself to death. I'll bet some homeless people are happier than some people who have a lot of money. Do you want some money? I'll give you some.

178

You can have it all. I need to talk to my attorney. Set that up, will you?"

Surprised by his burst of energy, Byron chuckled at the thought, then broke out in loud laughter. "I don't want your money. I wouldn't take it. All the talk about how bad it is to be rich sounds like you're a democrat."

"I'm no damned Democrat. Not a Republican either. I'm an independent American. Isn't that what Americans are supposed to be?" he bellowed. "Politics is an ugly business. As bad as television news guys. TV news guys spend hours in makeup and read from a teleprompter and think that makes them an expert. They're both more about serving themselves and each other. Little honor among thieves, they say. Politicians just want to be elected, spend money to make it a career, and will do anything: scare old people, poor people, and black people all to protect lavish lives and suck up to the Hollywooders.

"Don't get me started on Hollywooders. Now there's a group of people who live in La La land and can't think for themselves. They all seem to go to the same church. And there ain't no God in their churches."

His words hung there. There was so much wisdom in this man, lost on a generation who didn't care what old people thought. There was anger there too, and remorse.

Henry began coughing as he tried to clear the mucus from his lungs. The doctor warned him to watch for pneumonia, and he would order an antibiotic. Byron sat and stared, paralyzed, not knowing what to do. Henry's face turned red as he gasped for breath between coughing spells.

When the coughing subsided, Byron stood beside him and held out a glass of water. Placing a hand on his shoulder, he asked, "If you…well, if you get really sick, are you sure I shouldn't call an ambulance, get you to a hospital?"

Henry perked up, and a smile broke out. "You asking me that now? I thought we were becoming friends. Don't you dare. My attorney has all the papers. It's all laid out… be sure to set up that phone call I asked you to."

Byron never forgot he was a man on the run, and Christmas would have been a good time to move on, but the season passed, and he was still trapped. Presiding over the end of life was a bigger challenge and more complicated than expected, and there was nothing more important.

Instead of smiling, Byron nodded. Responsibility closed in and gripped him tightly. At first, the attic was his refuge, a hideout, then the comfort of a bed and shower, warmth, food, drink, and even loaned clothes of Henry's he found in the attic; now, it was a noose around his neck.

Minutes passed as they silently shared contemplations of the new friendship pact before Byron said anything. "You afraid of dying, Henry?"

"Harumph, there's a secret nobody talks about. In all the deep conversations with best friends in our card games, well into the sauce, nobody ever asked, 'You afraid to die? Why is that? Too afraid of the question? The answer? Well, I'll tell you, anybody who says they never thought about it is a liar.

"I used to think I would die in an accident, maybe a plane crash. When I was young, nobody flew. We never even had a radio for the longest time. Remember, I lived in the stone ages. Hell, I remember when we got our first television. I'm still amazed I can plug a box into a wall and outcomes real talking people. When Grandma Steele died, she still thought there were people inside the little black box. So, do you know how it works?"

"Not really. There are a lot of things we just accept. Kinda like faith."

"Anyway, I remember when I first started to fly on business trips, always thinking the plane was going to crash. I never thought I'd hang around like this. Never like this— dying from the inside out. My mind was always sharp, and I never put the weight on. Then my shoulders got sore, my knees so bad it was hard to walk, my hips creaked, my back twisted like a pretzel, my skin shriveled like a prune. Not a single one of those ailments was going to get me, but then they ganged up, staked out new claims, found hideouts, and slowly tossed me onto the dump heap. Dust to dust."

Byron leaned back and looked over at the clock on the nightstand. They had been talking for nearly an hour. The old man's eyes were red and glossed over. People rally right before the end. Was this a rally? Yesterday he worried he might not make it another night. Now he was standing on a soapbox and letting wisdom fly like a kite on a windy day. He still wanted someone to hear him, value him one last time.

Henry continued, "I used to think what a blessing it was to grow old, reap the rewards of a life well-lived, but then I lost Maj, then Babs—not such a good life lived after all. Now, when I pee on myself, I want to die.

"You know I refused chemotherapy. I didn't want to die with a chemical drip line plugged into my arm or end up like so many old people, stockpiled in a warehouse, out of sight, out of mind, trapped in my memories with no one to share them with—too old for anyone to believe I knew a few things, had any value, had something to contribute. Young people think they know it all, but they will grow old and irrelevant too and then wonder if they knew so much after all. Funny the people who have it all figured out are the dumb ones, and the really smart people keep trying to learn and understand."

"I care, Henry," Byron said. He was right. Nobody listens to old people. "You religious, Henry?

"I have faith, all right. And dying, it's gotta be better than this life, huh? I've seen plenty of church people whimper to their graves. Where's the faith in that?

"You Catholic, Jewish, Mormon? What are you? Buddhist? I don't figure you for that."

"Prop me up, Byron. I want to sit up."

After helping him sit up, Henry answered. "None of those. I have faith, but not the church kind. I tried the church scene and couldn't get used to all the praying to Jesus. I couldn't tell who God was and who Jesus was. And then all my Jewish friends seemed to make such a big thing about Jesus, too. Even the Muslims get all steamed about it. It all sounded like one big argument about Jesus. Like my prophet is bigger than your prophet."

"Kind of sounds like a man thing, doesn't it?" Byron reflected.

"I figured if we all lived like one of those prophets and weren't killing people in his name, we'd be a lot better off. Hell, I don't know. I just settled on the world not being an accident. That's about all I understand about it. There's more blind ignorance in saying this all just happened by chance but are unwilling to look at the science. So, how about you? You religious?"

"Used to be. But then I couldn't figure out why God let such awful things happen to really good people?"

"So, if something bad happens, you stop believing? Hell, I figure he cares less about our earthly bodies than we do."

"But why, if you got to take people out, why make good people suffer? Like kids, why make them suffer?"

How amusing, Byron felt like a small child being lectured to by a wise grandfather. Henry smiled before he answered. "It's not like he's just sitting there choosing who gets the gold and who gets to be homeless. It took me a long time to understand that. I was pretty mad when I lost my Maj so young, and then when Babs stopped talking to me. But then I finally figured he probably wasn't even listening to me. Why would he? I wasn't listening to him. I figure he set it all up to work on its own, and most of us don't pay any attention to the setup and never listen and along the way go against the rules, try to change them to fit our lives, stop listening, then wonder why we can't hear."

"How'd you get to be so wise?" Byron wasn't sure he heard him. His eyes were closed. Henry smiled, no longer in his bed, in his room, maybe young again. What a blessing for sleep to come so easily.

Byron waited. A half-hour passed before he opened his eyes. "I thought you left,"

Henry must have been mulling over their conversation because he jumped right back in. "Tell me about your wife."

"My Sybie was special like your Maj." She had cancer. Surprisingly, it came out easier than he thought but had no desire to discuss it further.

Henry responded, "I wish Maj had had cancer."

Byron understood what he meant.

After repositioning him, Byron asked, "Henry. Hope you don't mind me holding up here, weather being so bad? Maybe until you get better."

"I ain't getting better. You can stay as long as you want. Like I said before, take the bedroom upstairs."

"Was it special like it was with me and Maj?"

Byron didn't have to think about an answer. "Oh, it was special. We often talked about growing old together." Byron stopped and reconsidered, "At least, I talked about growing old together. Always in love, holding hands and feeling like we were strolling along an endless beach, no end in sight, a beach that stretched to eternity—a vast, all-powerful ocean at our shoulder following us. She was a beautiful woman, like your wife, so full of life. She understood life so much better than I did. You would have liked her, Henry. She was only thirty-three years old. She died too young."

Henry's head slumped down awkwardly as he watched Byron out of the corner of his eye, too worn out to lift his head. "I am so tired." He began to cry. Byron pulled a Kleenex from the box on the nightstand and wiped his eyes. "My Maj was a beautiful woman. Whatever didn't click in her brain never came between us. Never. We were so in love. She was full of life. I'll never understand how she had so much, be so full of life, and could kill herself. Do you know what I mean?"

Sad endings. Why did she have to die? Why did Sybie? Byron fought back the tears. "Yeah, I know what you mean." Taking a deep breath, holding back dammed-up tears, he turned away. "Well, I don't want to wear you out. I need to fix something to eat. Anything special you want?"

Too tired to lift his head, he smiled over to me. "I'm so tired," he mumbled.

Byron moved beside him and pulled the cover-up under his chin to keep him warm. Henry closed his eyes, defeated.

Chapter Nineteen

As Byron fixed a macaroni and cheese dinner, the way his mother made it, browning the top layer, he noticed Barbara's telephone number in the kitchen by the phone. Henry kept it right there all these years, but they never talked.

A woman's voice answered and said, "Why are you calling again? I told you I wasn't interested. Take me off your list."

Startled, Byron wanted to check the number but couldn't on the older push-button phone. "Err, sorry. Are you Barbara Ryan? Is your father Henry Steele?"

"Is he dead?"

"No." Byron hesitated. This wasn't the way he wanted to start the conversation. "But he isn't …hello. Are you still there?"

He could hear her breathing heavily. "Yes, I'm here. Who are you?"

"My name is Byron Kelly. I'm…'err, I'm with hospice. I am caring for your father. He'd like to see you."

"He would, would he? Thanks for calling."

He wasn't sure if her last comment was sarcastic. After a long awkward pause, he said, "Should I tell him you will be coming?

"I won't be coming. Tell him you couldn't reach me."

"He doesn't know I'm calling. I know you've not been on good terms, but he loves you and talks about you, and, well, he's so filled with regret. I hope you'll change your mind."

He thought she might be crying and waited. "I'll bet. I'm hanging up, and I won't be coming."

The phone line went dead.

He hung up, dissatisfied with how the call ended. Retreating to the attic, he pulled the printed pages from his messenger bag and laid them out on the floor. There was one page for each account he transferred. He didn't have a calculator, but with his mastery of numbers, he could easily hand-add the account summaries. They added up to 26,346,209.36—the total amount he transferred. The screenshot summary for each account had a control number tied to the Seven Continents system that all traced back to McDermott and a handwritten number of the corresponding offshore account, not the amount the FBI reported. The difference was 2,390,360 dollars. He found one account that exact amount.

In the beginning, Byron was so convinced McDermott was hiding those accounts that he transferred the money to a protected offshore account. Then he moved the money again to a different country. He wavered when McDermott unexpectedly called in the FBI. Now his hope was renewed.

McDermott was holding out from the FBI, making it tough on them. No, he wasn't holding out. He wasn't a suspect and was just monitoring things. Byron was convinced if McDermott was guilty, he had somebody inside working with him. Someone with easy access to the computer system and high-level security clearance. It wasn't anybody Byron worked with. They weren't smart enough. Oh, Alfred was, but he didn't seem the type.

Rejoining Henry at dinner time, it was unpredictable which Henry he'd find. He wasn't eating, and Byron was running out of ideas. "I made macaroni and cheese and a fruit smoothie. And you have to take your pills."

"Smoothie?"

"You're going to like this. You gotta try it."

Henry took a drink and politely said, "That's good," but pushed his hand away.

Picking through his pills and holding out a small orange-colored one, "You need to take this." Henry pushed it away. "You know they have a pill for everything. This one here makes you younger. Take years off your life. Here try to get this down. Reluctantly, Henry put it in his mouth but began to cough and spit it out.

"Come on, Henry, let's try it again." This time he swallowed it with a drink of the water. He gave him a minute before offering another pill. "This one here is for building up your muscles. You'll be able to hit home runs like Barry Bonds with this one."

Henry's mouth turned up at the corners as he took the pill and a drink. "I'm not going to grow breasts like a woman, am I?"

Byron chuckled, and they exchanged smiles.

"One more. Hey, this one is in case you get lucky with the girls today. You gotta take this one."

Henry swallowed the pill and, this time, took a larger drink.

Satisfied, Henry laid his head back on the pillow. "I sure miss Maj. More than ever. I bet you're sick of hearing that. It's just that I can't shake it like I used to."

Byron left the room without comment and returned a minute later with a picture of them. They were on a beach. It looked like Hawaii. Their toes in the sand, smiling at the stranger snapping the picture, they held each other like they were stuck together.

As Henry reminisced, Byron watched. Aging was so cruel; Henry said the worst cut of all was lying still in bed and thinking he was still young until he tried to move or roll over on his own. "Worse yet," he said, "was when I sold out to humiliation as an acceptable way of life—being bathed by another man, unable to control my bladder." Henry's mind was sharp; maybe the worst cut of all was that his sharp mind lagged behind crippling joints, and his best memories lost the battle against the bad ones when he outlived his friends, and there wasn't even a family member left to bury him.

Henry pleaded for understanding. "I keep hoping Barbara will understand and see me again. Does she hate me so much?"

"I doubt if she hates you at all. Sometimes people are just stubborn. It's hard to let go sometimes, and it can turn into regret. But then, I guess everybody has some regrets."

"Regrets? Regrets, huh? Sure, I wish I had a daughter who cared. I wish Babs knew. I wish I had told her the secret...secrets I'll take to my grave."

The next day, the house was especially hot—hotter than he would have it, but Henry was always cold. Mid-morning, Byron drank his fourth cup of coffee and made a grocery list, then decided to try and reach Barbara again.

When she answered the phone, he blurted out, "Please don't hang up. This is Byron..."

Barbara interrupted firmly, "Yes, I know who you are, and I know what you want."

"I know you don't have to talk to me. But I wanted to give you an update and well...honestly... try one more time. He's going downhill. He is still in good spirits...sometimes...but he...well, he probably only wants one thing before he dies, to see you."

There was a moment of silence, so he took advantage and continued. "I don't know much about your life, or probably even his, but I know he has regrets, and he feels he's let you down, and maybe he wasn't the best father, but I also know we all want different things out of a father, and it's hard for a father to measure up sometimes...and I also know sometimes we do things we don't want to, and they turn out okay, and sometimes they turn out not to be good for us and well, there might be another side...I also know..."

Barbara interrupted. "I know what you want. You don't need to go on."

He knew he was rambling. "I'm sorry. Maybe I shouldn't have called. I guess I've taken to your father and..."

"I got it," she said.

"I've gotten to know...".

"Stop. I'll come. But I won't stay long."

"I'm glad. Should I tell him?"

"I don't care." Then on second thought, she corrected, "I guess you should. I'd hate for him to die when he sees me."

****

The sun was out, perhaps in celebration of Henry's special day–Barbara's arrival. Byron knew there would be awkward moments but hoped it worked out.

Henry didn't sleep well, and neither did Byron, so he let him sleep until nine o'clock. "Time to get up. Big day. Let's clean up."

"Today, huh? I must be going fast."

"Yep…no, not dying…I mean Barbara's coming today. You know what I mean. She should be here at noon."

After eating half of his oatmeal, and a half glass of orange juice, Byron gave him a sponge bath, changed him out of his sleeping clothes and into fresh underwear, and a pair of gray trousers, shirt, and sweater, which were now three sizes too large. Judging by the size of his feet and large bony hands, at one time, he was a strong athletic man. Helping him to the chair, Byron turned the television on while he stripped the bed and threw them in the laundry. The old man's mood and health were always unpredictable, but today he was in good spirits.

At eleven o'clock, Byron asked if he wanted to get back in bed.

"I want to go to the living room," he answered. "Can you start a fire in the fireplace? There should be a good stack of firewood beside the garage. I have a guy who checks on it and keeps it stacked."

Before moving Henry, Byron went outside and added a hefty stock of firewood to the wrought iron log holder and on the hearth. It was near impossible for Henry to use the walker any longer, so he carried him to the living room. After propping him up on the sofa, he opened all the shutters in the living room and let the light in.

Being the coldest day of the winter season so far, Byron built a fire. Henry looked on. "I could always tell when Maj was happy to see me," he reflected. "She would wait up for me after a road trip. She often had a roaring fire going. We laid on the sofa together, and…we loved to listen to the crackle and sizzle of the burning logs, fall asleep and wake to dying embers."

Henry drifted off. The fire was warm and mesmerizing, and soon Byron was lost in his memories.

***

Byron recalled the day she made her dying announcement. That place on the Discovery Trail would always mark the begging of the end. Surrounded by happy people celebrating their lives on their evening walks, who had no way of knowing the tragedy that filled the air. *I was lost for words at a time when words were insignificant anyway. I asked what we were going to do and she said, "I know what I'm going to do." A piece of me died at that very moment.*

She knew what she was going to do. Her words thundered in his head. She was going to die.

Every time Sybie saw Byron's sadness, she always said, "I've expected it all along and was built to handle this." When she was a little girl, she knew she'd never reach old age, never have a daughter to see off to her first day of kindergarten.

They lived like she was dying. Of course, Byron never said that. She never said it either, but she lived that way. They took slow walks along the Sound, stopping along the way to breathe in ice-capped mountain views. They kissed their greetings and goodbyes in the morning before getting out of bed and the last thing at night. In the mornings, when daylight crept into the room, their eyes still closed, resisting the new day, she would roll over and put her head on Byron's chest as he held her in his arms.

No matter what their days were like, they always shared dinners. Her artistic talents extended to the culinary arts, and he too liked to dabble in the kitchen, so they combined their skills to create special meals and memories. And, routinely, on Friday nights, they still went to their favorite restaurant, Viva la Italia, where they had their first date.

190

Chapter Twenty

The sound of a car door woke him from his daydream. Taking a deep breath, he shuffled to the front door and met Barbara on the porch steps, and took her bag. She wore a hooded fur-lined winter coat, black tights, knee-high black leather boots, the hood pulled back resting on her shoulders, her butter blond pixy hairstyle bounced in the blustery wind as she bounded up the steps.

Reaching out for her suitcase and computer bag, they exchanged uncomfortable glances. "Hello. You must be Barbara. I'm Byron. Byron Kelly."

Her blue eyes sparkled in the bright sunlight, but her smile was tight-lipped. "Thanks." Handing Byron her bag, she said, "I traveled light. I'm not staying long."

Once inside, she slipped off her coat, hung it in the closet, and sneaked a peek back at Henry asleep on the sofa. The dying fire reflected flickering shadows off his face. She looked away immediately. A petite, pretty woman, wearing a white bulky snowflake turtle neck sweater, she looked so much like the photos of her mother at her age. It must have been a treasure for Henry but now an undesirable affliction.

Byron walked over to the fireplace and threw a log on the fire, then turned to Barbara. "He wanted to be out here."

She looked back at her father. He was motionless, laying on his back with his mouth open, as white as the blanket covering him. It was shocking to see her father so frail, such a stark confirmation he was dying. He looked more like a holocaust survivor. She paused momentarily, her mouth agape. "Is he asleep?"

"Looks like it. He does that a lot."

Hesitantly, she added, "Is he…is he okay?"

"Okay? Sometimes he's okay, but his days are…he's been up and down…maybe your visit will perk him up."

"I doubt it, but I'm glad I'm here. It's the right thing to do." Byron thought she wanted to say more but seemed to think better of it. "I think I'll freshen up while he is asleep."

"Where do you want me to put your bag? Which bedroom? The place isn't very clean, but I did clean the upstairs bedrooms. Take your pick?"

She looked puzzled. "Is that part of the service? Do you stay here?"

"I have been. I don't have to, though. Since you're here, I can leave."

He carried her bag up the stairs, and she followed. "So, you're with Sisters of Mercy Hospice? Do you often get so attached to your patients? Live with them?"

"Yes and no." he lied. "Can't help but get a little attached." More than overseeing Henry's demise and the tension between father and daughter, Byron dreaded the questions she might ask—even more than what he faced outside of the house. This was about life and death. "More than a little with your dad. I got attached and sort of just got stuck here in some bad weather, and he went downhill, and I stuck around. He refused help from anyone else, and I couldn't leave. It has worked out okay. Really, if you mind…"

Her thoughts raced, a bedroom away from a total stranger, a nice-looking man but oddly living there. Hospice? He must be okay. *I should check him out.* "No, it's probably good you're here."

Barbara returned to a roaring fire and smothering hot room. She took a seat next to Byron in the other club chair across from her dad, who was still asleep on the sofa. In the awkward silence, they avoided eye contact. She was there out of duty and for Byron for a secret reason, trapped, and with the added pressure of being caught in a lie and the whole thing blowing up and ruining Henry's dying. Adding to the tension, he didn't know much about her, and no doubt she worried too, not knowing what to expect from a stranger, now a resident in a bedroom a door away from hers.

Henry began to stir, tried to open his eyes, and blinked rapidly to focus on his surroundings. For all he knew, when he opened his eyes, he might be on the other side with Marjorie. He looked over and saw Barbara.

His eyes moistened. Clearing his throat, he finally offered hoarsely, "Well, hello."

Looking away from her father and to me, she answered. "Looks like Byron here is doing a good job of taking care of you."

Winking at Byron, he said, "I can't seem to get rid of him." Looking back to Barbara, he added, "You look nice."

Smiling, she chortled, "You look like hell, you know." She let her comment sink in, then added. "You look like you're hanging in there pretty good."

Byron had learned a new language and could interpret Henry's groans. "Do you want to be on your side?" he asked.

Byron went to and put his arms around him in a bear hug and rolled him onto his side, then returned to his chair. Barbara watched, her mouth agape, facing the naked truth of sticks of bone covered over by loose, sagging flesh, affectioned by a stranger.

"Does he need anything?" Barbara asked uncomfortably.

Henry responded quickly. "I've been through it with Byron. I don't need a thing. "How do you like Cor d'Alana…Cordale…damn it, I can never pronounce the name of that town?"

Barbara pronounced it phonetically for him, "Cor da lane. It's pretty there. Sure, beats the big city life."

Rising to leave, Byron said, "I'll leave you guys. Any thoughts about dinner?"

"You a chef too?"

"He's not demanding. But yeah, I know my way around a kitchen."

"We can order in. That Chinese place down the street still open? Woos, I think that's the name. If you want to order something, I'll just take something veggie and brown rice. Does Dad eat…er, what do you do about him?"

"I'll take care of that. That's a bit of a challenge."

Later, when Byron entered the kitchen with Henry's dishes, Chinese takeout containers lined the counter. She acknowledged him but went about washing the dishes.

Byron broke the silence. "Is it Mrs. Ryan or Miss? How should I refer to you?"

She laughed, part giggle and part relief, no doubt as tense as him. "It's Miss. But, please call me Barbara." She pulled her bangs back and said, "See, no horns. I'm not a bad person."

"I'm glad you came. He wanted to see you, and your being here has already raised his spirits. He has talked about you a lot."

"That bastard would," she said coldly. "No doubt. I shouldn't be here. Not sure I can do this."

The sudden shift in the conversation caught him off guard.

"Don't worry, no matter what I think of that man, I don't want to make it worse. He already looks like he's stepping into his grave, and I don't want to give him a shove."

As cold as her words were, her eyes were soft and sad, not angry. "Sure. Well, I am going to bed. I have to get up often in the night."

As he turned to leave, she had more to say. "I see you've done a lot for him, and he cares for you. This seems to be so much more than your job requires. I need to thank your employer—Sisters of Mercy, right?"

He hoped she didn't see him flinch. "Just doing my job."

"So, shouldn't he be in a hospital or nursing home somewhere?"

"Yep. Should be, but not for your dad. I wouldn't recommend saying that to him. He almost kicked me out of the house for making that suggestion. He refuses any help. He wants to be at home. A few good memories left, I guess."

"Good memories. BS. Yeah, he's a stubborn bastard who thinks about himself. Good memories for him."

Barbara shifted nervously, "I shouldn't be here," she repeated. "I'm going to take the next plane back if he starts sharing his good memories with me."

"I'm sorry. Maybe it was a bad idea."

Byron turned away, but she continued. "Is he like… soon…does he have long?"

"Not long. I couldn't say for sure."

What do you do anyway? To help him…?

"Not much. I just hope to keep him comfortable and well, be with him at the end. That's it. Don't want him to be alone. I'm not sure what else to do."

Barbara drew back with a puzzled expression on her face. "Not sure what to do?"

Byron felt panic stirring, took a deep breath, and smiled nervously, worrying she wasn't afraid to say what she was thinking. "He could get more help if he'd let me. Like you said, he could be in a facility with around-the-clock nursing. He doesn't like the idea of strangers helping him, and he isn't very cooperative." Trying to shift the conversation, "There is one thing you can help with. When the time comes, there will be questions about next of kin, legal matters, funeral arrangements. When you leave and when your father, well…when he crosses over, I'll call you. He has an attorney, and I hope you'll talk to him and leave me instructions. I am uncomfortable dealing with his affairs but will if I have to."

Her expression went blank as she squinted at him inquisitively. "You want me to talk to his attorney and make arrangements?"

"I think arrangements are made. I just want you to give me instructions...or if I can just call you and…you'll take care of it when…"

Cutting him off, she said, "So, you're going to be with him when he dies?'

"Probably. I'd like to be."

She looked away uncomfortably before she spoke. She had a pained expression. "You want to be with him?"

"No one should die alone."

"Don't judge me," she snapped. "You weren't there. I'll do my part and be gone." She hesitated and shook her head. "Don't get me wrong; I appreciate you'll be here. She smiled and asked, "Have you been doing this for a long time?"

"No." He hoped to avoid any more questions and again tried to shift the conversation, "He's right in a way. I'm not sure if there's a right way to die for everyone. I know in a facility, they would fill him up with drugs. That's what he said to me."

She looked at Byron, hoping for more information.

Byron felt closed in and wanted to avoid any deep conversations. Easing toward the kitchen exit, "I'm glad you're here, but I'm not trying to do anything but get him through this. He wanted to see you, and now you're here. He didn't think that would happen. He's happy."

He had one step out of the kitchen into the hallway when she said unconvincingly, "Yeah, I guess it was the right thing to do. Do you have a business card?"

Byron's mind raced. He wanted out of the kitchen and out of this conversation. "I don't have one. I'm new." Prepared for more questions to avoid being trapped, she would probably ask about his previous career and where he worked. Schoolteacher was his story. He thought he could easily cover the lie, having had enough teachers to know what they do. He could pick a school in Seattle, use the mom got sick story he used to land the job at Seven Continents. "Look, if you are ever uncomfortable with me, I'll get a replacement. I'll call them tomorrow. He needs round-the-clock care, and he won't agree to a facility. I won't force it. I wish he would, but he won't. I admire his resolve. He knows what he wants. He is ready."

"New. You're new, huh? No. No. I'm sorry. No way. He trusts you. That's important. Sorry."

***

The weekend arrived quickly. Playacting him or not, she added time to his life by fulfilling a dying last wish. He seemed to be willing himself not to die on one of these last treasured few days. As near as Byron could tell, there were no serious conversations between them. For his sake, there didn't need to be. And she avoided displays of anger or obligation. If he detected any, Henry ignored it, a blessing for both of them. But it pained Byron to know her act was just a front as he watched her look away when Henry talked about Maj and called her Babs. On one occasion, she stormed out of the room.

As perplexing as a rainstorm on a blue-sky day, she hadn't talked to her father for years, hated him, but there were lighter moments, too, when she could be so charming. Not around him, though. For his benefit, she played the role of loving daughter beautifully—an Oscar-worthy performance.

On Sunday, the eve of her departure, Byron cooked dinner to show his appreciation for her being there and to enjoy her company one last time. He had a twinge of regret seeing her leave tomorrow, not just for Henry, but he would be alone again. She filled the house with her perfume and laughter, and at times she trusted him and more and more treated him like a friend.

They ate at the kitchen table, a simple meal of baked Fettuccine and Caesar salad, but enough to impress her. "You do know your way around the kitchen. That was delicious."

"Good to have someone to cook for, share a meal with."

Throughout dinner, he detected she had more questions. Finally, as they were cleaning up, she asked, "I can't put my finger on it. You don't seem to be the hospice type."

"What is the type?"

"You seem... well, I don't know, sophisticated, passively controlling. I don't mean it in a bad way. Shrewd....I don't know...like a UN negotiator. Sometimes I feel you're controlling me."

"Yeah. Probably. I'm on pins and needles between you and your dad."

"Sure. I get that. No, it's like you have another calling, like maybe you paint masterpieces in your spare time or were a former executive. You do have another life, don't you?"

"I can't even draw a stick figure. Nothing wrong with what I do. Your dad asked me once why I chose to do this, and I told him, it's the best job I ever had."

Barbara drew back. "Really? Taking care of a dying old man?"

"Like I said before, what higher calling is there than taking care of a dying fellow human, not just anyone. Henry. Barbara, taking care of your father has meant as much to me as it has for him. One night I found your father on the bathroom floor. I thought he was dead. Life is precious. No one should die alone on the bathroom floor."

Barbara's gaze narrowed as her smile dissolved into a frown. "I've told you before you don't know him."

"I'm sure you're right. I don't know him well, certainly didn't know him when…I know you're mad at him about something, and that's none of my business. I'm sorry. I'd better get to bed. Sometimes my nights are short."

She ignored him and pressed on. "So, this is your life?"

"Yes, it is."

"No wife, or wives, children, girlfriends, boyfriends, what? Just this?" Her warm smile took the edge off the question. "So, I take it you aren't married, or maybe she kicked you out of the house."

"No. There is no one to kick me out. I was married once."

"That's it? That's all there is? Married once?"

"She died."

Chapter Twenty-One

Monday, in the early morning, Henry wet himself again, so Byron helped him into the bathroom, changed him into fresh clothes, and washed his sheets. Barbara walked in on them as he was changing the sheets. He had forgotten this was the day she was leaving. She had a puzzled expression, her mouth open, as she stood gawking at the scene. Comfortably back in bed, Byron pulled the covers up to his chin and returned to the kitchen.

Henry wasn't eating again and sleeping more. Byron usually left the television on, thinking the familiarity of sassy girls, rough talking cowboys ordering whiskeys, the sounds of ricocheting bullets and thundering hoofbeats provided some comfort. When he wasn't in his bed, he liked to be on the sofa in front of a fire.

When Barbara joined Byron in the kitchen for coffee, she announced she decided to stay longer. She didn't explain why or when she was leaving.

Barbara was the owner of an investment company in Coeur d'Alene, Idaho, which given Byron's background, piqued his interest. Setting up her desk at the dining room table, every morning, she reviewed and sent emails, called clients, read financial news, and watched the markets. Byron wanted to know more about her career and learn what was new in the financial world but thought better of it.

She became more attentive to Henry and played her role as well as any actor could. Always strained, unpredictably, at times, they laughed and shared quiet, contemplative moments and when her dad was lucid, even, occasionally about old times. Without failure, they took a family vacation every summer, and Byron eavesdropped as Henry described loading up the Cadillac and driving across the country to California or Florida. "That was so boring," Barbara said.

"How could it be boring? You slept through every state. You used to put pillows on the backseat floorboard hump to make a bed there."

"Yeah, because it was so boring."

"I know you liked Disneyland because you cried when we left."

Barbara snapped like a power line in the wind. "Yeah, mom cried too. She cried all the way home. She said she didn't want to go home. I'll never forget. Barbara stood up and eased away from her father, and tightened her jaw. "When she was sad like that, you always got mad. Told her to quit crying."

Henry was at a disadvantage in the thinking department. Past events and conversations circled slowly in his mind, searching for recollection, anything to connect past events, then find an answer and formulate words and, harder still, sentences. With a shake of his head, all he could muster was, "She was sad. I didn't…sad…I didn't want her…"

Barbara's face contorted grimly, and she left the room.

They made it through the rough times, and Barbara stuck to her commitment of playing the role of dutiful daughter to a dying father, albeit at arm's length. Byron had mixed emotions and never took sides but worried about a major blow-up. So far, she was content to be the good daughter and add life to his.

To pass the time, when she wasn't on her computer, or Byron wasn't tending to Henry, they played board games in front of the fireplace. She taught him how to play canasta, a game her father and mother used to play, and cribbage on a board Henry bought in Costa Rica. One afternoon, she found an old Scrabble game in one of the cabinets. She was a spirited Scrabble player. They both came up with outrageous challengeable words, bluffs that led to belly laughs, and, in the end, he got her on the word zak, and she won the game on jonquil—triple letter J and triple word.

When the Scrabble game ended, Barbara abruptly rose and walked away to check on her dad. Byron couldn't judge her feelings harshly since he understood only one side of the story, but to her credit, she didn't let her feelings stand in the way of being human. Byron recalled a quote he read in the Emerson book, 'First be a good animal.'

When she returned from checking on him, the howling bitterly cold wind outside rattled the windows and shook the house, adding an additional element of warmth to the crackling fire and accentuated the silence. Her face glowed in the dim flickering light. "I appreciate what you are doing for my father," she said reverently out of respect for the serenity. "I'm not sure I could do what you do. Not even for my father. Maybe especially."

So far, Byron tiptoed around the topic of her mother and father, worried he might open deep wounds. After spending so much time with her, he wondered if he had inched his way up her trust scale. "I wish you could forgive him."

Barbara drew back. Her bubbly smile turned serious, but then she surprised him with her warm response. Placing her hand over Byron's, she said, "Me too. I stayed here thinking it was the right thing to do, so maybe I wouldn't have any regrets, maybe forgive him. I don't think I ever will. We just need to leave it there."

"I'm sorry. It must have been hard."

She shrugged her shoulders and flashed a dismissive smile. "I have an idea. Let's get out of here—go to dinner. My treat. You haven't been out for a while. There's a popular neighborhood Italian resultant nearby. I'm sure they're open. Do you think he'll be okay?"

His initial impulse was to say no. He hadn't been out for what seemed like forever, and part of the time, he was isolated in an attic. It did feel safer now, given his new look and the passage of time. The authorities were still after him, but he also had the feeling they had searched the area thoroughly.

"I don't see why not," he answered cautiously. "You know we don't have a car. I assume your dad's car is dead. He said he hasn't driven it for a year."

Barbara responded enthusiastically. "We'll bundle up and walk. If you like Italian food, it's worth the walk. After you take care of Dad tonight, it's just down the street. I'll make a reservation."

After Byron fed Henry some cut-up oranges, toast, and a protein shake, Barbara entered dressed for dinner. She wore the same designer jeans and the white snowflake turtle neck sweater she arrived in. Looking back to Henry, "You had a good day. Think I could let Barbara take me to dinner?"

Barbara moved next to Byron. "I'll bet you're tired of seeing me in the same outfit every day. I didn't think I'd be here a week later."

"You'd look good in a throw rug," he jested. Looking away, embarrassed, "You look fine."

Henry nodded weakly. "I'm sure I can do without you guys for a while. Allow me to get some sleep," he chortled then began to cough

Barbara chimed in. "We're going to Richellie's. We won't be long."

Henry rallied. "Tell Guido to pull a bottle of his best wine. Maybe a Saccardi Chianti. How's that, Byron? Impress you?"

Leaning in close, laying his hand on his chest, smiling fondly, he answered. "Impressive indeed. Tuscany region wines are some of my favorites."

Henry wanted to laugh but coughed instead and struggled to get the words out, "Now I'm impressed."

Byron changed the channel to ESPN and departed.

Richellie's was dimly lit by tabletop candlelight. The tables were draped in red and white checkered tablecloths. Guido, the owner, had black wavy hair, a mustache, and wore a black sports coat and a white shirt. He recognized Barbara immediately and threw his arms around her. "Praise mother of Jesus, how long it has been. Still, you are such a beautiful girl." Pushing back to look at her, "Wow, you are so grown up." Looking over to Byron, "And you brought your boyfriend, or is he… do you have something to tell me? Celebrate?"

Waving her hand, "No. This is Byron…Kelly. He is taking care of Henry."

"How is my friend Henry? He doesn't come anymore."

Henry is not doing so well. I'm afraid…he is…"

Guido interrupted and genuflected, "You tell Henry I'll bring him a special meal. Would he enjoy that? Tell him I will cook him a veal parmesan and bring it to him."

"He couldn't eat that; he'd love to. I am afraid he is dying. But I'll tell him. He will appreciate the offer."

Guido raised his hand to his face and covered his mouth, then dabbed a tear.

Honoring Henry's wishes, Guido brought them a bottle of Saccardi Chianti. "This is Henry's favorite." Before they finished dinner, they ordered a second bottle.

After dinner, as the waiter began to clear the table, Barbara's expression turned serious. "This is all very awkward for me. You think I'm such an ogre. I know you don't understand. You can't."

"This is hard for you. Of course, I don't understand what happened. We all have stuff. It can be hard to forget. I know about that."

Byron picked up the wine bottle and filled her glass, then his.

She grimaced. "Oh well, it's best we not talk about it. Not now. This is so nice. How about I tell you about the shortest marriage in history. My so-called marriage didn't last six months. I was young and stupid and fell for a professor. I loved how smart he was, but it turned out he wasn't interested in my mind. Just wanted someone who would admire him."

"So, you never tried again?"

"I guess I want to find someone the exact opposite of that jerk."

"You mean stupid?"

Barbara swallowed hard and began to laugh, almost choking.

Since they arrived, the restaurant had filled up, and patrons were sitting at tables all around them. Byron worried someone might recognize him and hoped being bald helped but knew it didn't make him invisible.

Barbara picked at her food like she wasn't hungry. "You told me your wife died? I am so sorry. Was it an accident?"

Other than his parents, he hadn't discussed Sybie with anyone else and wasn't sure he was ready or knew what to say or how it would come out. They were so close to the other tables he leaned in and almost whispered his response. "She was too young. When I first met her in high school, she was disabled, afflicted by NPS—nail-patella syndrome. Kids called her Tic Tock. We met up again later, both well into our careers."

It took willpower to keep his emotions in check, and he stopped several times to collect himself. "She overcame her disabilities and turned herself into a very successful, beautiful woman. Her name was Sybie. Thing is, it wasn't the NPS that got her. It was her mixed-up DNA that caused cancer to ravage her body. It consumed her. I wasn't prepared for her to die."

Barbara wiped a tear from her eye and placed her hand on top of his. Diners nearby turned to her. Sorry, she lamented, and then didn't know what to say. "My God, that's so tragic. I'm so sorry. Where were you? What were you doing? Hospice?"

When he looked away to avoid eye contact, clenching his teeth to avoid his own tears, he was startled to see two men in dark suits enter the restaurant. He recognized the two men as the FBI agents. They showed a picture to Guido.

Guido shook his head and pointed to the back of the restaurant.

Pushing back from the table hastily, he said, "Would you excuse me for a minute? I'll be right back. He poured the remainder of the wine into her glass and looked over her shoulder, and saw agent Barnes walking toward them.

When he arrived in the back hallway, he watched agent Barnes weave his way between the tables. Agent Galinski stood alone near the front entrance. To his right was the men's room, and behind him, an exit with a sign posted that read, 'Alarm Will Sound.' Darting into the restroom, he entered the only stall and lowered his pants and sat on the toilet, and watched through the crack in the stall door as agent Barnes entered and looked around. After the agent washed his hands, he retrieved a tube of salve out of his pocket and leaned in close to the mirror, and began to apply it to a very large cold sore.

When Byron exited the men's room, he waited until the two agents left the restaurant before returning to the table.

"You okay?" Barbara asked.

As he patted his sweaty forehead with his napkin, he said, "I'm fine. Must be the Chianti."

Outside, the wind had swept away the clouds and uncovered a full moon. As they walked in silence, it felt colder than when they arrived. They were still looking for him and right there in the neighborhood. How long would it be before she saw his mug shot on the front page of the newspaper or the television? What a close call. It felt like just a matter of time before he was caught.

Still, he couldn't tell her he was Army Bendorf, the notorious embezzler—the Houdini bandit. There was no good reason he could think of—he wouldn't even know what to say. He tried to look at it simply but found it complicated when he thought about explaining it. Why explain? Henry would die, and he would never see her again. She would leave the area. They would go their separate ways, and he would go—where would he go?

Byron broke the silence. "That thing back in the restaurant, I haven't talked about it. Guess all the emotions are still right there. Kind of surprised me."

"I get it. We all have stuff, don't we?"

She had no idea how good it felt to be called Byron. Byron. Byron Kelly. He needed to be him again. "C'est la vie," he said."

Barbara giggled. "The wine's got you speaking French."

"And, it was an Italian wine."

She laughed. When she laughed, it felt like the sun breaking through storm clouds, like a baby bird taking flight. When the laughter stopped, the quiet returned and left them with the crunching sound of footsteps on the frozen walkways. Not a single car passed on the street. The sidewalks were snow-packed, except for one small icy stretch where he reached out for her hand as they moderated their way. As they neared the house, Barbara asked, "So, who were those men?

"Men?"

"The men in the restaurant."

"It was nothing."

"You looked like you saw a ghost."

"Yeah, I thought I had. Just some old demons. I'm fine, and everything's okay."

Chapter Twenty-Two

Tuesday was the beginning of a new normal deathwatch day. "All of this waiting is hard. How do you handle it?" Barbara asked over the top of her book. Byron brought one of the boxes of books down from the attic. She was reading, *The Thorn Birds*, a novel by Colleen McCullough, and he was reading *Shogun,* by James Clavell. The bitter cold kept them inside and in front of the fire. Neither felt like a board or card game, and there was no television to distract them.

"I'm not sure. Never thought about it."

"Never thought about it? You must deal with this all the time. How come you never go anywhere, never call anyone or check in with the hospital?"

"I'm checked out. Offline. I wanted to stick with this, and I'm not full-time," Byron stammered. "More of an on-call employee. I didn't feel like another assignment right now. How could I?" He had a twinge of regret lying to her. But she seemed comfortable with him being there, and Henry refused to let anybody help him. Sure, a real hospice nurse would have handled things differently, but probably not the way Henry wanted it.

"Not much we can do, huh?" Barbara reflected. "It's a waiting game now. He isn't much for talk anymore, and when he does, he babbles and is hard to understand. At least maybe he knows what he is saying, and he knows I'm here. We're here."

"Yeah. He doesn't seem to be suffering or want anything. I got him that picture of your mom, and he sleeps with it like a teddy bear. He sure loved her."

Laying his books aside, he rose and said, "I'm cooking dinner tonight. Something special. Let's dust off the dining room table. It'll keep me busy, and we have to eat."

When dinner was ready, he found her sitting with her father, staring at him. He looked so peaceful; the comforter pulled up under his chin, so just his face poked out. Byron touched her arm to announce dinner was ready.

The dining room table was formally set, two candles burned in the middle, an old radio resting on the dining buffet tuned to a country music channel, the volume low.

"Wow, this is so nice." Barbara was wide-eyed and smiling like he hadn't seen her since their dinner at Richelle's.

As he poured her a glass of wine, he said, "Your dad has good taste in wine. I don't think he'd mind if we drink another bottle. There are two bottles of Beringer Private Reserve Chardonnay and two Plantenta Roses remaining.

"Mind? I think he'd be pleased. His wine drinking days are over." As she took her first drink and admired the candlelit pasta in the blue Florentine ceramic bowl, she asked, "What's for dinner?"

The song *Stardust*, sung by Willie Nelson, came on the radio. "Oh, just a little something. Penne Amatriciana—of course, you know the popovers."

"You are a surprising man. Popovers? They're so puffy, so perfect. What's your secret?"

Smiling, Byron answered, "Don't open the oven door until they are done. It's simple. Popovers weren't my first choice, but making focaccia would take too much time."

The dinner conversation was somber and thoughtful—something bothered her, and something was certainly on his mind too. He wanted this to end, not for him to die, but his life back—he wanted to go home and longed to see his folks again. Life moves quickly and never waits for anyone or anything, or it can crawl at a snail's pace. Right now, he was stuck. Looking across the table, he detected sadness, maybe some regret. He tried to comfort her. "This will all end soon?"

"Yes. It will," she said. "Soon." She looked serious, alone in her thoughts. Their gazes connected and held there. In a soft voice, she said, "Maybe it will be a beginning."

"Are there ever beginnings without endings anyway? I'm sure of it," he said. "I'm moving on after this. Too much sadness, too much dying. Too complicated." He took a minute to reflect then rose to clear the table.

The song, *We Danced*, by Brad Paisley came on the radio. She rose and stood before him, "How can two people not dance when a song like this comes on?"

She opened her arms, and they came together and began to sway to the music. As the song finished, they parted, only a whisper apart. She placed her head on his chest, and he pulled her closer.

"I'm glad I'm here. Thank you." She sighed.

Byron nudged her away and gazed into her eyes. Transfixed, under the spell of candlelight, the warmth of a woman, their gazes screaming out, but what were they saying? He had forgotten what it felt like to be in the arms of a woman. Barbara was everything a man could ask for, gorgeous, brainy, and bubbly, and beyond her rough exterior, so caring. "I'm glad you're here too."

Seconds ticked by as their gazes held each other and flickered nervously. She moved up to him, their lips millimeters apart, longing to meet but hesitant. He yearned to feel this way again, so warm, the fragrance of her perfume, feel her soft lips pressed to his.

He pushed away, then pulled her back and held her close, firmly in a never let go embrace. Fighting back the tears, it was Barbara he was holding, not Sybie. It felt so lonely, two wounded people clinging to each other, isolated, on an island of hope and loss. He thought about Henry, a room away, dying, the estrangement of father and daughter, both loving, good people.

Byron pushed back but held her hands, narrowing his gaze, trying to lock onto her eyes. "There is something I have been wanting to tell you. I know I'm betraying your dad, but I don't agree with him, even though it's not my place."

Her eyes flashed with anticipation, her mouth open, her eyes wild with anticipation.

"Your dad has been burdened with secrets, and time is running out. Did you know your mom was bipolar? Not just depressed."

"Well, I guess…yes…I know she was depressed. She couldn't stand it when he left her home alone. He was gone all the time. It bothered her, and she couldn't tell him."

"Your dad knew her condition was more complicated than depression. No amount of hand-holding could have cured her. No amount of love. Your mom knew if she didn't take her meds, she would be worse, but taking them made her feel worse in other ways. Your mom made him promise…made him swear."

Speechless, Barbara steeled her unblinking gaze as she searched for understanding.

"Did you know your mom's mom, your grandmother, committed suicide? It was a family secret that only you didn't know. And your aunt, too, her sister. She made him promise to never tell you about her disease, and your father was duty-bound to live with the secrets your mom left—to protect you."

"Why would she do that?"

"Because she loved you. It was her way. She hated her disease and didn't want you to know. She didn't want you looking over your shoulder, worrying a spat of sadness was a death sentence. I know what it's like. Sybie hated her condition and would never have kids for fear she would pass it on. She might have done the same thing." Byron hesitated, hoping to see understanding, but Barbara remained stone-faced.

Byron continued, "Your mom was everything to your father, so much he endured the loss of his daughter. No matter how much he loved you, your mom was his very heartbeat, and it was devastating to lose her, and you, and every day the secrets were locked away while he only saw his Maj in your face."

Byron swallowed hard. There was one more thing he had to tell her. "Your mom killed herself, too. Your father found her."

Barbara's face turned red like she was holding her breath. Unsure how she would react, she eased back, trembling, the pressure building like a bubble about to burst. Suddenly, she yowled like the sound of a wounded animal. Tears gushed forth. He opened his arms to invite her in, unsure if she would accept. She rushed into his arms, and he held her.

Henry was dying with his secrets, loyalty to the promises he made, and a touch away from his daughter's rejection. Byron held Barbara in his arms, his heartbreaking, while warm memories of Sybie crowded his thinking. All he could think to do was hold her as tears streamed down his face.

Reaching out for the table napkins, he handed one to her and dabbed at his eyes with the other. Through her sobs, she cried out. "Damn her. Why did she have to do this? I knew about bipolar, but maybe not so much. Why would she keep all these secrets…why keep Dad from talking to me about it?"

Taking a step back, an arm's length away, she continued. "The biggest secret of all, even in her happy times, she was considering suicide and may have been plotting it all along— smiling, loving me, cheering me on all the time contemplating suicide. Dad never talked. He seemed so uncaring. What was I to think? Why couldn't I see?" It's too late."

***

Barbara stayed with Henry through the night. No telling how long Henry would hold on. When Byron joined them in the morning, Henry looked to be at peace. Maybe she released him from his anguish – told him she understood, that she loved him. He seemed so content. He could die in peace now with his daughter home and at his side. Byron woke her and encouraged her to go to bed, or at least to the sofa. "I'll let you know if there are any changes."

Mid-morning, Barbara was asleep on the sofa and Byron with Henry when the doorbell rang, and he heard the shuffle of slippered feet move to answer the door. He moved to the hallway outside the kitchen, where he could observe. He

211

could tell by the silhouette images of a tall and short man, the relentless agents Barnes and Galinski were back.

A rush of cold air swept up the hall when she opened the door, sending a shiver up his spine.

The agents held out their credentials. "Hello, I'm FBI agent Barnes," he said in a deep, commanding voice, "This is Agent Galinski." As you may have seen in reports, a man living in this neighborhood is wanted in connection with embezzling a large sum of money from Seven Continents Financial Group. We are recanvasing the neighborhood. He lived a block from here." Looking down at his notes, "Is this the residence of Henry Steele?"

"Yes. I'm his daughter."

"Is your father at home."

A gust of wind blew snow into the house at her feet. "Please come in."

The agents were visible through the crack in the kitchen door he was standing behind, so close he could hear them breathing, their backs to him.

Agent Galinski held out a picture, the same one seen on television. "We are looking for this man. His name is Army Bendorf."

Relieved to hear they were still looking for Army, relieved it was the picture of him in straggly hair. "Without hesitating, Barbara said, "I haven't seen him. But I haven't been here long."

"We are recanvasing the neighborhood. We think he could still be in the area. Or at least there is someone who knows something. Maybe your father has seen him? Is he available?"

"I can assure you my father hasn't seen him. He is barely able to speak." In a hushed voice, she added, "He's dying."

The agents exchanged glances. Agent Galinski filled her in. "We were here before. He must have been the older man we talked to. We are sorry. He seemed so alert then, but then…do you live here with him?"

"Could I see the picture again?" Barbara requested.

Agent Galinski pulled the picture from his suit coat pocket. Byron was bald now, but no doubt there was a resemblance. His heart raced.

This time Barbara took a long look at the picture of Army.

Shifting from foot to foot, after a long delay, she said, "No, I haven't seen him."

Holding out the picture again, Agent Galinski said, "Would you call us if you see him?" Agent Barnes handed her a business card.

As soon as they left, Barbara turned and met Byron in the hallway. He shrugged apologetically, lost for words, not knowing if she recognized him in the picture, but sensing she had.

Her gaze locked on his blank expression, processing what just happened—unbelievable on the one hand and the truth of the picture on the other. As she studied his face, she recalled the picture she had just seen. She furrowed her brow and pressed her lips together in a grimace. "What the hell is going on. That's you, isn't it?" She stood cautiously, an arm's length away.

After a long pause, Byron finally spoke. "I need to tell you…I'm so sorry. First, Barbara, your father has taken a turn." Silently, pleading for understanding, or more a reprieve, he said. "We need to get through this, then I'll explain."

He was committed to bringing an end to the whole thing, but not how. Originally, he hoped to escape from the area and stay informed through newspapers, television, and internet searches. The FBI should have solved the case before now.

Barbara disappeared into the bedroom. Later, when Byron returned to the bedroom, she was sitting on the edge of the bed, her head on his chest. He stood back and waited. After a few minutes, she looked back, "He hasn't awakened. Not once." Whatever makeup she had applied was caked and runny. "I'm not sure he knows how I feel."

"No, it's not too late. Never." Reaching out, he helped her rise. "Your dad can hear you, and he already knows you love him. He told me so. He just felt bound by his promise to your mom. He's a lucky man to have had you guys."

Barbara moved closer and laid her head on his shoulder, then abruptly pushed away. "God, it's so painful. I loved my mother so much. Why did she have to? I loved my father. God, why couldn't I see this?"

Throughout the day and into the evening, they stood to watch over Henry. Occasionally, she looked to Byron and wanted to say something but thought better. He wanted to tell her everything, but this was not the time. Henry was at peace; sometimes, his mouth turned up in a smile like he was dreaming, maybe of his wife and happy times, maybe he was with her already. At times it seemed he had taken his last breath, only to continue. Byron suggested they take turns throughout the night. "This can go on for hours."

He had seen mailing envelopes and stationery on Henry's desk. What he didn't have was postage. Agent Barnes's business card was still on the kitchen counter—the one he gave Henry.

Retreating to the attic, he retrieved the messenger bag and composed a letter.

Agent Barnes,

Regarding the Seven Continents Financial Group investigation, enclosed you will find original screenshots of accounts under investigation with tracking numbers that identify the controlling source— McDermott. This should make it easy to reconstruct what happened, who was responsible for the embezzlement, and what changes were made in the system to cover it up. Also, you will find a print-out of a Belize bank account with access numbers, user names, and passwords. I never intended to keep this money but was convinced of the fraud and thought this was the best way to expose it. I thought you would have solved this by now. You will discover McDermott had help in changing the system to cover up the existence of these accounts. No doubt this is why it has been hard for you to figure this out.

Best of Luck,

He added the rhubarb and sage remedy his mother used when his dad got cold sores.

Byron checked on them at 2:00 am. She had fallen asleep in the chair. Henry hadn't moved since the last time he checked. He still looked to be at peace.

There was an all-night market a mile and a half from the house. It hadn't snowed for two days and the sidewalks, for the most part, were clear, but it was officially the coldest day of the year. Wearing Henry's parka, mittens, and a turtle neck sweater from the attic, a scarf around his neck pulled up to cover his face to protect him from well below zero temperatures and the added cold of the wind that drove the temperatures to over twenty below. The good news was there was no traffic—nobody crazy enough to be looking for him.

When Byron returned, he found Barbara still sleeping comfortably in the chair next to Henry's bed, but he seemed agitated, clinging to the bed cover like he was struggling to breathe. His skin was cold and had a blueish tint. It wouldn't be long. He woke Barbara. Watching Henry, he thought there was so much nobility in the way he chose to live, ever faithful to his wife until his death.

How long had he been standing there? He put his arms around Barbara and whispered, "He has passed on."

She jerked her head like awakening from a dream. For fifteen minutes, they couldn't find any words, but she allowed Byron to hold her. It felt cliché to say at the time, "He's at peace. I'll bet he's with your mother right now."

Chapter Twenty-Three

They moved to the living room. Barbara's tears were quiet, her pain palpable. Byron felt like he had found a wounded animal in the woods and didn't know what to do before it died. He remained silent and waited.

She finally spoke. "Do you believe they are together?"

"I'm sure of it. If love has anything to do with it."

"Yeah, I hope so. When Dad called me about Mom, it was the worst day of my life. I was just divorced and still in college. Dad warned me about him. Thad, that was his name. I hadn't talked to my dad for months. I married him against my dad's wishes …and now…I wish."

Byron cautiously took her hands and said forcefully, "Barbara, quit it. I've known you for such a brief time—your dad too, he was lucky to have you, lucky you were with him when he passed on."

Pulling her back into his arms, processing the next steps. "First, we need to call someone for your dad."

Barbara interrupted, "Halliburton's. That's what he told me. That's where mom was interred."

He continued. "You should call Doctor Woods. He likes your father and wants to know. Later this morning, you need to reach out to his attorney and see what instructions he left. I think your dad had everything worked out."

Swallowing hard, summoning up the courage to tell his story, weighed down by secrets in such a heavy-hearted moment, he knew things could blow up and easily end in bitterness and distrust. Before he could say anything, she blurted out, "I almost forgot who you were. Before I do anything, you need to tell me what is going on."

On winter days in Chicago, nights come early, and it was nearly dark. "You no doubt already know I'm not with the Sisters of Mercy Hospice. Henry wouldn't let anybody take care of him. Even doctors. He stopped treatments. He wanted to die just like this. He allowed me to just be his friend. I feel fortunate to have been here, but…"

"I wondered about that many times," she interrupted, her mouth agape. "I even thought about calling Sisters of Mercy. But I know how stubborn my father is and how I could have made things worse. I could see it was for the best."

"There is a lot more." Barbara backed up a step, then another. "I am the guy the FBI is looking for, but you know that, too." Byron was drowning with no expectation of being saved.

Backing up further, she gripped the stair banister. "God, I couldn't believe it." Shaking her head, she blurted out, "I would have never thought you were a bank robber? What else can you tell me? That you're gay? I can't believe this. You…a bank robber?

Her expression didn't change, and he couldn't tell if she was listening. He felt naked. "Well, I'm not. They think I am. A bank robber, I mean…I'm not that."

"Are you going to prison?"

"No. I don't think so. Not for this. I'll be cleared."

"Really. Not for this? I don't know what to say. You're not hospice, living in my dad's house, wanted by the FBI…and yeah, I saw you in the picture, a druggie Rastafarian. I couldn't believe the tender man caring for my father, with a big heart, was a criminal. At first, I thought I should turn you in. My father's hospice nurse, who wasn't a hospice nurse, was wanted by the FBI," she repeated. I had to look at the photo twice. There was all that hair?"

Byron ran his hand over his bald head. "That was a different guy, to be sure. I do have hair, just not right now."

"What if I had asked you to talk to those agents? That would have been something. All hell would have broken loose…what a shootout? God, it's hard to see you as a bank robber…you're not the type."

"Thanks. I am telling you I'm not a bank robber. It will all be cleared up. It's a long story."

She turned and slowly, haltingly, ascended the stairway and disappeared from view.

Byron realized he had feelings for her. Circumstances pushed them together in synchronous heartbreak, vulnerable, longing for an understanding of the past and the present.

Endings. Henry's wish to see Barbara one last time came true. Byron didn't know what was said, but he died a happy man, and as for Barbara, she reconnected just in time and gained the bittersweet knowledge of secrets and truth—and the nobility of her father and his undying love.

***

Byron put more logs on the fire, pulled the leather chair up close, and let the warmth wash over him as he recalled his own endings and beginnings.

Wedding days are supposed to be filled with joy and promise. What was intended to be the glittering crown of their uncommon love and a bold statement of winning and conquest and future turned into a never forgotten misunderstood wedding. Byron's folks tried to talk him out of it. At the time, it was the right thing to do—the ultimate consummation of love. What could be a greater tribute to love than marriage? Besides, Byron felt if they stood boldly in the face of the unavoidable, unthinkable and kept producing memories, they might delay the inevitable.

When Sybie and Byron woke up on their wedding day, they were greeted with the beginning of the rainy season and the promise of gloomy days ahead. Thoughts of enjoying a view of snowcapped Mount Rainier on the drive to the wedding were dashed.

Marcy, his assistant, with the help of her husband, Quinten, a Seattle homicide detective, volunteered to help coordinate the whole affair and make it upbeat. Byron didn't want the celebration of love to become a sad observance of perseverance.

Byron's folks supervised the church preparation and the clean-up afterward. Improvements were made to the Grange church—a fresh coat of white paint inside and out, repaired front steps, fixed two broken windows, cleaned the three windows on each side, and cleaned pews.

In her healthy days, Sybie and Byron often shared Sunday dinners with his folks—fried chicken or pot roast, always mashed potatoes and gravy, with pie for dessert. And, Sybie always gifted them one of her watercolors. His folks didn't remember her from his high school days and never heard of Tic Toc. They only knew her, as she wished to be known, Sybil Kobak. Being a small town, they knew her folks had died a few years apart, and of her disability.

No formal wedding invitations were sent. Sybie invited her friend and boss, Sally McSally. It struck Byron there wasn't another person in the world she invited. She told him she didn't have any high school friends and didn't go to college. It seemed so lonely.

Three Oreves senior partners, who had so willingly covered for Byron, attended with their wives. His high school and college friends were scattered around the country. That felt a little lonely, too. Sybie wore an ivory evening dress, and Byron a dark business suit. He remembered that dress, the one she wore when they reconnected at the Seattle Sound grand reopening ceremony. When he complimented her dress, she said, "It's the only nice dress I own. If you ever run into me again at another formal occasion, I'll be wearing this one."

Standing outside the church, waiting for the music to cue their entrance, he squeezed Sybie's hand and started to lift her soft tulle veil to kiss her, and she rebuffed him. "No. Isn't that bad luck or something?"

"I just saw you in the car on the way over," Byron argued.

"But now we are at the church," she said as she playfully slapped his hand away. They could hear shuffling, and muffled conversations inside the church as guests took their seats. Five minutes passed.

Sybie leaned back against the wall, breathing heavily. "I don't feel so good."

She slept all morning, hadn't eaten anything and was nervous. The past few days, she had gone downhill but refused to go to the doctor, and at the last minute, he suggested they cancel the ceremony. She rallied at the suggestion, saying it was important. No matter what, she wanted to become Mrs. Kelly. She said it was going to be a Banff day.

"Should I get you some water?

'No, I'll be okay in a minute."

"Are you sure?"

"Yes, we're going to do this."

He studied her cautiously through her veil and thought how lucky to marry such a special person, such a beautiful woman. "Remember what I told you about this church. Built for miracles, every sawed board, every hammered nail, was muscled in place with love. Legend has it hundreds of lives were saved. We have to keep the faith."

When everybody was seated inside, the sound of violin finger plucking silenced the chapel, followed by the warble of Jill Barber's voice, as recognizable to jazz aficionados as a Patsy Cline was to country music fans, singing, Never Quit Loving You.

They opened the double doors of the church and started up the aisle toward the chancel. A raw wooden cross cocked to one side hung on the wall behind the pastor, looking to be made of fence post wood. Well-wishers sitting stiffly on crudely constructed straight-backed pews solemnly watched them pass by and listened reverently to the words of the song:

As long as this world keeps on spinnin' around, I'll keep hangin' on to this love that I found I won't let go, cause I know I have something that is true And I will never ever quit loving you.

The Work New Hope Presbyterian Church minister, Michael Thrixon, casually dressed in a black shirt and tan slacks, stood with his arms folded behind a small unfinished pine single pedestal lectern. In his early eighties, his full head of thick white hair and oversized black glasses framed a smile often mistaken as a grin. By reputation, he was a jokester, so Byron's mom told him to keep it short and not to tell any of his religious golfer jokes.

As soon as they took their place, Pastor T began, "Welcome. Today is a celebration of the love of two beautiful children of God, Sybil Kobak and Byron Kelly. To love one another is His most precious gift." Gazing around the room, he added, "looking at all the open umbrellas drying out around the church reminds me that marriage is one great big umbrella that shelters love from the elements."

Pastor T paused and surveyed the faces of the guests. "It takes faith for us to join together in marriage, unaware what our futures hold except the going forward in love. In the word of the prophet Kahil Gibran, "Love is everything and forever. Love isn't something you say; it's something you do." Looking first at Sybie, then Byron, he said, "I invite you to exchange your vows."

Byron and Sybie appreciated he kept his remarks brief. They delivered their vows in unison. "I take thee, Sybil Kobak, as my wedded wife…I take thee, Byron Kelly, to be my wedded husband…"

The chapel went stone silent as every ear strained to hear their soft voices deliver their vows. The wind rustling through the trees increased as it began to rain harder. "… in sickness and in health, to love and to cherish, till death do us part."

Byron clenched his teeth so tightly Sybil bristled. Through her vale, she appeared to be calm, but emotions roiled—stuck in her throat. Byron placed the ring on her finger as they continued in unison, "I give you this ring as a symbol of my love…"

Pastor Thrixon smiled and held his hands out, "Now that Sybil and Byron have given themselves to each other by solemn vows, with the joining of hands, the giving and receiving of rings, I pronounce they are husband and wife." He continued, looking out to the well-wishers. "Having witnessed their vows of love to one another, it is my joy to present you, Mr. and Mrs. Kelly, husband and wife." Looking toward Byron, he said, "You may kiss the bride."

Beaming with pride and filled with anticipation, Byron leaned in and lifted her veil. The beauty of the moment was gobbled up in the terrifying reflection she was dying, shocked like it was the first time he accepted the thought. Until that moment, he knew she was dying, but on another level hadn't accepted it. This was a church, a place for miracles after all, but suddenly it felt like the place miracles died. The financial whiz, the maker of deals, the great communicator, always quick to see where the deal was going before everybody else, had missed the whole thing. Had denied it. Her face was white as cracked porcelain; her eyes were sunken, dull, and gray. Byron couldn't breathe and thought he was going to faint. Just a minute ago, through her veil, he saw only the healthy Sybie, the fighter, confident, flashing her smiling eyes.

Byron looked back at the faces of family and guests, stoned knowing faces, holding their breath, then back to Sybie. A solitary tear dripped from her eye and rolled down her cheek. He plucked it with his two fingers, using them like tweezers, and put her captured tear to his lips. A tear rolled down his cheek as their gazes locked lovingly. The poignancy of the moment was punctuated by the collective sigh of well-wishers.

Byron mouthed, "I love you."

She smiled and said, "I love you."

A congratulatory reception of coffee and shortbread followed the ceremony at the back of the one-room church. Marcy's husband turned the music back on and played a mix of love songs by jazz artists including Sinatra, Fitzgerald, Connick, Bublé, Nat King Cole, and Natalie.

The rain beat against the windows and pounded the roof so hard it shook the church and reverberated in his head. Surrounded by well-meaning friends and family, the chapel hot and closing in, Byron stood on wobbly legs. Each handshake and congratulations saddened and angered him equally. He never anticipated the wedding would unveil the stark sad truth, so completely, without a breath of compromise, the cover was pulled off to reveal the great obvious—a broken masterpiece. He could tell with each handshake they were reading his mind, projecting their sadness, sending out waves of pity.

How were they going to escape?

Louis Armstrong was singing 'It's a Wonderful World.' Sybie could hardly stand on her own, forcing smiles, pushed beyond her limit to get through the wedding. Looking up to Byron for support, she no longer found confidence in his voice. Rather she could see the panic in his forced smile and doubt.

Melting away, she leaned on Byron. All along, he thought it would be all right, but she was in no condition to be getting married. How could he be so wrong, for what purpose?

After the wedding, they agreed to stop by Viva La Italia, not for dinner but simply to deliver on a promise. Giovanni couldn't leave the restaurant to attend, so he made Byron promise to stop there for one final celebratory act. Byron had briefed him on her battle with cancer—he assured him she would win.

Byron and Sybie went directly home, and he called Giovanni to explain they weren't coming. "You better not start crying," Byron half-jokingly admonished him when he called and told him they couldn't stop by. The last time they were there brought tears to his eyes. Even in her better health days, he always made it seem like he wouldn't see her again. Every time they came in, he said, "Sybie,"—he was the only other person who called her that, "you are the most beautiful person in the world." Sometimes he would add, "Are you Italian?" With sweat rolling off his face from the hot kitchen, he would add, "I love you."

He could tell Giovanna understood, and before they disconnected, he said, "I hope God gives her a big hug."

When they arrived home, he carried her into the house and put her in bed, and she quickly fell asleep.

***

It was a sleepless night. The rain had diminished, but still, Byron could hear the pitter-patter of raindrops falling on the deck and could feel the oppressiveness of the gray turned blacker than black. Only the hallway light slanted dimly onto the bedroom wall. He laid close to her and listened to each breath like it was a ticking clock marking the passage of time, life itself. He couldn't help thinking; like a clock, each breath she took counted down the seconds of her life, their life, allocated so much time, so many minutes until the clock stopped telling time.

How did his life come to this? At the core, all they had was each other. He wondered what it would be like to live without her. They spent so much time together, connected at the hip, breathing in unison, reading each other minds. His love for her devoured him in small loving bites. Byron lost interest in work, devoted every waking minute to her. He told her, "Us is all I need."

Even as he dozed off, her inhaling and exhaling was the cadence of their life together and several times startled him to fully awake when he couldn't hear her breathing. Then she would take a deep gulp of the night air and begin breathing again. People find love in the most surprising ways, he reminded himself. *I'm so blessed she was my first love, my last.*

In the early morning, a last-minute yielding to weariness, Byron dozed off and was awakened by Sybie's soft voice calling out his name, "Byron. Byron, are you awake? I'm scared."

Stroking her hair tenderly, "I'm scared too, but …" Words stuck in his throat. He wanted to say they would fight this together, but he didn't know what they were fighting. The fight seemed to be over.

224

"I didn't think I could do it. Get through it."

He knew she was talking about the wedding. "We shouldn't have. I see that now."

"I'm Mrs. Kelley, right? I always wanted to marry you. You know that, right? Even when I kept saying no, my heart was crying out yes. Thank you."

"Thank you? Don't say that. This was you and me becoming us. That's it."

"I love you, Mr. Kelly."

"I love you, Mrs. Kelly."

Byron pulled her close and held her for several minutes.

She gently pushed him back and said, "I had a dream that our baby lived. It was a girl. We named her Sophie. It was so real. Did you ever have a dream you thought was real?

"Not often."

"She was taking her first steps toward my outstretched arms."

"That's a nice dream. Sophia. Her name was Sophia?"

"I don't know if it was a girl. That was my dream, though."

For a minute, the silence embraced them. "That's a nice name."

"That wasn't all. Sophie stopped and began to back up. I panicked and pursued her. When I reached her, she was waiting for me with open arms. Funny, it wasn't her taking her first steps; it was me."

A few minutes later, she said, "Byron, are you going to be okay with the company? What are you going to do?"

It struck Byron she was worried about him. She knew what happened in his last conversation with Valentin, at least his version of it. He told her Valentin was mad because a deal, an impossible one, fell apart. He didn't tell her he punched him or that he was going to be sued. "It'll all blow over."

Byron also didn't mention he had to appear in court for attacking him. She didn't need to know everything. Nothing was ever all right with Valentin. He would blow up his own company if it made him look important. He also didn't tell her he didn't care. It was just a job. "I need to move on. I've come to realize I don't want my life wrapped up in that stupid job. Taking care of you is the most important thing I do. I don't want to fail at that."

"You're so good at taking care of me, so good at what you do. After all, you've worked for."

"I'll be okay. I'm good at what I do. It comes easy for me. The hardest parts of my job are the easiest for me. I think everybody's job looks harder than mine. When you master what you are good at, like a great quarterback, the pace of play slows, and the field of play comes into focus. Like you and your watercolors. It's easy for you, even as you strive to improve with each painting. As I told you, I can't even draw a stick figure."

Sybie went quiet, just the rhythm of her breathing in and out and the chatter of rain pelting the deck. He waited to see if she had fallen asleep.

Several minutes later, she said, "I remember. I remember that time in the hallway when I had fallen, and you helped me. Do you remember?"

"Of course, I do. Like it was yesterday." She had often recalled the special moment. "That was when I fell in love with you. I saw what a beautiful person you were. Inside and out. Never forget that moment."

Sybie sighed and closed her eyes. "I love that version of the story."

He continued, "But we went on with our lives. I moved on but never forgot. And then when fate brought us together again, that feeling came back to me in a rush. Remember, like going back in time…beam me up, Scotty." he chuckled. "And I rematerialized into reality."

She strained to laugh and then began to cry softly. "Why did I have to fall in love with you, ever meet you that first time." She had said that before. "Sometimes I wish we hadn't met, but then I wouldn't have lived. I wouldn't be Mrs. Kelly.

Oh, Byron, hold me. Why does my life have to be so short? Our life? Why were there so few days?"

"You know what we say; we'll always have Banff."

In the morning, when Byron awoke, she was in his arms; her head was on his chest where it was when she fell back asleep. He rolled away, trying not to disturb her. Her arm was stiff and cold. Alarmed, when he sat up, she looked to be sleeping, smiling, like she knew secrets. She wasn't asleep. He pulled her close, "Oh, Sybie, don't leave me. Please don't leave." But she didn't hear his appeal. She couldn't. Sometime in the early morning, laying there in his arms, her soul passed through him. "I love you," he whispered.

It wasn't long ago he thought she still had some fight left—that there were more days ahead with the woman of the sculpture, with the steel rod of perseverance.

Chapter Twenty-Four

Unprepared, not knowing what came next, he called Doctor Payne and left a message. Looking out to the deck, he watched the dawning of another gray, murky day—a perfect match for his expectations as he waited for his return call. When he called, Doctor Payne sympathetically said calling him was the right thing to do. He could make things easier for him.

He said to pick out a funeral home, and they would pick her up. He would call the medical examiner's office and explain what happened. A half-hour later, someone from the medical examiner's office showed up along with a policeman. They were there less than a half-hour. An hour later, two men from the Isley Funeral Home, not too far from him in Queen Anne, showed up.

It started to rain harder. From the covered deck, he watched them carry Sybie, now a lifeless covered lump shifting back and forth as they struggled to make the turn out of the bedroom— then out the front door. Another ending.

He dreaded calling his folks, Sally and Giovanni. It was all over by mid-afternoon, left alone in the quiet, lost in the sound of rain, unsure what to do next. He laid on the couch until the day passed into darkness and reflected on what duties lay ahead. What would he do when his duties were finished?

Plan a funeral. What to with her things? His things? This condo? No job, he was going to be sued, show up in court and listen to Valentin tell lies about him. He knew how it worked. His attorney would be expensive, and Valentin would spare no expense to destroy him. *How could he destroy me any more than this?*

After two days of sleeping on the couch, Byron ventured into the bedroom. Every corner of every room was her: her watercolors, her art tools, canvases, finished paintings, clothes, slippers, shoes, the Nicholas Sparks book,

The Lucky One, open on the coffee table, the unfinished smoothie he made her. Everything reminded him of her. The plan he had been contemplating crystallized.

He wasn't going to go through her things. He'd hire someone. Surely there were people out there for a job like this. He also decided which of his possessions he wanted to keep. Everything else had to go.

He went to work on his future and the whole sorting out, clearing out, and putting the plan in place. The plan had its genesis sitting in the attorney's office. It took the rest of the week to put in place. He wanted to put this phase of his life behind him, get lost somewhere where nobody knew his name. A hot dog stand on some Caribbean island sounded good, where nothing reminded him of Sybie.

Byron knew banking and finance better than most. He paid off his bills, a few in advance, then closed his bank account and asked for cash. He then went to his investment advisor and told him to close his account. He hated to do it to him; he had been good to Byron, and, of course, he would lose a good client. To avoid discussions, he told him, "I'm leaving the area." He requested a certified check be sent to him when all the transactions cleared. He knew it could be done by Monday.

Next, he needed an untraceable place to deposit his money. He was familiar with banking in the Cayman Islands since he had used them to avoid taxes for a couple of his clients. It was perfectly legal. He also made an advance payment to the IRS in an amount to cover future liability. The last thing he wanted was the IRS looking for him.

Listing his Condo was easy. The realtor who handled his condo purchase was eager to list it. Byron told him he had a great overseas opportunity and didn't have a forwarding address at this time and needed to leave soon. Byron met with the real estate attorney and signed over his power of attorney, and instructed him, "Just put the proceeds in a bank account, minus your fees, and we'll settle up later."

When the day of the funeral arrived, on the first sunny day in a while, he picked out a white coffin and adorned it with white roses. Pastor T officiated a brief graveside ceremony, but his words were lost in the gentle breeze. If the words were for his benefit, he wasted his time. Sybie didn't hear either.

A gift from God, from a young age, she knew she was going to die and lived with it every day. Everyone dies, but not like she did. Looking back, the thought of dying didn't pick away at her. Sure, there were periods of sadness when she would say dying was more about missing Byon. "Missing us," she always said. She complained about the short time they had together. She said it was her greatest regret. In the end, cancer ripped away at every organ and died along with every other cell in her body. The pain survived in Byron.

When the graveside service ended, clouds gathered on the horizon. Rainy days ahead again. Byron's thoughts about his own death idled away on distant shores.

The casket was closed. He never saw Sybie in the light of day since the wedding day and wanted to leave it that way. His last recollections of her were snippets of early morning whisperings, her dream about Sophie reminisces of Banff and the Tea House, and the covered lump being carried out of the condo.

After the graveside funeral, he took his folks back to his place. They were surprised at how bare the condo was. The few remaining pieces of furniture, a sofa, bed, television, one lamp, even the bar stools, were donated to a local charity. The Salvation Army eagerly took everything he didn't want.

There were a few watercolor paintings of Sybie's he had put aside, which his folks agreed to keep. "Someday, I'll send for these." Byron did take his favorite watercolor with him, which fit easily in his suitcase, the 'A Lonely Cloud and Field of Daffodils.'

He explained he had to leave the area for a while and left out any hint it could be forever. He provided scant details of his troubles with Valentin or his plans. Previously, he shared Valentin wasn't sympathetic when he took time off to care for Sybie and explained he wouldn't go back to the company. All the time, Byron worried what they might read about the blowup in the newspaper. His mom locked up any discussions about the evil, uncaring company Oreves when she said, "Good for you, Byron. You don't need them."

After they said their goodbyes, Byron moved to the back deck and sat in one of the chaise chairs. The Seattle-style drizzle obliterated the trail running behind the condo. The fiery maple, with leaves as large as a man's hand, leaned low, amply saturated, generously bestowing life juices to the roots below. As he stared over the top of one of the big strong arms of the 100-year-old tree to the rough dark peeling flakes of the trunk, the drooping leaves had opened up a clear view of a large knot he had never noticed before. The knot moved, and the shape of a large owl revealed itself. For so long, every night, he heard the hooting of an owl but never saw it.

The owl watched unblinkingly. Byron slumped back, curious about the owl as much as he was about him. "Goodbye, Mr. Owl."

What few items remained would stay, left to whoever purchased the condo. He packed two suitcases with casual clothes, no suits or sports coats, no dress shoes, just golf shirts, plain shirts, and two pairs of khakis pants.

He removed the picture of them from its frame, the only photographic reminder of her, taken in Banff at the top of Sulphur Mountain. They were clinking glasses of wine in the background, just a wisp of clouds caught on the mountain peak behind them.

Done with this phase of his life, he wanted to start over, get lost in a new life, come what may. Nothing to stay for, except bankruptcy, unemployment, and even worse. What did he care for wealth, power, pleasure, recognition, being the best at anything, the successful deal? Nothing made up for not having Sybie in his life. He had been living in alternating layers of hope and loss, gives and takes, the best days and the worst, the past and the present, now just the future.

The morning of his scheduled court appearance, the day of his disappearance, he called his attorney told him he wouldn't be there. The attorney began to explain the consequences, and Byron cut him off, "I plead no contest." He called him so he wouldn't look like a stood-up date trying to explain to the judge he'd be there any minute.

As he left the condo, he cleared all information off his cell phone and took a hammer to it, and discarded it in a brimming full dumpster.

On the way out of town, he stopped by Viva La Italia. They weren't open, but Giovanni was there. He told him he was leaving town and wouldn't be back. He didn't say forever, but they exchanged looks that knew the truth.

Chapter Twenty-Five

What a difference a day makes. The night before Henry died, Byron walked sideways against the wind-aided twenty below zero arctic cold. Today, the dark and cold of yesterday had turned to a balmy sunny day. Midwest days can be like that. The snow melted so fast the sidewalks and streets flooded. The house was dark and gloomy, so he moved the television to the living room to add noise and monitor the news and opened all the shutters and curtains in the house.

Barbara kept busy making arrangements for her father. She made it clear she could stay one more week to sell the house, so Byron stayed busy cleaning. He dusted, vacuumed, and scrubbed the floors, wiped down the baseboards, and contacted local consignment shops and charities.

Barbara let him use her computer to search for information on the investigation, his old company, Oreves, Inc, and his troubles with them, a reminder he should tell her about that too. The company was still growing, and Valentin was doing okay without him. It had also been a while since he poked around in the financial market. He sent an email to his folks, thinking it would be an interesting test as to whether the FBI knew his true identity.

That night Byron couldn't sleep knowing she was a bedroom away. He sensed when they called it a night, she wouldn't mind if they kissed, she the proper woman to be sure, not wanting to be too obvious, and he the grieving widower. That he wanted to take her in his arms and make love indicated he might feel differently someday.

After a breakfast of scrambled egg whites and toast, they moved to the living room, and Byron started a fire; they sat across from one another and watched the fire take hold. He turned the television on to protect him from more silence.

"So, you said you were married?" She started.

"Yeah, I was married. The wedding was a beautiful disaster. We married in a small white abandoned church in

Work Washington, a small town in the shadow of Mt Rainier. It was a private ceremony, just for friends and close associates. Her name was Sybil. Sybie. Her body was riddled with cancer.

"We had been together for quite a while—knew her in high school. We talked about getting married, but she…well, she knew all along she was going to die of cancer. She had a genetic predisposition for things to go haywire. While she battled cancer for all it was worth, I convinced her we should marry, consummate us. We were in the battle together. And I wasn't going anywhere. We were like a married couple anyway.

"The wedding was nice, but that night, she passed away. I saw it on her face as the minister pronounced us man and wife. The battle was over. She was a tough woman who went through a lot in her life."

Barbara wiped a tear away. That's so sad. I'm so sorry. So, you ran away?"

Byron couldn't help not smiling. "Remember when you asked if I was going to prison, and I told you I didn't think so. Not for this."

"Yeah. Good God, there's more?"

"A little more. No, it wasn't her death that drove me away. Not entirely. When my wife, well, she wasn't my wife yet, was losing her battle with cancer…" For a long minute, he considered what to say. "I still thought she would win her battle. I was so blind. I no longer tried to keep up with business. At the time, I was still responsible for a big nightmare deal, and it was going nowhere—a waste of time.

"Right before the wedding, Valentin, the CEO, my boss, began to send me cryptic emails and threatening voice mails. I wasn't naive enough to think he was powerless, him being the owner. He had all the cards, but I wasn't going to let him bully me from taking care of Sybie. Then he showed up at the house.

"I knew I was being insolent, but he wouldn't listen to me. I also understood he had a business to run, and I was out of control from his perspective. He said he wasn't going to fire me, me being a senior partner and all, but he was going to sue me. Told me his attorney said I had abandoned my position, causing the company irreparable harm. Said he would make sure I never work in investment banking again."

Rising, Byron walked over to the fireplace and put another log on the fire. "He should have stopped there and left, but it wasn't enough to sue me. He never could shake me, and I'm sure it irritated him to see me smiling. He wanted to hurt me more than sue me. He launched into a tirade about Sybie, how she was dying, and…for God's sake, she was just inside the house." Nodding and clenching his jaw. "I should have hit him harder. I have thought about that punch and how I should regret it. I can't get there. No regrets. When I play it over in my mind, I should have hit him harder."

"And, so you left?"

"He filed charges. Lawsuits were next. I decided to leave.

***

The day of Henry's funeral arrived.

Byron half-heartedly watched the television, hoping for a report on the FBI investigation, as he waited for Barbara to finish dressing for the funeral. He offered to get Henry's car running so Barbara could use it. He still had his car parked in his apartment garage. The rent paid up, so unless it had been impounded, it was still parked there. He decided it would end up in a police auction someday if lucky enough, never have to face them.

While waiting, he wandered into Henry's bedroom. Barbara wanted to leave the house fully furnished while being shown for sale. Arrangements were made to donate all the furnishings and accessories to charity after the sale. They boxed up the memories she wanted to preserve and shipped them to Coeur d'Alene. It was hard to shake the image of Henry lying there, hoping to live to see Barbara again, be with his Maj.

Henry's car was a 1994 navy-blue Cadillac Deville Concours with a little over 36,000 miles, top of the line in its day. The battery might be rechargeable but was unreliable, so he had it replaced. Henry had dutifully paid his OnStar fees, so he called for roadside assistance. They were eager to help and sent someone out to replace the battery. Given the mileage and the tire tread, it looked like they were new 10,000 miles ago. Barbara had plans to sell it. Byron had other plans.

"It's time. Is there anything of Dad's you want?"

"There is one thing. Could I buy your dad's car?

"You can have it. I'll sign the title over right now."

"I want to pay for it."

"No. Someday, you can bring it to me. Okay?"

She drew back and observed he wasn't dressed for a funeral. He was back to wearing the khakis and flannel shirt he came therewith. "I'm not going to the funeral."

"Why?"

"I'm leaving," he said regretfully.

"Where will you go?"

Preparing to answer, it struck him she meant something to him and already regretted they were about to become a brief memory. He would always wonder what might have been. It seemed his life had become a procurement of memories, maybe, in the end, one of the few guarantees in life—memories.

"I guess I can't go back to work for Hospice."

"They'd love to have you."

"I'm sure my old company won't have me, either?"

"Is there more to the story? Another secret?"

"I hope not. We've both had a lifetime of secrets. Two lifetimes. I hope the whole thing can be cleared up, but I'm not anxious to face up—but will have to eventually. I'll head west. I've gotta get out of this town and forget about Army. I won't forget Henry, though." Swallowing hard, "Or you." Smiling awkwardly, he continued, "My first stop is to see my folks. Let them know I'm okay."

Her face lit up in a smile that flooded the room. "And, what about this bank robber thing?"

He returned her smile. "I explained what happened. That too. I hope it's over soon."

"Me too. I don't think you'd look good in an orange jumpsuit. Where'd the name Army come from anyway?"

"Just a made-up name. Wanted to be left alone. My co-workers thought I was crazy. Thought I was a bomber."

"You looked like one," she smiled. "Do you need some money?"

"I'm good there. You know I was pretty successful before all this happened."

"So, you're still running?"

"I hope it is already over, but I'll stop running and face up after I see my folks."

Barbara rose out of her chair and went to him, sat on the arm of the chair, and reached out for his hand and covered it with hers. "Byron, I hope I see you again."

She was so close he could smell her perfume, feel the electricity, and the gravitational pull between them. Taking a deep breath and about to say, 'I'm not sure when,' the special moment was interrupted by a news alert.

Simultaneously, they turned back to the television to see a male news anchor sitting behind the news desk with his female co-anchor. "There is breaking news on the Seven Continents Financial Group embezzlement story. For the report, we go to Angela Hume."

Angela was blond and cute as a bunny. Being a beauty queen must have been a requirement of her job. "I am standing in the lobby of Seven Continents Financial Group. Last night Robert McDermott, CEO and President of Seven Continents Financial Group, was arrested for embezzling millions of company dollars from his own company." The picture on the television shifted to film footage of McDermott being led from his home handcuffed.

The picture shifted back to Angela. "The FBI has recovered 23,956,001 million dollars. This is the largest company financial fraud since Bernie Madoff made off with billions and was sentenced to 150 years in prison in 2009. This is the largest Chicago bank embezzlement since 1998 when First National Bank employees stole 70 million dollars."

The screen shifted back to the news anchor. "Thank you, Angela. Looks like Bernie may soon have a roommate."

Barbara turned to him and smiled. "I guess they got their man."

The News Anchor continued. "We have also learned the FBI is no longer searching for Army Bendorf. He is now seen as a whistleblower that led to the arrest of Robert McDermott."

Barbara turned back and tenderly kissed him on the forehead. "Congratulations." She stood up and straightened her dress. She wore a simple funereal black dress of her mom's. "Do I look okay?"

"As I said before, you'd look good in a throw rug." Byron wasn't so embarrassed this time.

She shrugged off his comment with a side glance and a smile. A brief awkward silence engulfed the moment. "How about you bring the car to me in Coeur d'Alene. I have a job for you in my firm if you want it. A partnership, if you'd like."

"Thanks, I need to find a job, for sure. Not sure I could get a license right now."

"I can help…maybe someday then?"

Barbara disappeared to put the finishing touches on her make-up and returned with her coat on, ready to leave. "Well, this is goodbye. I'm trusting you to bring me that car, or I'll report it stolen."

Byron snickered and moved closer, taking her hand in his.

A mischievous grin appeared. "If I see you again, you'll have hair, right?"

Running his hand over his bald head, he could feel bristles of hair poking through. "Yes, but not dreadlocks, that's for sure. That was so uncomfortable."

"You couldn't ask for a nicer place to live than Coeur d'Alene, you know."

They came together and kissed, a slow lingering kiss, as natural as if we had known each other for years. When she arrived at the door, she turned back to say one more thing when another news announcement story caught her attention.

"Today, the Shriners Hospital announced they received an anonymous donation, the largest ever of 2,390,360.00 dollars. The donor specified the donation designated for Nail Patella Syndrome. NPS is a rare genetic disorder that strikes children.

Barbara backed away from the door and looked at him. "Was that…did you? Isn't that the disease your wife had? What just happened?"

Stifling a smile, trying to look surprised, he tried to keep the tone of his answer even and unrevealing. "Yes, that's what my wife had. What a nice gift."

Turning back to the door, she hesitated and turned back again. "Byron. That's some coincidence, don't you think? Are there more secrets?"

"Barbara, there are good secrets and bad ones. Let's just leave it that this might be a good one."

Smiling, tilting her head inquisitively, "So I'll see you in Coeur d'Alene?"

Epilog

Byron hit the road right after Barbara left the house. He planned to drive as far as he could until he could no longer keep his eyes open, his destination Work, Washington, to see his folks. On a whim, he drove by Buster's to see if they were open. Buster had no regular opening times, sometimes at seven in the morning. The neon beer sign was lit.

It was 9:30 am when he entered. There were only two people in the bar: Buster washing glasses and Gabby in her regular place nursing a beer. Gabby only gave him a circuitous glance as he took his regular seat. Buster quickly set up a draft Budweiser in a frosted mug on a coaster. "Hey Army, it's good to see you."

Byron was about to tell him he was getting ready to hit the road and pass on the beer but instead said, "Just one. One for the road."

Gabby joined in when she figured out who he was. "Well, look who's back. We've been watching the news and had a small bet on what happened. I won."

"Yep, Gabby got it," Buster added.

Gabby smiled at her victory and seemed happy he stopped by. "Frosty said you were gonna do time. Said the FBI would crack it and find you before Christmas. They never found you, did they?"

"Nope. I'm a free man. It's Byron. My name was never Army."

Buster looked surprised. "Byron, huh." Looking over to Gabby, "You got that right, too. Said Army wasn't your real name?"

"Yep and Buster here said you were already on some island somewhere."

Buster added, "that's what I figured. Hoping anyway. Gabby said you weren't going anywhere. She figured you for too honest. She said there was more to the story."

"What did she win?"

Buster grinned and said, "A date with Frosty."

"That's not winning," Gabby countered with a soft giggle. "Nope, I won free beers for a week."

"What would have you won, Buster?"

He answered with a grin. "A date with Gabby."

Byron looked over to Gabby and her smiling face. It took him a minute for it to sink in. Buster and Gabby—he never saw it coming. He recalled Buster always went out his way to be nice to her and watched his language when she was within earshot. He always thought Buster was much younger than her, with all that black hair, but he might have been wrong. "I wish Buster had won. I'd be on some island with all that money, and Buster would get the girl."

They all had a good laugh. It was good to be on his barstool in his personal dive bar.

Buster looked at Byron quizzically, "So, Army…I mean Byron…She got the fake name right, too. So, what's the story?"

Talking a deep satisfying gulp of his beer, he began to tell them the story, leaving out the part of holding up in an attic and taking care of a dying man and meeting his daughter and how good it felt to reunite father and daughter. It was the best part of the story, but that part of the story had too many tentacles connected to memories of Sybie. "McDermott got greedy. I'll never know why a man who has everything has to have more. Maybe it's the feeling of invincibility that money grants as if wealth proves a man can do and get away with anything."

Buster started polishing the bar, and Gabby leaned forward over her beer, not wanting to miss a word. "McDermott is the worst kind of human," Byron told the elevator story and how he humiliated one of his junior executives. "When I figured out he was doing the embezzling, the best way to prove my theory was to steal the money from him. He would either keep quiet or call in the Feds and try to cover it up. I figured he had some inside help and might try to cover things up if he had time."

Buster looked over to Gabby. "Didn't we just hear a report on that?"

Gabby jumped in, "Some guy named Alfred…not sure of his last name. He's been indicted too."

Sad news, but not unexpected it was Alfred. "Alfred wasn't a bad guy. He had big dreams. He just got caught up, I guess."

"You lost all your hair."

"That was a cover. It'll grow back. Not dreadlocks, though."

"Where are you heading?" Buster asked.

"West, to the other side of the mountains." He instantly thought about adding, 'to where the sun shines.' "Did the FBI ever come here?"

Gabby was quick to respond. "No. We would have covered for you. We were rooting for you, whichever way it turned out."

"Thanks."

Byron drank the last swallow of beer and set the mug on the bar. He could see Buster poised to refill it and Gabby looking on to see whether he would let him. Funny, the dive bar was a part of his life—a refuge in a dark time. He would never return. He pushed aside thoughts about what he faced—he had plenty of car time for such ruminations.

Pushing back from his barstool, he looked around, paused, and without a word walked to the exit. Gabby wished him good luck. Buster leaned against the bar; a white towel draped over his shoulder. Not wanting to turn back again, Byron waved his hand in the air and took a deep breath. "I'll miss you guys. Stay safe."